MALCHUS

WRITTEN BY

MICHAEL DAWSON

Michael Dawson

2 Co. 5:7

ISBN: 978-0-9995245-1-0

TABLE OF CONTENTS

Dedicated to my dad and mom who taught
me early to love the stories of Jesus and
by their lives, made the stories real.

————————

Thanks to my oldest son, Joshua Michael, for his
idea for this book. I don't think I would have ever
thought of trying to do a story like this on my
own. I learned more from this effort than I can
tell. Also, thanks to his wife, Erika, who patiently
formatted the book for print and eBook.

FORWARD

It is impossible to do an original story of Jesus. So much has been written about His life.

As someone born and raised in a missionary family, I heard these stories all my life. I still retain an undying love of listening and learning about Jesus.

One of the men who has blessed me with his songs and writings is Michael Card. In his book, *Mark: The Gospel of Passion*, he encouraged his readers to "engage with the Scriptures at the level of the informed imagination."

I may have carried his encouragement a little far, but this is what I have attempted to do with this story.

This book is not intended to be an exhaustive work on the teachings, miracles, and life of Jesus. I have purposely left out some stories as I felt it was not possible for one man who was living in Jerusalem to be a constant shadow of a Rabbi who primarily did His ministry in Galilee. I have attempted, however, to put the included stories in their right order and setting. This is harder than you might think, as each of the writers of the Gospels told things in their own order as they remembered and wanted to share with their readers.

This story was an adventure to write. There were times I felt I was walking the dusty roads watching, listening and being with Jesus -- even if it was only in my imagination.

PROLOGUE

John, James, Levi, and I were walking along the rocky beach on the Sea of Galilee. I tried to visualize it as others see it: supposedly one of the most beautiful bodies of water in the world. But I just wanted away from here. I was tired of the poverty, tired of the squalor. I craved excitement. I kicked at a stone and sent it skipping down the beach.

James was the oldest at 15. He was quiet and deeply religious, always studying. Levi and I were 14 this year, and John was just past his 10th birthday. James was already working with his father, fishing. Levi's father owned his own shop, and it was expected that my friend would follow in his father's footsteps. John, although still too young to do much, was James' shadow. I was the only one with nothing here.

My folks had decided to move to Jerusalem. Looking at the poverty all around us, I thought if I never had to return to this place it would be too soon! "I can't wait to get to Jerusalem," I told my cousins and friend. "My father has already found me a place in the High Priest's house. I hope I never have to smell another fish again!"

I

I walked in behind the High Priest as he marched into the room. Many of the priests were already assembled. I had not seen my master so agitated before. He quickly silenced the men and went right to his point.

"That wild man, John, is back at it again. We have got to stop him! He is undermining our authority, and I want him stopped." He glared around the room at the assembled men. They nodded their heads. My master went on. "You, you and you," he said, pointing at some of the men, "are going to go and find out what he wants and why he is dressed in such crazy attire. What is he hoping to accomplish?"

Their heads bobbed again, and they rose to their feet. My master turned and stalked out of the room. I quickly took my place behind him and, with my head high, followed him out of the room.

He paused as if remembering something and motioned me closer. "Malchus," he commanded, "I want you to go and listen to them and to John. I want you to remember everything they say and what he says in return. This is very important; I have to know what he is thinking. This is extremely serious. I have to be able to stop this rabble rouser before the Romans step in."

I nodded, proud to be singled out with such an important mission, and hurried from the room to catch up to the priest, who had already started toward the Jordan River. Even with an early start, it would take us all day and part of another day to cover the long miles to where it was reported John was baptizing. It was hot and dusty, but we made good time. Soon we began to catch up and pass multitudes of people heading out to the area around Bethabara— beyond the Jordan, where John was speaking. Anticipation was in the air. Even while still a little distance from the crowd, I could hear a gruff voice bellowing out his call.

We stood out on the fringes of the crowd and listened for awhile. I looked around at the multitudes: they were eating it up. Their faces were held in rapt attention to what he was saying. To be honest, I felt sorry for them to be so taken by this nonsense. Finally catching a break, the priests I was with stepped forward. The crowd parted in respect for them.

I held my breath as the self declared leader marched right up to John and demanded: "Who are you?" His arrogance did not affect John. The wild man, hair flying everywhere, seemed to understand the question behind the question.

"I am not the Christ," he declared.

"Who are you then? Are you Elijah?" He asked.

"I am not," he answered.

"Are you a prophet then?"

"No," he shook his head.

I looked at the priests' faces. It was easy to see they were only getting angry at John's mild answers.

Harsher now, they pushed, asking, "Who are you, that we may give an answer to those who sent us? What do you say about yourself?"

He said, "I am 'the voice of one crying in the wilderness: Make straight the way of the Lord,' as the prophet Isaiah said." His answers bothered the priest even more. "Well, why do you baptize if you are not the Christ, nor Elijah, nor The Prophet?" they questioned.

John's answer was cryptic. "I baptize with water, but there stands One among you whom you do not know. It is He who, coming after me, is preferred before me, whose sandal strap I am not worthy to loose."

I tried to make sense of his words so I could know what to report to the High priest, my master. Trying not to be obvious, I looked around to see if I could find whom he was talking about. No one stood out in the crowd. I watched for a while, wondering about all the people who came up to John and were put under the waters of the Jordan. I heard different ones refer to it as being baptized for the forgiveness of sins. Sounded like nonsense to me, but I tried to understand them so I could give a good report.

As I trudged back over to the small town where I was staying while on this assignment, I was baffled by the fact that my master was so worried by this ridiculous wild man. Why would he send a delegation all the way from Jerusalem to the back side of nowhere just to listen to what he had to say?

The next day and the next, however, found me still in the ever-growing crowd. This was getting tiresome. I wanted to go home, but my Master, Caiaphas had insisted we stay, listen to him, and see if we could find something of which he and the other Temple authorities could accuse him. But by John's own admission, he was nothing. Not the Christ, as if He was ever going to come, not Elisha, and not The Prophet either. But here I was again, on the muddy banks of the Jordan, listening to John whip up the crowds, telling them they had to repent.

I was standing fairly close to John when all of a sudden I saw him turn and look at an approaching man. He must have recognized Him, because John raised his thunderous voice even louder and yelled. "Behold! The Lamb of God who takes away the sin of the world! This is He of whom I said, 'After me comes a Man who is preferred before me, for He was before me.' I did not know Him; but that He should be revealed to Israel, therefore I came baptizing with water."

Everyone turned to look at the man. He was rather nondescript. I certainly could not see anything in Him for John to be carrying on so. But the man walked up to John and stood before him. "Why are you coming to me? You should baptize me," John insisted. But the man gently shook his head no.

"You have to do this, so that all righteousness is fulfilled."

Had the world gone crazy? Here is this wild-looking man, wearing a camel's hair coat and a belt made out of some kind of hairy leather, hair overgrown, dunking this mild mannered young man under the water — and it is for righteousness? I couldn't wait to give my report to the High Priest this time. It was all just too much!

I heard someone say His name was Jesus. There were many people milling around and waiting for John to baptize them. The noise was raucous, like you would expect with any crowd of people, but it was as if Jesus were all alone. Just Jesus! As He started to make His way back to the bank of the river, He was walking toward me. Then, out of nowhere, a beautiful snow white dove came and landed right on His shoulder. Now, if that doesn't top it all! The man was obviously a charlatan and a magician. Why else would He have had trained this bird to come to Him like this? I'll tell you, it was a great effect, but did not impress me. The riffraff were sure impressed, though. And as if that were not enough, there came a clap of thunder out of a clear blue sky and what almost sounded like a man's voice. I could have sworn I heard the voice say, "This is My beloved Son and I am well pleased with HIM." I wasn't sure if I would include all that in my report to my master or not. Quickly, I was realizing this job might hold some dangers for me as well. I wanted to give a good, truthful report — but the High Priest had to believe it or he would think I'd gone mad.

As Jesus continued walking toward me, He climbed the bank, stopped for just a second, and looked right at me. Talk about a piecing gaze. For some reason, His look really shook me. I turned and made my way out of the crowd.

Larger and larger crowds were attracted to John's preaching and yelling. He certainly was a one-man show, that is for sure. Again, I just could not see why my master was so adamant about finding something to take him out.

The next day and the next day and the next, there I was, listening to everything he said. I found myself looking around for the man with the dove, but He was gone.

Then one day, while trudging back over to the bank of the Jordan, I was surprised to see someone I did recognize. "Hey John," I yelled. No, not the Baptizer, but a cousin. We were not that close, as his family were fishers and did not mix in many of the same circles I was in now. Poor family, they had bought into the story that the "Glory of Israel" was going to be revealed. "The Messiah was coming." I knew one thing. If — and just between us, that was a huge if — if the Messiah was coming, it wouldn't be back here in the middle of nowhere. He would be revealed right in the Temple — to my master!

Despite our differences, I was happy to see my cousin. "What are you doing here?" I asked him.

"Malchus, what are you doing here? I walked up from the sea where we were fishing, but you?" His eyes were serious as he looked at me. "You? Why are you here?"

I mumbled something. Needing to hide my true purpose in this place, I changed the subject. "You should have been here a few days ago. Craziest thing you ever saw. A man was baptized, and a beautiful dove flew right down and landed on Him! Then you should have heard the thunder! Almost scared me to death. Right out of a clear blue sky! Sounded for all the world like a man's voice!"

John looked at me funny. "Actually, that is the man I am looking for. His name is Jesus. But He has disappeared. No one has seen Him since that happened."

"Well, sorry cousin, I am here to see the one-man show that the Baptizer puts on every day. I shook my head, frowning. Personally, all I wanted was to be done with this whole thing. I longed to be back in the cool shadows of the Temple, listening to the old priests arguing about some forgotten manuscript as if it were important.

I knew the Baptizer had disciples. I looked intently at my cousin. "What are you doing here? Don't tell me you have fallen under the spell of that wild man too? Leave it alone, John. This man is trouble! Remember who I work for?" I did not want to tell him I was a spy or anything, but at the same time, he needed to be aware of the possible danger he could be in. So I added, "He is making some high-up people very unhappy and angry." Figuring he was family and I owed him something I went on. "They are not going to put up with him much longer."

My cousin frowned. "I don't know, Malchus, sometimes you have to follow your intuition. I just feel something big is coming, and I want to be on the right side. The Baptizer looks wild, but cousin, you should know what the prophets said about the Messiah! How there would come one 'crying in the wilderness before Him.' Well, this is the wilderness, and I can't imagine anyone crying and yelling louder that the Baptizer! And have you listened to his message? 'Repent for the Messiah is coming.' That is who I am looking for. The Messiah."

"Well, I still don't think you are going to find Him here." I said, and turned to go.

John the Baptizer was in fine form that day! He no sooner spotted the delegation of priests coming then he ran up to us, looking even wilder than he had in the past. I tell you, the man was unhinged! He ranted, and I can tell you exactly what he said. For my reports, I'd taken to carrying around a small scroll with me. Here are his words: "You brood of vipers! Who warned you to flee from the coming wrath? Produce fruit in keeping with repentance. And do not think you can say to yourselves, 'We have Abraham as our father.' I tell you that out of these stones God can raise up children for Abraham. The ax is already at the root of the trees, and every tree that does not produce good fruit will be cut down and thrown into the fire." How absurd! I will have to make sure my master is sitting down when I give him this report.

The Baptizer continued on with his rant, then — exactly what we were waiting for — he turned political. He started blasting Herod the king with having stolen his brother Phillip's wife! Now I know he is crazy! Either that, or he is the bravest man I have ever seen.

Just as the sun started to peek through the sky, we started on our long journey back to Jerusalem the next day. After a long, dusty, hot trip I was glad to get back to the coolness of the Temple. It was not long after I got back and had given the report to my master that envoys were sent to Herod. A short time later, Herod had the Baptizer thrown into prison. No one I knew thought for a minute he would ever be released.

The calm and peace of the Temple quickly dissipated as the priests debated over what happened with the Baptizer. I have never seen such a searching of the old prophets. My master was firm. "The Baptizer got what was coming to him. Enough of all this nonsense! The only thing important is the Temple and the sacrifices!"

My master does not have time to worry about anyone coming. The only thing he is concerned about is his standing and trying to keep the Romans in their place. The Temple is divided. One of the older priests, for whom I also serve as a bodyguard when my master sends me, is an old man by the name of Nicodemus, a righteous, powerful, and wealthy member of the Sanhedrin. He is also a Pharisee, and he is clearly one of the ones dreaming about and searching the Scriptures for signs of the coming Messiah.

I had heard whispered rumors that about 30 years ago some magi came from the east and asked Herod where the king of the Jews was born! I asked Nicodemus about it and his face almost glowed as he nodded his head. "Yes, not rumors, it was true! They had been searching because of a passage found in our ancient writings:

"I see him, but not now;
I behold him, but not near.
A star will come out of Jacob;
a scepter will rise out of Israel."

According to Nicodemus and older priests here, when those magi came with their entourage and possibly even some Persian cavalry asking about the birth of a king of the Jews, their appearance and questions set off old Herod the Great (who was the father of this current Herod, Herod Antipas). He about went crazy! Herod sent for the priests and asked them where the Messiah was to be born. It did not take them long to come back with an answer. They quoted the passage to Herod:

"But you, Bethlehem Ephrathah,
Though you are little among the thousands of Judah,
Yet out of you shall come forth to Me
The One to be Ruler in Israel,
Whose goings forth are from of old,
From everlasting."

The Messiah was to be born in Bethlehem.

"So Herod the Great," Nicodemus went on, "called the Magi and sent them to Bethlehem to find the Messiah. Then he asked them to come back and tell him where the child was, so that he, Herod, could go worship Him as well." The old man's eyes were sad for some reason.

"Did they find Him, this child?" I asked, interested in spite of myself.

"The story gets miraculous now," Nicodemus said, shaking his head. "They found someone. They gave the gifts they had brought, from all accounts, gifts fit for a king. My sources told me there was gold, frankincense, and myrrh, all of this stuff, very expensive. I tried to get more information, but Herod went crazy with anger. He heard the magi had gone home after worshipping a child there. Since they did not come back and tell him which child they had worshiped, he, in his rage, sent his soldiers to kill every boy-child two years old and under based on when the magi had told him they had first seen his star."

"So Herod had the Messiah killed?" I don't know why I was so interested.

Nicodemus shook his head. "Hard to say for sure, but I don't think so. According to someone I talked to, Joseph the father had a dream, got up in the middle of the night, and left with his family for Egypt. The very next day, the soldiers came slaughtering the babies. Funny thing, my boy," the old man went on, "but even that fulfills prophecy. We are told in our Scriptures by the prophet Jeremiah there would be a weeping in Ramah, another name for Bethlehem. The words of Jeremiah were fulfilled that terrible night. Here is what Jeremiah wrote so long ago:

'A voice is heard in Ramah,
mourning and great weeping,
Rachel weeping for her children
and refusing to be comforted,
because they are no more.' "

Now I was sure I saw the gleam of a tear in Nicodemus' old eyes. "Why is this important, Teacher?" I asked him.

"I thought," the old man paused. "Well, I really had thought it was possible our Messiah had come. I spent years looking and talking with people, but there was so much chaos. You would not remember, as it was before your time, but it was right when the whole world had to be taxed. In order to tax everyone, they ordered a census to be taken. You talk about confusion! Everyone had to go back to the city and place of their forefathers. Back to the roots of their family.

"I know it sounds strange now, but there were whispered rumors right here in the temple that one of our priests, Zechariah, while burning incense to the Lord, saw a vision of an angel."

Nicodemus went on, "From all accounts, it about gave old Zechariah a heart attack. I heard about the vision and tried to ask him about it, but the vision scared him so badly, it caused the old man to go mute. I heard later, months later in fact, that his wife--and she was an old, old woman—had in fact given birth to a son. Funny thing was, his relatives wanted to name him after his father, but both he and his wife Elisabeth refused. When asked what to call him, Zechariah asked for a tablet. On it he wrote. 'His name is John.' The house was full of people sharing the old couple's joy. They had wanted a child forever but they could never get pregnant.

"Well, everyone had to be happy for them in spite of the fact they were both stubborn about the name." Nicodemus grinned. "Surprisingly, as soon as he wrote John's name, the old man started singing a praise to the Lord. His muteness was gone, just like it had never happened!"

Nicodemus continued his story. "When I again saw Zechariah, I had to ask him about his vision. He grabbed me by the arm and stared intently at me. 'It is true, my young friend. I was paralyzed with fear. But the angel said to me, "Do not be afraid, Zechariah; your prayer has been heard. Your wife Elisabeth will bear you a son, and you are to call him John. He will be a joy and delight to you, and many will rejoice because of his birth, for he will be great in the sight of the Lord. He is never to take wine or other fermented drink, and he will be filled with the Holy Spirit even before he is born. He will bring back many of the people of Israel to the Lord their God. And he will go on before the Lord, in the spirit and power of Elijah, to turn the hearts of the parents to their children and the disobedient to the wisdom of the righteous—to make ready a people prepared for the Lord."'

"The old man looked down sheepishly. 'I hate to admit it, but I did not believe the angel. I mean, Elisabeth is old and let's face it, I am not young any longer myself, so, a baby? Come, let's be practical! But the thing that really caused me to doubt was our nation has been waiting for the Messiah since the days of Abraham and actually, since the days of Adam the first man. God promised Adam's wife that from her seed would come the Messiah, and we have come all the way to now. I am not a gullible, young fool any longer, so I doubted the angel.' His face flushed with embarrassment. 'You should have heard the angel when he told me, "I am Gabriel, who stands in the presence of God, and I was sent to speak to you and tell you this good news. Now listen! You will become silent and unable to speak until the day these things take place, because you did not believe my words, which will be fulfilled in their proper time."

"'So that is why I was struck dumb. It was not because of fright, but was because of my disbelief. I refused to believe him, so to show me his word was true, the angel told me I would be dumb until the baby was born. But that is not the end of the story, my young friend.'

"Zechariah looked around as if he were hesitant to finish his story. 'You know, I have mentored you and instructed you since you came to the Temple. I hesitate to tell this to anyone else because it sounds so crazy, and it is something I have never told a soul. When my Elisabeth was pregnant, in about her sixth month, she had a frightened visitor from Nazareth. It was her cousin, Mary, just a young little thing.

"'She called from outside the house and Elisabeth hurried, well, hurried as fast as a very pregnant old woman can hurry, to open the gate for her. She told me that as soon as she heard Mary call her, she felt her baby move and kick like crazy! My Elisabeth took her young cousin in her arms, and said loudly. "You are blessed among women ... why is the mother of my Lord coming to visit me? How could this happen to me, that the mother of my Lord should come to me? You see, when the sound of your greeting reached my ears, the baby leaped for joy inside me! She who has believed is blessed because what was spoken to her by the Lord, will be fulfilled!"

"'Mary had seemed frightened and shy when she first came to the house, but it seemed after hearing Elisabeth's blessing, somehow it eased her heart as she also started praising the God of Abraham, Isaac, and Jacob. You should have heard her, Nicodemus! How it thrilled my heart to hear this young girl praising our God. Here is what she sang:

"Oh, how I praise the Lord. How I rejoice in God my Savior!

For he took notice of his lowly servant girl, and now
  generation after generation forever shall call me blest
  of God.

For he, the mighty Holy One, has done great things to me.

His mercy goes on from generation to generation, to all
  who reverence him.

How powerful is his mighty arm!

How he scatters the proud and haughty ones!

He has torn princes from their thrones and exalted the
  lowly.

He has satisfied the hungry hearts and sent the rich away
  with empty hands.

And how he has helped his servant Israel!

He has not forgotten his promise to be merciful.

For he promised our fathers — Abraham and his children
  — to be merciful to them forever.'"

"'After things had calmed down, Mary told us her story. She
was engaged to Joseph, a godly man, by all accounts. But an angel had appeared to her. He was the same angel who had talked
to me. Remember, I told you his name was Gabriel? His greeting
startled Mary.

"Congratulations, favored lady! The Lord is with you!"

'Confused and disturbed, Mary tried to think what the angel
could mean.

" ' "Don't be frightened, Mary," the angel told her, "for God
has decided to wonderfully bless you! Very soon now, you will
become pregnant and have a baby boy, and you are to name
him 'Jesus.' He shall be very great and shall be called the Son of
God. And the Lord God shall give him the throne of his ancestor

David. And he shall reign over Israel forever; his Kingdom shall never end!"

" 'Mary asked the angel, "But how can I have a baby? I am a virgin."

" 'The angel replied, "The Holy Spirit shall come upon you, and the power of God shall overshadow you; so the baby born to you will be utterly holy—the Son of God. Furthermore, six months ago your Aunt Elisabeth—'the barren one,' they called her—became pregnant in her old age! For every promise from God shall surely come true."

" ' "I am the Lord's slave, I told him," said Mary. "May it be done to me according to your word." Then the angel left me.'

"Zechariah shook his head. 'That little girl had more faith than I did.' But then he smiled, 'She stayed with us for three months, and right before our John was born, she left to go home to Nazareth. She was worried about Joseph. What was he going to say? Would he believe her? Would anyone? Because by this time, there was no hiding the fact that she was pregnant and still was not married,' Zechariah whispered. 'But I believed her ... "Behold a virgin shall conceive..." Is it possible Nicodemus? I think we are living the Promise.' "

Nicodemus looked at me. "Remember, this was during that confusion I told you about, when all the world had to be taxed. Well, Joseph did marry his Mary. It was a big scandal and everyone was shocked, as they were sure he would put her away, but he insisted on marrying her. She was hugely pregnant, and they had to go to Bethlehem. Such a chaotic time."

Nicodemus continued with Zechariah's story: "'Something else I have never told anyone. Do you remember Simeon?'

"I shook my head.

"'No, you would not have. I think he died before you came to the Temple. But Simeon was an old man. He was very righteous and loved God. He had told someone that the Spirit of the Lord had told him he would not die until he had seen the Messiah. I remember some of the priests used to joke that he was probably going to live forever, because you have to understand, very few of the priests still had much hope or belief that there would ever be a real Messiah. The Messiah had almost become legend now. But not to Simeon! He really believed. One day I was walking across the Temple Courtyard, and I saw Simeon standing near a young couple. Simeon was holding a baby close to his chest. Recognizing Mary and Joseph, I walked up until I was just a few feet away, but decided to give them some privacy. There were tears in Simeon's eyes. I could hear him clearly as he said:

"Lord, now I can die content!
For I have seen him as you promised me I would.
I have seen the Savior you have given to the world.
He is the Light that will shine upon the nations,
and he will be the glory of your people Israel!"

"'His face had such a peaceful look on it. I found myself staring at him. Simeon pronounced a berakah, a blessing, on the young family, but then, his next words chilled me as he said to Mary standing beside her proud husband. "A sword shall pierce your soul, for this child shall be rejected by many in Israel, and this to their undoing. But he will be the greatest joy of many others. And the deepest thoughts of many hearts shall be revealed." By this time the old man was almost whispering.

"Zechariah continued his story. 'I looked at Mary's face. It had gone white, and I saw her lips tremble and tears start in her eyes. I remember being almost angry at Simeon for scaring her like that, and actually thought to step forward and say something, but then an old lady came up. She was Anna. We in the Temple recognized her as a prophetess. She has been in the Temple almost forever. Rumor has it that she had been a beautiful woman and had only been married for seven years when her husband died. Since that time 84 years ago, she had never remarried and never left the Temple. She spent her time praying and fasting for the nation of Israel. She walked up as Simeon was talking. She too, took the baby in her arms and raised her face to God and began to praise the Lord, thanking God that His promised Messiah had finally come. I heard later she told everyone who came to the Temple that the Messiah had come. Soon the story was all over Jerusalem.

"Zechariah gripped my arm again and grinned. Now he had tears in his eyes, but his smile lighted his face. 'Nicodemus, I really think we are living the promise!' he told me again."

As Nicodemus seemed to remember he was only retelling the story, not actually back there in time with Zechariah, he slowly shook his head and lowered his voice. "Do you know who Zechariah's John is?"

I had a sinking feeling in my heart. "Do you mean the Baptizer?"

He slowly nodded. Turning, he walked back into his room at the Temple. He looked fragile and weak, as if the telling of the story had taken a lot out of him. I shook my head. No wonder Nicodemus was so sad. Now I felt I understood a little more of the history, even though I was unsure how much of the story I could believe. My master had never told me any of this. He had to have heard it as well. If my master was not convinced, why should I let an old man's memories bother me? I stood there thinking about all I had heard. If John was Zechariah's son, what had happened to Mary and Joseph's baby?

With John the Baptizer in prison, my job of shadowing him ended and my life settled down a bit. I found myself drawn to old Nicodemus, and I really did not know why. I knew he was sincere, but not for the life of me could I force myself to believe his farfetched tale. Sure, I really believed he believed it. He was not lying, but somehow I felt he had been deceived. As I said, I was drawn to him, and I had thought about his stories. But how did they tie into anything for me?

One day, after arriving at the Temple, my master beckoned me over.

"You will be with Nicodemus for the next couple of days. My old friend is not well and has asked me for your assistance as he would like to see a healer," he directed.

My head bowed in obedience. I left the room, partly happy for the chance to see the old man again, and a bit nervous. His words were still bouncing around in my head.

I found him perusing some old manuscripts. I quietly set down so as not to disturb him, but it was almost as if he had been waiting for me. He looked up, mumbling, "This is even more fascinating than I had originally thought. But can it really be? Could it really be Him? Has He finally come?"

I looked around. Who was he talking about? Surely he did not expect me to answer him. What did I know?

Nicodemus smiled. "Excuse me, my young friend. I find my-self talking to myself more and more these days, but I realized I had left you hanging as I was telling you about my search for the Messiah a few days ago." He motioned for me to get comfortable.

"Remember the child my old friend Zechariah had told me about?"

I nodded.

"The other day as we were looking through our Holy Scriptures, my friend, Joseph of Arimathia, told me a story that ties in with my search. He does not remember the date that well, but he is quite sure we could be talking about the same child. He said one day about 18 years ago, he was in the Temple when he became aware of a young boy of about 12 years old listening intently to one of the teachers expound on the many subtle points of a particular law. He remembers the incident because the boy was there in the circle of listeners and teachers for three days. Joseph remembers that He had many very insightful, deep questions. He also remembers that the teachers of the law were amazed at His questions and answers when He responded to their questions.

"He remembered that they were all a little disappointed when, at the end of three days, a harried young couple rushed into the Temple complex, obviously searching for something or someone. One of the Temple guards, having seen the young boy there with them, pointed in their direction. The couple rushed over and seemed shocked to see their son sitting with such a dig-nified group of Temple leaders. Joseph told me he could not help overhearing the mother cry, 'Son, why have You treated us like this? Your father and I have been anxiously searching for You.'

"The boy's answer perplexed Joseph, because so many years

later, he can still remember His exact words. 'Why were you searching for Me?' He asked them. 'Didn't you know that I had to be in My Father's house?'

"He says he remembered the boy being about 12 years old, so that time frame would be about right for him to be the same baby born in Bethlehem during the time of Herod the Great."

Nicodemus looked down, frowning. "Joseph believes. I just don't know. I keep searching our Scriptures for answers, but it seems I find more questions than answers. Like this passage. Listen to this. This is found in the first book of our Torah.

'Before they came to Ephrath, Rachel began giving birth to her baby. She was having a lot of trouble with this birth. She was in great pain. When her nurse saw this, she said, "Don't be afraid, Rachel. You are giving birth to another son." Rachel died while giving birth to the son. Before dying, she named the boy Benoni. But Jacob called him Benjamin. Rachel was buried on the road to Ephrath (that is, Bethlehem). Jacob put a special rock on Rachel's grave to honor her. That special rock is still there today. Then Jacob continued his journey. He camped just south of Eder tower.' "

The old man was almost trembling. "Boy, there is so much symbolism here. I became fascinated with Bethlehem back when the magi came. I have tried to find out everything I can about it. Rachel means ewe, a female sheep. She died in Bethlehem giving birth to a baby boy, she called him Benoni, meaning 'son of my sorrows.' Her husband changed his name to Benjamin, meaning 'son of my strong right hand.' I have just been reading in Isaiah, this passage here:

'He is despised and rejected of men; a man of sorrows, and acquainted with grief: and we hid as it were our faces from him;

he was despised, and we esteemed him not … He was oppressed, and he was afflicted, yet he never said a word. He was brought as a lamb to the slaughter; and as a sheep before her shearers is dumb, so he stood silent before the ones condemning him.'

"These passages are confusing, but at the same time, interesting to me. We know they are talking about our coming Messiah, but I can't reconcile what they seem to be saying with the picture we have all had of our Messiah King. What did you say the Baptizer called that young man when he saw Him?"

I thought back to the wild man on the river bank as he stared intently at a man walking calmly towards him.

"Oh, I remember," I said. "He proclaimed, 'Behold! The Lamb of God who takes away the sin of the world!' "

The old man grabbed my arm. "That's right! Can't you see it? The Lamb of God. Can it really be true?"

I had no idea what he was so excited about. I had not seen a lamb, only a quiet man walking up and talking with the wild man, John. As far as I knew, no one had seen Him since that day over a month ago. The wild man was in prison, and as far as I was concerned—end of story!

The old man continued his story as if he were convincing himself.

"Ok," he said. "We know the Messiah has to be born in Bethlehem. We know that my good friend Zechariah sees an angel and the angel tells him he is going to have a son. He is to call him John. Zechariah thinks that Mary's baby was supernaturally conceived, fulfilling the prophet's words, 'Behold a virgin shall conceive…' We know Mary was in Bethlehem because of the census and her baby boy was born there. We know magi came saying the king of the Jews had been born. We know shepherds were out in their fields as it was the time for the birthing of their lambs. There is a story still told there by old shepherds, who said one night, about 30 years ago, an angel appeared to them and told them not to be afraid, that he was bringing them good news of great joy. The angel went on to say that on that very night the Savior of the world was born in Bethlehem, and they would find him wrapped in swaddling clothes and laying in a manger."

The old man smiled. "My boy," he said. "Do you know that all sacrificial lambs for the Temple worship are birthed in Bethlehem? Do you know that the best of the best that will be used for the Passover, will be wrapped in cloths and placed in troughs carved into the floor of the Tower of the Sheep, for their own protection? Passover lambs have to be without spot or blemish, so they are wrapped to keep them from hurting themselves. Isn't it interesting that John calls the man 'the Lamb of God?' The shepherds say the angels said He would be wrapped in swaddling clothes and they would find Him laying in a manger. We know Bethlehem was a mad house as everyone was coming in to be counted in the census. So as the young couple were looking for a place to get in for the night and they could not find any room, maybe they found their way to 'Migdal Eder.'

"So when the shepherds were told they would find the baby wrapped in swaddling clothes, laying in a manger, maybe they knew right where to go to find Him? Doesn't it make sense that they would look for someone wrapped in swaddling clothes laying in a manger, or a trough in the floor, where they, so many times, had put their own little lambs? Right to 'Migdal Eder' — the Tower of the Flock!

"The reason I don't think this is so farfetched, my boy, is because of this forgotten passage in the prophet Micah's scroll, the same scroll the priests used when they told Herod where the Messiah was to be born. In this passage it names Migdal Eder, the Tower of the Flock, as being the birthplace of our future King. Listen to this:

'And you, O Migdal Eder,
The stronghold of the daughter of Zion,
To you shall it come,
Even the former dominion shall come,
The kingdom of the daughter of Jerusalem.' "

I still could not see where the old man was going with all this. "So what? Why did he think it was important?"

Nicodemus must have seen the doubt playing across my face, for he said, "Don't you understand, Boy? The wild man is the son of my old friend Zechariah. I think the man he called 'the Lamb of God' is Mary's baby, born in a sheep's stall in Migdal Eder, whom the shepherds and magi worshiped and whom Herod tried to kill. I think our Messiah has finally come!"

II

The next few days passed quietly, yet there seemed to be something hanging over the whole temple. I had never seen my master so agitated. I was surprised he was still in such a foul mood. John was in jail, after all, and the country was quiet. But he was up pacing way into the night, and I did not know why.

It did not take long to find out, as rumors started flying again. Now, instead of John, it was the man Jesus drawing the crowds. I could not help but wonder where He had been. It has been well over a month since I last saw Him, and I never even heard His name mentioned. I had not even thought of Him since my last conversation with Nicodemus. But my premonition had been right: something big was coming up, and my master was in a dark mood.

Summoning me into his quarters, He waved his hand indicating he needed to finish something before giving me my orders. Finally, he looked up and motioned me closer.

"Malchus, I need you to go and shadow the Rabbi from Nazareth. You will need to figure out where he is currently located
and go listen to Him. I want reports on what He does, what He
says, and who He is with."

My heart sank. I had not enjoyed listening to the Baptizer.
Something about his talks stirred something deep in me that I had
no desire to listen to. But, my master's wish was my command,
so quickly getting ready, I walked down to the marketplace to see
if I could hear if anyone was talking about this Rabbi. I had no
idea where to even begin to look for him.

Once I arrived at the marketplace, it did not take long to
hear talk of this Jesus, the Rabbi from Nazareth. Seems everyone had heard Him speak or was planning on going to hear
Him. From all I gathered while there listening, it seemed my best
bet would be to head to Nazareth. If the Rabbi was not there,
I was sure I could find out where He had gone. I will tell you
one thing: the last place in the world I wanted to go to was to
poverty-stricken, backward Nazareth. I still wished I knew why
my master was so upset and determined to know all about this
lowly Rabbi. I mean, there were rabbis all over the place and, for
the most part, they lived their quiet lives with their few disciples
and fewer possessions. Why would my master care what a Rabbi
did—and in Nazareth?

It took me four days of hard walking to get to Nazareth from
Jerusalem, and I had not wasted any time. The road was very
crowded. It seemed everyone was trying to get to Nazareth, too.
I found myself walking beside an intent young man. I glanced at
him. He nodded his head in acknowledgment, and we fell into
step. We talked of this and that during the hot, dusty day and
were grateful when we found a shady spot beside a nice, cool,

hurrying brook for our midday rest. My friend shyly introduced himself as Nathanael, and I told him my name. We continued walking together for the rest of the trip, sharing as people do who are thrown together.

On the night before we would finally arrive in Nazareth, we began talking about our reasons for our trip to this little, out-of-the-way town, where no one even had two denarii to rub together."

"I am going to see and hear the Rabbi Jesus," Nathanael told me. He looked like he was just dying to tell me about Jesus. By this time, I was getting used to people wanting to divulge the latest story about Him. I, on the other hand, had to be careful. People would not be happy to know I was basically a spy for my master. I looked up.

"Have you met the Rabbi?" I asked.

Nathanael nodded. "Yes, I did." He smiled sheepishly. "To be honest, my real name is Bartholomew, but the Rabbi called me Nathanael and for me, this is now my name. But about the Rabbi, it was funny. I have been searching the Scriptures for information about our Messiah for a few years now. I spent hours each day begging the God of our fathers Abraham, Isaac, and Jacob to honor His promises and send our Messiah. I have a large fig tree in my yard where I go out and pray under the shade of its branches. One day, just a few weeks ago actually, I was out in the shade of my fig treeing begging God to send us our Deliverer. All of a sudden, I felt like God was telling me He had already sent the Savior, and I would meet Him shortly. I was still under my tree when a good friend of mine, Phillip, came running into my yard. He rushed up to me and grabbed me by the arm. 'Come with me!' he exclaimed. 'We have found the

Messiah! We have found Him of whom Moses and the prophets
wrote. He is Jesus of Nazareth, the son of Joseph!'

"I was skeptical. I am from Galilee as well, and to be honest,
knowing the apathy and moral decline of our entire region, I
was not impressed! 'Can any good thing come out of Nazareth?'
I asked him with raised eyebrows. Again, Philip tugged on my
arm. 'Come and see!' he begged. I rose to my feet and followed
him. As we walked up to a group of men, one of them looked at
me intently and said, 'Now, here is a true Israelite in whom there
is no guile.' I stared at Him, wondering what His motive was for
this strange greeting. Phillip whispered. 'This is Jesus!'

" 'Where do you know me from?' I asked. Jesus' face lit up
with a smile. 'Before Philip called you, I saw you under your fig
tree.'

"My morning prayer time came back to me with a rush. I
remembered feeling like my prayer was being answered. I stared
at Jesus. He nodded at me and I knew, I just knew HE was the
answer to my prayer for our Messiah. It was all I could do to
stop myself from getting down on my knees before Him to hon-
or Him right there. But I did say to Him with my whole heart,
'Rabbi, you really are the Son of God! You are the King of Israel!' Again, Jesus' face lit up. 'You are convinced just because I
said I saw you under the fig tree? Well, let me tell you, you have
not seen anything yet!' "

Seeing the devotion in Nathanael's face, I swallowed, afraid
he would see my guilt. But looking at me, he asked me, "What
about you? Have you ever met the Rabbi?" I shook my head no,
and thankfully, he let it drop. I decided I did not wish to travel
any more with him. I could imagine his reaction if he knew I
was only looking for his Messiah just to spy on Him. So on the

outskirts of Nazareth the next morning, I mumbled something about my business, and we split up and each went our separate way into the small town. It was the day before the Sabbath.

The next morning, I found myself seated near the back of the synagogue for the Sabbath. I was told the Rabbi Jesus was going to be speaking here this morning. I was glad to get this chance to hear Him and get the information my master wanted. Once the Sabbath had passed, I could make my way back up to Jerusalem and my quiet house.

All talk died down as the rabbi made His way to the front of the synagogue. A scroll of the prophet Isaiah was given to Him and He took it, kissed it, and, unrolling it, He found the place where it is written:

"The Spirit of the Lord is on me,
because he has anointed me
to proclaim good news to the poor.
He has sent me to proclaim freedom for the prisoners
and recovery of sight for the blind,
to set the oppressed free,
to proclaim the year of the Lord's favor."

After He finished reading the short passage, He rolled up the scroll and, handing it back to the attendant, sat down. Every eye in the place was on Him, and there was not a sound in the entire synagogue. I realized even I was holding my breath.

The rabbi was very calm. Finally He spoke again. "Today this Scripture is fulfilled in your hearing," He said. We looked at each other. This is it? His voice was so beautiful to listen to we had hung on every word, but this was it?

Finally someone said, "Isn't this Joseph's son?"

Jesus turned around and said, "I know you will quote the proverb that says, 'Physician, heal yourself!' And you will tell Me, 'Do the miracles here in your hometown that you did in Capernaum.' But in reality, no prophet is welcomed in his hometown. I am sure you know there were many widows in Israel in the time of Elijah during that great famine when the sky was shut for three and a half years and there was no rain. Yet, Elijah was only sent to a widow in Zarephath in the region of Sidon. There were many lepers in Israel during the time of the prophet Elisha, but none of them were cleansed, only Naaman the Syrian."

We were all furious hearing Him compare the children of Abraham in an unfavorable way to worthless Gentiles. As one man, we rose up, pushed Him out the door of the synagogue, and rushed Him on up to the top of a cliff. We were about to push Him off the cliff when, all of a sudden, He turned and looked at us. I thought He was looking right at me, into my eyes and into my soul — only me — but I heard others say the same thing. In the silence that followed, He turned and walked away, leaving us staring after Him.

In my report to my master, I decided to leave out the part about almost participating in a mob killing. I had no idea why I was so angered by this man. His voice was beautiful to listen to, but I was not fooled. Something was not right. He seemed to have a hypnotic hold on the crowds, but not me. I was no simpleton.

Later on that same week, in the small town of Cana of Galilee, I caught up with Jesus and His disciples — yes, He now had about a dozen burly men following Him everywhere He went. Our family was very embarrassed that our own John and James joined this band of uncouth men. Because of my desire to avoid being associated with my cousins, I chose not to go to a wedding to which almost the whole town had been invited.

I wished, after I heard what had happened there, I would have gone. Not that I believed it. I was becoming more and more convinced this rabbi is a common magician and a charlatan. But the story floating around was that the bridegroom ran out of wine. Jesus' mother, Mary, was helping with her relative's wedding and ran up to Jesus all agitated that they had run out of wine. She felt the family would be humiliated about this. From all accounts, Jesus tried to distance Himself from everything, and His response to her is a bit harsh, it seems. While my source was telling me this story, I wrote them down, so I do have His exact words here. "Woman, what does your concern have to do with Me? My hour has not yet come." But Mary's response is even harder to understand. Again, according to my sources, she turned to the servants and said, "Whatever He says to you, do it."

Here is why I wished I would have gone. According to all the reports, Jesus told the servants to fill six large pots with water. Just plain water. They obeyed Him, and before too long, the pots were filled to the brim with clean water. Jesus never even went near the pots according to my source, but only told one of the servants to dip some water out and take it to the master of ceremonies.

The master of ceremonies, not realizing he had just been

given water, tasted it and declared it to be the best wine he had ever drank! He was so impressed he even called the bridegroom over and gave him a hard time over it.

"Mazel Tov! Congratulations!" he said. "What are you doing? Normally, people put out the best wine first, and when their guests are drunk, then, he puts out the cheap stuff, but you have saved the best for last."

"...And all these drunk guests are saying that this man Jesus did a miracle. They are saying He turned the water into wine." After giving the report to my master, I held my breath. I knew my master's terrible temper, and I was afraid he would make a big deal of this and somehow, he might even blame me for something. The Rabbi Jesus was getting under my skin. I found myself almost terrified of Him without knowing why.

"Oy! Well, it has started! I was afraid of this!" my master ranted as he paced back and forth. "This man is going to be harder to control than the Baptizer! Oy!" He slammed his fist into the palm of his other hand, causing me to jump with the smashing sound it made. I was nervous and jumpy enough without this now. Finally, I was dismissed. Backing out of the room, I turned to go to my own place, but before I got too far, I heard my master call me back.

"Yes, Master," I said, bowing.

"Tomorrow you will go and help my friend Nicodemus. He has asked for your assistance again." I nodded and resumed my departure.

The next morning, I made my way over to Nicodemus' place. I found him as agitated as my master, but he was much more curious about all I had seen and heard than my master was. My master seemed angry and almost frightened. Nicodemus' interest appeared much more personal in some way. When I told him the passage of the holy writings Jesus had used in the synagogue in Nazareth, he slowly nodded his head. "Yes, yes, that makes sense!" he mused. But then, when I told him about our attempts to pitch Him off the high cliffs there near Nazareth, he frowned.

"Why?" he asked me. I hung my head. I did not know myself. "I heard Him speak and His voice was beautiful, but I am not fooled by His words," I muttered.

Nicodemus choose to drop it. "I asked my friend if I could have your services as I need to go out tonight. It is a private matter, but it is important to me. I trust you, and I know you will not fail me." Without understanding fully, I nodded.

"I asked for your help as I have to go out tonight, late. It is a personal matter," Nicodemus told me again. His repetition grabbed my attention. I looked at him. He seemed strangely calm and yet, at the same time, like he was afraid of whatever he was facing.

"I will be here," I told him. He nodded, and I turned to go. The rest of the day passed quickly as I tried to compile a list of the stories and rumors involving the Nazarene. I had heard someone refer to Him as such, and the name stuck. It was easier than having to say Jesus. I did not want to think of Him like that. I certainly didn't need to be saved from anything.

I looked at my list again. There was a report of Him casting out a demon in Capernaum, a town in Galilee. It seems the man, supposedly under the influence of an evil spirit, cried out when the Nazarene came near, "Go away! What do you want with us, Jesus of Nazareth? Have you come to destroy us? I know who You are—the Holy One of God!" (I wonder how much He had to pay that man to say something like that?) Obviously it was some kind of an elaborate setup to delude all those fools running around the country after Him.

Levi, my friend who told me this story, reported that Jesus looked at him with compassion, whatever that is, and then spoke directly to the demon, "Be quiet! come out of him and leave him alone!" Levi shuddered. "You should have seen it! The demon-possessed man was flung down with such violence I thought for sure he was dead. But then he slowly stood up, his face was calm, and he was in his right mind!" Levi looked at my dubious expression. "Ok, I know you don't believe anything about this man, but I tell you, if that was an act, they are awfully good actors! Everyone there was very impressed. I heard many people saying, 'What words these are! With authority and power He gives orders to impure spirits and they come out!'"

Levi went on to tell me that after the demon incident, Jesus, I mean the Nazarene, went to one of his disciple's houses. He was a man by the name of Simon—wait, Levi also told me that this Nazarene changes people's names at a whim. He changed Simon's name to Peter and I remember Bartholomew's name had been changed to Nathanael. This Rabbi had some nerve! Why did He think He had the right to change someone's name? My goodness! I would like to have Him try and change my name, I can tell you right now!

According to Levi, Simon's brother Andrew met the Nazarene first. He and my cousin John had been standing with the Baptizer talking. Suddenly, John the Baptist pointed at a man approaching, "Behold the Lamb of God!" he said.

John and Andrew turned to look at the man walking by and as He passed them, they fell into step behind Him. He turned, stopped, and waited for them to catch up. "What are you looking for?" He asked.

Andrew looked at John, so John said, "Rabbi, where do you live?"

"Come and see," He answered.

The sun was a golden orb on the western horizon when they arrived at the little place in Capernaum where Jesus was staying. It was so late, Jesus invited them to just spend the night. They talked way into the night. Levi did not know what they had talked about, but it must have been important, because early the next morning, Andrew went looking for his brother Simon. Finding him, Andrew ran up and said, "Simon, we have found the Messiah!" And he brought him to Jesus.

Jesus looked at him intently and said, "You are Simon the son of John, you will be called Peter, which means, a stone."

Peter's house was just a short way up an alley from the Capernaum synagogue. According to Levi, Peter's mother-in-law was almost dead from a high fever when they arrived at the house. Jesus went to her, took her by the hand, commanded the fever to leave her, and the woman was instantly healed. She got up and served them food. This story sounds so false, I hesitate to even include it, but my master told me he wanted to know everything that was attributed to this false rabbi, so here it is.

Levi's stories were so exciting and miraculous that I wondered if I could even trust him anymore. I thought I could: first, because we had been friends for a long time, and second, because he worked for the Romans as a tax-collector. But I wondered if he was falling under the spell of the Nazarene. Before he'd had no interest in a Messiah, but now I wasn't sure I could trust his tales of the trickster.

Getting back to the story, Levi told me, "When the people

in Simon's neighborhood heard how Jesus had healed Simon's mother, although it was already late afternoon, they began bringing to Jesus all who were sick in that area. Jesus loved them and moving through the crowd gently touched each sick person instantly healing them. At His approach, demons came out of many people, shouting, 'You are the Son of God!' But Jesus rebuked them and would not allow them to speak, because they knew he was the Messiah." Talk about your delusions of grandeur. This guy will have textbooks written about Him, I can already see it!

I walked down the dark streets of Jerusalem. Nicodemus was quiet. He seemed preoccupied and concerned. I was acting as his bodyguard as the streets of the city this time of the night were not safe. I could not imagine what in the world we were going out for at this time of night nor imagine where we were going. But Nicodemus hurried along, determined to complete his mission. I kept looking around, worried but confident in my ability to take care of my friend and myself.

Nicodemus paused at a door and gently knocked. You could have knocked me over with a feather when my cousin John opened the door. He beckoned us in. John stared at me, and I stared back at him. I could not even guess what Nicodemus could be doing with John. An inner door opened, and Jesus stood framed in the doorway. He looked deeply into my eyes, then turned and welcomed His midnight guest.

Nicodemus nodded at me, indicating that I was to wait in the outer room with the others. I bowed and took my place against the wall near the door in case my charge needed me. I purposely looked at the men lounging around the room, either asleep or almost, so I could recognize their faces if I needed to later on. A few were speaking together about the day's events. Bits and pieces of their conversation drifted my way, and I found myself interested in spite of myself. John seemed hurt by the fact that I had not even acknowledged him nor recognized him in any way. He kept trying to catch my eye, but I had no desire to talk to him. I kept wondering what my master would say if he ever found out I was meeting with the enemy. I did not know most of the men in the room, but I did know John and his brother James. James walked over and greeted me, but possibly sensing my uneasiness, left me and made himself comfortable against the far wall, soon appearing to fall asleep.

I realized from my place by the door I could hear the conversation taking place in the other room. Not wanting to listen in on the old teacher, I almost moved away, but then could not help myself from listening. I heard Nicodemus' high-pitched voice as he said, "Rabbi, we know that You are a teacher come from God; for no one can do these signs that You do unless God is with him."

Jesus' calm deep voice came easily through the door, and I had no trouble hearing His answer. "Honestly, I have to tell you, unless you are born again, you will not see the kingdom of God."

Now what in the world? I thought, What does that mean? Why couldn't He at least acknowledge the fact that Nicodemus was trying to be friendly? What does "born again" have to do with anything? He is talking to an old man! I clenched my fists in frustration. He needed to show some respect. Then, it was as if the old man had read my thoughts, because his next question was telling.

"How can a man be born when he is old? How could he enter into his mother's womb and be reborn?" My old friend sounded confused, as if he had not heard right.

The Nazarene was not put out by my charge's question, and He calmly answered, "Why are you surprised when I tell you one must be born again? Because honestly, unless one is born of water and the Spirit, he cannot enter the kingdom of God. What is born of the flesh is man, and that which is born of the Spirit is spirit. The wind blows, and you hear its passing, but you cannot tell where it came from and where it goes. So is everyone who is born of the Spirit."

Boy, none of this made any sense to me. Born again? Water? Spirit? The wind? This guy is a bigger charlatan than I was even giving Him credit for. I was disappointed that someone close to and respected by my master was even in there listening to this nonsense. What could Nicodemus possibly be thinking? I mean, he was a Pharisee and a respected teacher of the law! What could have caused him to meet and talk to the Nazarene? My master, Caiaphas, the High Priest, and all the other priests along with the scribes of the Temple had made it clear: this man had nothing in common with us.

I had to smile when I heard Nicodemus' answer, because I could still hear the bewilderment in his voice. "How can these things be?" I almost felt sorry for him. But I still could not figure out what he was doing in there. My master would be furious and with reason. Now, finally I understood why the old man had insisted twice that this was a personal matter. I listened in unbelief as the Nazarene, sounding more the teacher than Nicodemus, asked him a question.

"Are you the teacher of Israel, and do not know these things? Honestly, I say to you, We speak what We know and testify what We have seen, and you do not receive Our witness. If I have told you earthly things and you do not believe, how will you believe if I tell you heavenly things? No one has ascended to heaven but He who came down from heaven, that is, the Son of Man who is in heaven. And as Moses lifted up the serpent in the wilderness, even so must the Son of Man be lifted up, that whoever believes in Him should not perish but have eternal life."

I don't mind telling you that I could not have been more confused. I heard His words, but they held no meaning for me at all! "Son of Man?" "Ascending to heaven?" "Coming down from heaven?" "Lifting up snakes to heaven?" Then, "lifting up the Son of Man?" Who was this "Son of Man" the Nazarene kept referring to anyway? He almost made it sound personal. But like I said, I could not make heads or tails of it. He might as well have been speaking Gaul for all I could understand.

I could still easily hear the Nazarene's voice through the wooden door. "For God so loved the world that He gave His only begotten Son, that whoever believes in Him should not perish but have everlasting life. For God did not send His Son into the world to condemn the world, but that the world through Him might be saved.

"He who believes in Him is not condemned; but he who does not believe is condemned already, because he has not believed in the name of the only begotten Son of God. And this is the condemnation, that the Light has come into the world, and men loved darkness rather than light, because their deeds were evil. For everyone practicing evil hates the light and does not come to the light, lest his deeds should be exposed. But he who does the truth comes to the light, that his deeds may be clearly seen, that they have been done in God."

Hearing him say all that, I remembered His name Yeshua meant "God saves." Did this lowly rabbi really think that just because He bore the name Yeshua He was the "only begotten Son"? Did He think He was the Light of the world? Please! I did pause a bit when I heard Him say "they like darkness rather than light because their deeds were evil." Couldn't really disagree there. I could not stand to hear any more of this, so I moved away, putting some distance between me and the door so their words were no longer heard. I had no desire to hear of anyone condemning my world or trying to save my world, for that matter. I shook my head. Poor Nicodemus! He was getting caught up in all this Messiah talk. I knew my master would not like this!

I could no longer hear the conversation in the other room, but now I could not help but overhearing the conversation taking place between some of the guys that were still awake. John and a big, bearded man were telling the day's events to a couple other guys who must not have been with them that day. They were explaining about a run-in the rabbi had had a few days before with some priests and other religious men in the town of Capernaum. I had heard about it, but it was interesting to hear it from their point of view, if, for no other reason, it gave me a window into their way of thinking. The way I'd heard it told at the Temple was that somehow, and it was obviously planned beforehand, these four guys let a man pretending to be sick down on his bed through the roof in front of Jesus. The charlatan healed him, and everyone was happy except for some priests. They were the ones who ran to tell my master the whole thing.

But from the way John and the big guy were telling it, they

believed every word! Here is their story.

"When the people heard that he had come home (after He was almost killed in Nazareth, He very seldom goes there any longer, He has made Capurnaum His home now), they gathered in such large numbers to hear Him that there was no room left, not even outside the door. Jesus was inside preaching the word to them. Then four men came, bringing a paralyzed man, carried by them on his bed, trying to get him in to see Jesus. Since they could not get him close to Jesus because of the crowd, they climbed up on the roof and made an opening in the roof above Jesus by removing some tiles and then lowered the mat the man was lying on. When Jesus saw their faith, He said to the paralyzed man, 'Son, your sins are forgiven.' "

"And you should have seen the religious leaders!" interrupted the bearded man. "When they heard Him say, 'Your sins are forgiven you,' they really sat up straight with their eyes bugging out. They were obviously getting ready to open a debate with the Master, and you could just hear them thinking to themselves, 'Why does this fellow talk like that? He's blaspheming! Who can forgive sins but God alone?'

"It was as if Jesus knew what they were thinking in their hearts, and He said to them, 'Why are you thinking these things? Which is easier: to say to this paralyzed man, "Your sins are forgiven," or to say, "Get up, take up your mat and walk"?' "

"Of course, we all know both are equally impossible if you are not God." John again took the lead with the story. "Jesus was calmly staring at them, and you could see they were getting more and more uncomfortable under His stare. Finally He said, 'But I want you to know that the Son of Man has authority on earth to forgive sins.' So He said to the man, 'I tell you, get up, take your mat and go home.' He got up, took his mat and walked out in full view of them all. This amazed everyone and they praised God, saying, 'We have never seen anything like this!' You all should have been there!" finished up John.

"Yes," interrupted the big, bearded man again, "you should have been there to help me fix my roof!" Everyone laughed.

Listening to them talk, it was obvious they really were taken in by all this nonsense. I could not believe someone couldn't just go, find the man or someone from his family, and find out if he really had been paralyzed and for how long and even if it was the right man. Maybe someone just took his place. I was sure there had to be a logical answer for all this, but no, to hear them talk, not only did Jesus have the right to forgive his sins but also had the power to heal him. I could not wait to get out of the place. I think fanatics are the most dangerous people in the world, and I could hear fanaticism in their voices. My cousin John was gone!

Then, the big, bearded one (I finally heard someone refer to him as Peter) boasted that on their way to the city a man ran toward Jesus, the bell around his neck clanging, warning all who heard it that he had leprosy. The leper fell at Jesus' feet and actually grabbed Jesus by the legs, begging Him for healing. Because of his leprosy, he should have never gotten close to Jesus, much less touched Him.

"It was all I could do to keep from gagging. The stench was terrible! I can tell you that!" said Peter. "We were all backing up," he chuckled, and everyone laughed along with him. I was interested in spite of myself. "Well, all of us except Jesus," clarified Peter.

"What did the Master do?" one of the guys asked, wide-eyed.

"You should have been there!" Peter lowered his voice for

effect. "I was standing pretty close to Him, and when the man grabbed Him and said, 'Lord, if You are willing, You can make me clean.' Jesus did not even flinch. His eyes had such compassion in them, and He actually reached down His hand and touched the man. He touched him like He really cared for him and like He could see past the sores and smell. This very leprous, unclean man — Jesus touched him! Then, smiling, Jesus said, 'I am willing, be clean.'

"I have thought of this so often since it happened. You would have thought Jesus would have healed the man, then touched him. I have to tell you, I don't think I could have touched something so vile. But it did not bother Jesus. Thinking about it, I think Jesus knew the man needed to be touched. He knew he needed to be healed on the inside more than he needed to be healed physically. Anyway, He touched him. Amazing!

"You all won't believe this," Peter looked around at his audience. After listening to them for just a few minutes, I could tell one of their favorite and most-used phrases was, "You all won't believe this!" Or, "you should have been there!" Because it seemed that was how they started every other sentence.

Here it was again. "You won't believe this, but I was looking right at the man, and he was so eaten up, it was hard to even look at him, but while I was looking, the man's skin became like a young man's skin, bright and healthy. He was totally healed right on the spot. It still gives me goosebumps even thinking of it." Simon rubbed his arm and got a pensive look on his face.

"Funny. Normally if someone touches an unclean person according to the word of our law, the person touching the unclean person becomes unclean. But it seems with Jesus, when He touched that unclean, stench-ridden man, full of sores, Jesus' cleanness went out of Him and made the leper clean!"

"Then what happened?" His audience could not be satisfied but demanded more details.

"Well," Peter went on, "after Jesus helped the man to his feet, his next words surprised us. Jesus almost sounded angry — well, maybe not angry. Maybe frustrated would be the right word. 'Don't tell anyone,' Jesus said abruptly. Jesus' abruptness did not take the smile off of the man's face though, and then Jesus told the now smiling man, 'Go, show yourself to the priest and offer the sacrifices that Moses commanded for your cleansing, as a testimony to them.' "

I was glad to hear one of the guys ask Peter the same question I had thought of. "Why was Jesus angry? You would think He would be happy for the man!"

"Oh, he was! It took me a bit to figure it out as well, but I think what was happening is this: everywhere we went, Jesus would heal people, and that only brought more sick people. While Jesus loved healing them, He really wanted to be preaching the "good news" He kept talking about. The healings seem to get in the way of allowing Him to do that, as there were so many people needing to be healed. The healing is all they seemed to want Him for. Anyway, that's what I think," Peter finished.

I saw John nod. I could have added to his story if they would have asked me, but I did not say a word. The man had appeared in the Temple with his two turtle doves, which is the smallest sacrifice he was allowed to bring. He looked poorer than anyone I had ever seen, so he could not have brought much more than that, but I overheard my master shouting at the man, trying to get him to admit that he had really never been sick. I mean there were no scars, nothing! How were the priests supposed to know the man had ever been leprous? Anyway, it is because of all these people coming and showing themselves in the Temple that my master is always in such a foul mood. He just does not believe them, and he thinks the charlatan is somehow deceiving these people. My master is getting tired of it ... and of Jesus.

III

It was hard to believe things could get any worse, but reports kept pouring into the temple, and my master was in constant turmoil over this silly Rabbi. Just between me and you, I wished the High Priest would just ignore Him. That would probably do more to stop Him than anything else. I personally thought most of what the Nazarene did was just to get a rise out of my master. And if that was the case, whew! He sure got one this time.

I heard the Pharisees that were in the synagogue went out and began to plot with the Herodians how they might kill Jesus. And all this because Jesus told a man to stretch out his shriveled right arm and when the man did so, it was healed. They saw this as the Nazarene abusing their law of not working on the Sabbath.

So now, they wanted to kill Him. The worst part was they would not have to search far to find Him. If they were angry before, this particular morning infuriated them. Jesus came into the Temple, and when I didn't think things could get any worse, they did. My master almost had a heart attack. I couldn't believe the nerve the Nazarene had; He marched into the temple right before Passover. You should have seen Him!

I was there and still can't believe what I witnessed. He came in, with the usual crowd of His disciples, and it seemed like half of Jerusalem was with Him. The oral law the Pharisees follow mandates anyone within a certain distance of Jerusalem to physically come to the city itself for the three great feasts: the Shalosh Regalim. They are Pentecost, Tabernacles, and Passover. This Passover looked like it would be a wild one.

Because everyone has to physically come to Jerusalem, the city's population grows enormously. Well, I think most of those country people were following Jesus that morning. He came in, stopping right inside the Court of the Gentiles, slowly taking in the scene. I knew what He was looking at. The outer courtyard of the Temple looked more like a live marketplace than anything. There were cattle lowing, lambs bleating, and doves flapping in their cages. Seemed everywhere I looked, someone was buying or selling something. There were even tables of money, so people could come in and exchange their coins from other areas of the country for the Tyrian shekel, the only coin accepted by the Temple. The Temple accepted this coin because it was the closest in value to the old Hebrew shekel due to its higher silver content. The roar of so many people doing business was deafening.

I was watching Jesus, because, as someone trained in fighting, I can almost sense a problem or threat developing. Picking up some rope that had fallen near where He was standing, He tied it into a whip. Taking that whip, He went into action, and it did not take Him long to clear them out. You should have seen it! There were cattle jumping and running, doves flying, and sheep everywhere, with the moneychangers on their hands and knees trying to pick up their precious coins. It is a wonder none of them were trampled by some fool animal trying to get away, but it was a madhouse, I will tell you! My master and the other priests really have something to try and kill Him for now. As I said, they were already talking about it yesterday. The reason I was even in the Gentile Court of the Temple was because I was on my way to see my friend Levi. I wanted to see if I could add anything to the story that had them in meetings the entire day before at the Temple.

When I finally heard the whole story of the shriveled hand, I thought they were joking. It was just crazy! The story we have is that Jesus was in a synagogue on Sabbath, and there was a man with a shriveled right arm. From all accounts I heard, it would have been impossible to fake this one. The man's hand and entire arm were totally shriveled all the way to his shoulder, and it was really ugly.

Anyway, according to all the priests and Pharisees that were there, they were just waiting for the Nazarene to do something and break our law of not working on the Sabbath.

Then Jesus walked in, big as life, looked around at all the people, especially letting His gaze settle on the ones who thought they were going to trap Him. Finally, Jesus said to the man with the shriveled hand, "Stand up in front of everyone." Then Jesus asked them, "Which is lawful on the Sabbath: to do good or to do evil, to save life or to kill?" But they, realizing they did not have a good answer for Him, refused to answer.

It was obvious the Nazarene was terribly frustrated with their stubbornness, because He glared around, almost daring anyone to say something. No one said a word, so finally He said to the man, "Stretch out your hand." He stretched it out, and his hand was completely restored. That was it! He just told the man to stretch out his hand!

I kept wondering why the big deal, but I guess I don't know the Law. If the reports were true and everything happened just like it was told, I didn't think that Jesus did any work. I mean, all He said was, "Stretch out your hand." If anyone worked it was the man who stretched out his hand. I didn't see what the charlatan did. But who was I?

When I finally found Levi's tax-collecting booth that morning, I couldn't get through the crowd. I wondered what was going on. Oh! It was the Nazarene, and He was speaking with Levi. And what was Levi doing? It looked like he was putting all his tax stuff away and getting up. My best source of information against the Nazarene was following Him now! I couldn't believe it. What could Levi be thinking? How could a sinner and tax collector become a disciple? Who was this man?

They didn't appear to be in much of a hurry and headed in the direction of Levi's house. In the huge crowd, there was no way anyone would recognize me, so I tagged along to see what happened. I could not believe this! If you remember, I was getting concerned about Levi. It looked like my suspicions were right!

I was pretty sure we had lost Nicodemus, too. After his night visit with the Nazarene, he had not been the same. He was really wrestling with something. His mind was far away, and I saw him pouring over old manuscripts of our prophets. I had no idea what he thought he could find there. But I saw him at them from early morning until late at night.

My master also needed to watch a man called Joseph. He was from the town of Aramathia. I saw him and Nicodemus together all the time, passing manuscripts back and forth. I really should have let my master know about that night meeting and how funny Nicodemus was acting, but I liked the old guy, and I just couldn't force myself to say anything. And to be honest, as old as he was, what could he hurt even if he did think the Messiah has come? Anyway, with the Romans here, a lot of good a Messiah would do us now.

I did follow Levi and the Nazarene all the way to Levi's house. It was funny, first time I ever saw a place where a rabbi went in with a bunch of tax collectors and other riffraff and all kinds of sinners. I even saw some prostitutes in there. Ho boy! As you can imagine, the Pharisees were fit to be tied. By the time I got close enough to see anything, the Pharisees and other teachers of the law had gotten together and went up in a pack to demand an explanation from either the Nazarene or His disciples. I joined them, since many of them recognized me and knew who my master was; but I held to the back of the group as by this time I did not want John, James, or my friend Levi to see me.

You should have seen that crowd! What a feast Levi threw for the Nazarene. He had all his tax-collector friends there with him, and he had really laid out a banquet. Oh, I finally found out what the Nazarene said to Levi to make him leave everything. Are you ready for this? People, who were close said all Jesus did was stop and look at Levi for a minute. Levi half rose to his feet like he was expecting something. Then, Jesus said, "Follow Me." That was it! Just follow Me! The man must have some sort of hypnotic powers.

At Levi's, the Pharisees called for someone to come out,

because with all those sinners in there, there was no way any self-respecting Pharisee was going to go in that place. Finally, getting a disciple's attention, they asked him their question. Funny thing was, and I could hear it clearly from where I was standing, all that came through was a complaining whine from the Pharisees and the teachers of the law as they asked, "Why does your master eat and drink with tax collectors and sinners?" I think I could have thought of a better question than that.

By that time, Jesus had walked up and heard the question, and He had no trouble answering them. With a raised eyebrow He said, "It is not the healthy who need a doctor, but the sick. I have not come to call the righteous, but sinners to repentance."

Then He said something that galled them even further than His first answer had. Because Jesus told them, "Now, go and learn what this passage means. 'I don't want your gifts and sacrifices, I want you to practice hesed. I want you to be merciful.' "

As learned men in our Scriptures, every one of them knew He was quoting the prophet Hosea. This fact possibly made them even angrier, because if there was one thing they loved to do, it was throw Scripture around to bolster their own point of view--not have the Scriptures condemn them, which is how the entire crowd took what Jesus had told them.

I overheard a man standing next to me explaining that Jesus' family were on their way to try and take Him home with them. The man said His family figured He had become delusional, and they were embarrassed because of and for Him. So they wanted to take Him home. The man telling the crowd kept repeating, "They think He's out of his mind." Everyone nodded.

Hearing them, the Jewish teachers of religion who had not yet gotten over Jesus' rebuke, said, "His trouble is, He's possessed by Satan. That's why demons obey Him."

All of a sudden, toward the back of the crowd, a lady with four young men — whom I took to be her sons — came up and tried to push through the crowd. The man who had been explaining all of this looked around and said, "There is Jesus' mother and brothers now." I craned my neck to get a better view. She was still a pretty woman, but her face was drawn in worry lines.

She could not help but overhear the Pharisees and other teachers of the Law explaining that her Son's power came from Satan. I saw her face pale, and she put her hand up to her mouth. Her eyes glistened with unshed tears.

Jesus knew they were accusing Him of being possessed by an evil spirit, so, turning to them, He said, "How can Satan drive out Satan? A kingdom or a house divided against itself can't stand, so how could Satan oppose himself and stay strong? It is a fact that if you intend to enter and plunder a strong man's house, you first have to tie up the strong man. If I am able to cast out demons, it is because I have already tied up Satan. But you need to be careful what you say, as any sin a man commits can be forgiven except blasphemy against the Holy Spirit! This sin can never be forgiven!"

When He said the word blasphemy, you should have seen those Pharisees' faces. If there is one accusation they love to throw, it is telling someone they are blaspheming. Well, they knew exactly whom He was talking about, and they did not like it one bit!

I looked at His brothers. They stared straight ahead, like someone does when they are embarrassed to do something but they have to do it anyway. I could still hear people whispering

that His family thought He was out of His mind and had come
to take Him home.

About that time, I saw His mother gesture to someone she
recognized. This man quickly stepped to her side. From where I
was standing, I heard her ask him if he would ask Jesus to come
out. "Please tell Him His mother and brothers are outside," she
quietly directed him.

He nodded, and I saw him make his way through the crowd
until he was standing beside Jesus. You know those times when
everything is really loud and you are trying to be heard above
the noise, and then, while you are speaking, everyone goes quiet?
Well that is what happened in this case. Everyone clearly heard
the man say, "Your mother and brothers are outside looking for
You."

I was watching Mary's face when Jesus said, "Who are My
mother and My brothers?" Then He looked at those seated in
a circle around Him and said, "Here are My mother and my
brothers! Whoever does God's will is My brother and sister and
mother."

I think I am pretty heartless, and in my line of work I get
called to do things I am not proud of. But hearing those words,
that poor woman's face sank. I really felt badly for her and am
more convinced than ever after hearing this rabbi, this Nazarene, this charlatan say that—I am more convinced than ever
He is just a fake.

After the heartless way the Nazarene treated His mother, I
could not take any more, so I turned to go home. Walking up the
street, I came face to face with a guy who was grinning from ear
to ear. He grabbed me by the arm. My first thought was to jerk
away from him, but he had such an open, friendly face I decided

he could not be intending to hurt me.

"Have you seen the Nazarene?" he questioned loudly, almost yelling. I pointed back down the way I had been coming.

"But why do you want to see Him?" I asked.

He had already started down the street, but bounced back at my question. "Sir," he said. "I was born an invalid. For 38 years, I was taken every day to the pool of Bethesda, where I would lay waiting for the chance to get into the healing waters. Since I had no one to help me, I never made it and had no hope of ever making it. So each day dragged into another day as I lay on my mat and hoped for a break. Last Sabbath, I was laying there as usual beside the beautiful pool with its five cool white colonnades, when all of a sudden, a man was standing by my side. He looked down at me and said. 'Do you want to get well?'

" 'Sir, I have no one to help me get into the pool,' I answered Him. Even now, my answer sounds so weak. Of course I wanted to get well, but I no longer had any hope of that ever happening.

"But the stranger said, 'Get up! Take up your mat and walk!' Instantly, I felt power flowing through my body. I obediently picked up my mat and started walking. I walked right out of there, forgetting to even ask the stranger His name. My feet were barely touching the ground! But it did not last long. As I was still walking home carrying my mat, I caught up with a group of pious men, a bunch of Pharisees. They saw me with my mat, and I thought they were going to beat me up on the spot.

" 'You there, carrying the mat!' one of them yelled. 'What are you doing; don't you respect the Sabbath?' I did not know what to say, but just blurted out the first thing that came to my head. 'I've been an invalid for 38 years. But today, a man walked up to me and healed me. The man who healed me, told me to take up my bed and walk. So I did.'

" 'Who was this man?' a long-faced priest demanded. I don't know why, but they seemed very angry. 'I don't know. I have never seen Him before, and I did not think to ask His name. I just picked up my mat and started walking like He told me to do and here I am,' I blubbered. They glared at me for a moment longer but then continued on down the street.

"Having nowhere else to go, and since it was the Sabbath, I decided to go on to the Temple, which was just a short way from where I was standing. I was so thrilled to be healed, I wanted to go to the Temple to honor God with praise.

"I was still in the Temple when, all of a sudden, the man who had healed me was again standing beside me. 'See, you are well. Do not sin anymore, so that something worse doesn't happen to you,' He said. Someone in the crowd around Him called Him Jesus. But I was still so confused by all that had happened to me, I did not even think to thank Him. I just went and reported to the Jews who had yelled at me that it was Jesus who had made me well. When I finally got my wits about me, I realized I had never thanked Jesus, and, worse yet, I had turned Him over to people, that now, I understand, are trying to kill Him. I have searched for Him and have only just heard He is in the neighborhood. I have got to find Him and thank Him and tell Him I am sorry. I really appreciate what He did for me!"

Well, you've got a funny way of showing it! I thought to myself. A man heals you, then finds you and introduces Himself, and you run and tell the people who want to kill Him His name?

Again, pointing in the general direction I had been coming from, the exuberant man rushed off to find the Nazarene. Shaking my head, I continued on back to give my report to my master.

IV

As much as I wanted to be angry at my friend Levi, I only felt sorry for him. I kept hoping I could talk him out of doing something crazy. I couldn't imagine what he saw in that charlatan. But the last few times we met, we only argued. He was totally brainwashed by this crazy rabbi. I wished there was something I could do.

I headed over to Galilee, as Levi told me they would be there for a few days. Levis attempts to talk me into "believing on Him," as he put it, gave me some good material for the reports my master continually asked for. What did my master do with all these reports and stories? I, for one, just wanted to forget this man ever existed.

A huge crowd milled around the place when I arrived, but I could not find my friend Levi. I walked toward the seashore, assuming he would be somewhere around there. Suddenly, I saw the Nazarene approaching. As usual, He was followed by His close disciples. I saw my friend, but I decided to just listen as one of the crowd. Jesus walked on down toward the seashore with His disciples. Finding a nice level spot on the slope near the beach with the gentle hills forming a place for the crowds to sit facing Him. Jesus sat down. I watched as His disciples took seats on the grass around Him.

When the crowds saw Jesus sitting, they all looked for places on the grass to sit and listen. I sit down myself and looked around. Amazing! There were people everywhere, packed together tightly. From where I was sitting, I talked to people from all over Judea, from Jerusalem, and from the coastal region around Tyre and Sidon. They had all come to hear Him and to be healed of their diseases. Many people I spoke with claimed to be cured. It was crazy! Before we sit down, I had seen people trying to touch Him. I asked about this and I was told that if you were sick or bothered by an evil spirit, all you had to do was touch Him., as they said power was coming from Him and healing them all.

Finding a nice, level spot on the hillside, Looking at them, He said:

> "Blessed are the poor in spirit: for theirs is the kingdom of heaven.
> Blessed are they that mourn: for they shall be comforted.
> Blessed are the meek: for they shall inherit the earth.
> Blessed are they which do hunger and thirst after righteousness: for they shall be filled.
> Blessed are the merciful: for they shall obtain mercy.
> Blessed are the pure in heart: for they shall see God.
> Blessed are the peacemakers: for they shall be called the children of God.

> Blessed are they which are persecuted for righteousness'
> sake: for theirs is the kingdom of heaven.
> Blessed are ye, when men shall revile you, and persecute
> you, and shall say all manner of evil against you falsely,
> for my sake.
> Rejoice, and be exceeding glad: for great is your reward
> in heaven: for so persecuted they the prophets which
> were before you."

It is a good thing this man has such a beautiful voice, I thought to myself, because with this nonsense He talks, I don't think anyone would listen to Him. I mean, "blessed are you when they revile and persecute you"! If it weren't for my master insisting I get this material, I could not stomach it for very long!

For some reason, my master wants me to be able to tell him in detail what this man says. But I get so tied up in trying to understand Him, I forget I am only supposed to be trying to remember what He said. How am I supposed to handle words like this?

"You are to be the salt of the world to keep it from totally rotting. But salt that has lost its flavor is good for nothing and thrown out to be trampled into the dirt of the street. You are to be lights in a dark world. A city on a hill is there for all to see. You would never light a candle and put it under a basket. No, one lights a candle and places it on a candlestick so it lights up the entire room. So in the same way, let your lights shine before all so that they, in seeing your light, might glorify your Father who is in heaven. Now, don't misunderstand why I have come..."

Somewhere, I got to thinking about why He had come, and I lost most of His discourse. I have no idea what my master would do with this anyway, I couldn't imagine him really being interested in hearing much of this, so I am not that concerned. I, personally, can only take so much of Him.

He kept on talking, the sound of His voice echoing off the nearby hills. Like I've mentioned before, the man had an incredible speaking voice. It was just beautiful to listen to—but this next bit would set my master off! Whew, I hoped he read this section after I had already left the room.

"... Don't resist violence! If you are slapped on one cheek, turn the other too ...There is a saying, 'Love your friends and hate your enemies.' But I say: Love your enemies! Pray for those who persecute you! In that way you will be acting as true sons of your Father in heaven. For he gives his sunlight to both the evil and the good, and sends rain on the just and on the unjust too. If you love only those who love you, what good is that? Even scoundrels do that much. If you are friendly only to your friends, how are you different from anyone else? Even the heathen do that. But you are to be perfect, even as your Father in heaven is perfect. Heaven can be entered only through the narrow gate! The highway to hell is broad, and its gate is wide enough for all the multitudes who choose its easy way. But the Gateway to Life is small, and the road is narrow, and only a few ever find it."

Yes, I can see my master acting this out right now, I can tell you. No, I am sorry to say, I can't see my master letting someone slap his cheek or giving one of his enemies a big hug. Then this next bit.

"Take care! Don't do your good deeds publicly, to be admired, for then you will lose the reward from your Father in heaven. When you give a gift to a beggar, don't shout about it as the hypocrites do ..."

Well, that blew it for my master and any of the other high-up authorities I knew. They did nothing without planning it all out to get them the most recognition.

I was smugly thinking about how my master would squirm if he were here listening to the Nazarene when His next phrase hit me right between the eyes.

"Do for others what you want them to do for you. This is the teaching of the law of Moses in a nutshell." He talked on and on, but all I could think of was how I lived my own life. If this phrase sums up the entire law and the prophets, I was sunk! There was no way anyone could live like the Nazarene described. I mean, treating everyone like I wanted them to treat me? Impossible! While I was still wrestling with His words, I realized He had finished and the crowd was going crazy.

They were amazed at His teaching. I heard many of them commenting that He taught as one who had authority and not as their teachers of the law. I think what they meant was, Jesus did not quote any other source. He spoke using His own illustrations to convey His message. Other teachers in the Temple that I heard were always quoting other sources and seemed to get their authority from their sources. I had never heard Jesus quote any source other than our Holy Scriptures.

I kept having to shake my head to get His words out of it. He could sure work a crowd with His voice. He had such a beautiful-sounding voice! But of course, His words were nonsense. Who could ever do these things? Love your enemies, do good to those who hate you, bless those who curse you, pray for those who mistreat you. If someone slaps you on one cheek, turn to them the other also. If someone takes your coat, do not withhold your shirt from them. Give to everyone who asks you, and if anyone takes what belongs to you, do not demand it back. Do to others as you would have them do to you.

I could not wait to get off by myself with Levi. What in the world was this drivel? He smiled broadly when he saw me and hugged me exuberantly.

"My friend, it is good to see you!" He smiled. "What did you think of all the Rabbi had to say?"

"Levi, can we talk honestly? I have to tell you how concerned I am for you. How can you stand it? I mean, 'Blessed are you who are poor'? Does this make sense to you? As a poor man, I sure don't feel very blessed!"

Levi frowned in concentration. "Malchus, the thing is, He is not talking about a kingdom right here, right now. He is talking about the Kingdom of Heaven. We are promised an eternity with Him. He is talking eternal life!"

"Yeah, I heard Him say something about that the other night when He was talking to Nicodemus. He said some crazy things that night, like 'the Son of Man will be lifted up.' Then compared Himself to a snake that Moses lifted up. Then He said, 'All who believe in Me shall never perish but have everlasting life.' I mean, Levi, does this sound like a sane man talking?"

"All I know, Malchus, is that since I started listening to Him, down deep inside of me there is a contentment that I have never known," Levi explained earnestly. "I was not happy with my life, Malchus: cheating people, trying to get rich, and all that involved. I know you think I am crazy, but I am happier now than I have ever been in my life. Malchus, you should see the miracles He does! He has a supernatural power that you have to see to believe. I don't know. You know I have not been a good man. But since I looked into His eyes and He said, 'Follow Me,' my life hasn't been the same. I wish you could understand and really hear Him."

"Oh, I have heard Him. I just am not a blind follower like some people I could name." I frowned. I did not want to hurt my friend, I only wanted him to stop and think.

"Listen to me, Malchus," Levi demanded. "I don't think I am blind. When you look at Him with an open mind, I don't see how you can deny there is something about Him that is impossible to explain unless He is the Messiah. He has a power that is amazing. Take for instance the case of a few days ago. Have you heard about the Centurion's servant?"

At my negative shake of my head, he went on. "Well, this happened while we were in Capernaum. There, a Roman Centurion's servant was sick on his death bed. The Centurion valued this servant and wanted to help him, but nothing he did worked. The Centurion heard of Jesus and how He could heal the sick, so asked some elders of the Jews to go to Jesus for him, asking Him to come and heal his servant. When they came to Jesus, they begged Him to listen and heal the man. The elders obviously did not know Jesus personally. If they had known Him, they would have known all they needed to do was ask Jesus for compassion for the man. So they tried to convince Him it was the right thing to do. 'He loves our nation!' one said. 'He built our synagogue!' another pointed out. And Jesus did go with them.

"He was not far from the house when the Centurion sent friends to say to him: 'Lord, don't trouble yourself, for I do not deserve to have You come under my roof. That is why I did not even consider myself worthy to come and ask You myself. But say the word, and my servant will be healed. For I myself am a man under authority, with soldiers under me. I tell this one,

"Go," and he goes; and that one, "Come," and he comes. I say to my servant, "Do this," and he does it.'

"What did Jesus do?" I asked Levi.

Levi was silent for a minute. "In all the time I have been with Jesus, I have not seen Him surprised by much, but He was this time! He looked all around Him and I felt His eyes deep in my soul, and He exclaimed, 'I tell you, I have not found such great faith anywhere in Israel.' Then, turning back to the men who had come to Him, He told them to return to the Centurion.

I watched the men turn around without another word and head on back to the Centurion's house. Funny thing was, it was not long until someone came running back and told us the servant was well! Just like that, he was well!

Levi went on. "I know you refer to my Master as the charlatan or a magician, but have you ever heard of a magician who could fool someone in a house a good distance away without ever being in the house, seeing the servant, or even knowing his Gentile master? My Master is a teacher and a Rabbi, but He loves people, and I know if that Roman Gentile would not have come out, my Master would have gone in. That is the kind of person He is."

Levi continued, "I'll wager you have not heard about this one yet either. This just happened yesterday. We were coming to a town called Nain. We, His disciples and a large crowd following Jesus, approached the town gate. A dead person was being carried out—the only son of his mother, and she was a widow. Because she was a widow, as you know, she had to walk in front of the funeral procession. The poor lady was frantic with grief, guilt, and shame as she led the funeral procession to where they were going to bury her son.

"When the Lord saw her, His heart went out to her and He said, 'Don't cry.' I was looking at her face when Jesus said those words, and it was actually quite amazing to watch the light of hope dawn in her tear-filled eyes. She stopped. Jesus walked on by her and stood by the bier. By this time, the bearers and everyone else had also stopped. Those near Him shuddered when He reached down and touched the bier they were carrying him on." Here Levi lowered his voice. "Malchus, as you know, anyone touching a dead person is unclean by our Temple laws. But I have noticed that Jesus is never rendered unclean. The power flowing out of Him reverses the process. His power overcomes being unclean or defiled. The leper was healed, and now this dead boy, too. The power of Jesus is unbelievable!" Levi finished.

"Well, what happened to the boy? What did Jesus do?" I asked.

Levi grinned, "Oh, Jesus looked down at the dead boy and said, 'Young man, I say to you, get up!' The dead man sat up and began to talk, and Jesus gave him back to his mother." My jaw dropped.

"You should have heard the crowd. Remember, there was our big crowd of people and then all the ones from the town going out to bury the dead boy, but we were all filled with awe and praising God. 'A great prophet has appeared among us,' they said. 'God has come to help His people.' You can imagine, everyone is talking about this. I mean, Malchus, who has ever raised a dead man?"

I looked at Levi. His face was alive with his love of his Master. I had never seen my friend this excited about anything. It pained me that it was so misdirected and that my friend was becoming such a fanatic. I did not know how to continue the conversation, so I quickly said my goodbyes and left to head back and try and make my report to my master. I decided I would not mention my personal ties to Levi. I know my master would never understand. As I slowly made my weary way back to where I was staying the night, a thought hit me. Why did the Roman Centurion call Him Lord? I have never heard of a Roman respecting a backcountry rabbi before. Am I missing something?

The next day, Jesus was back teaching by the lake. This time, the crowd that gathered around Him was so large that He got into a boat and sat in it out on the lake, while all the people were along the shore at the water's edge. He taught them many things by parables, and in His teaching said:

"Listen! A farmer went out to sow his seed. As he was scattering the seed, some fell along the path, and the birds came and ate it up. Some fell on rocky places, where it did not have much soil. It sprang up quickly, because the soil was shallow. But when the sun came up, the plants were scorched, and they withered because they had no root. Other seed fell among thorns, which grew up and choked the plants, so that they did not bear grain. Still other seed fell on good soil. It came up, grew and produced a crop, some multiplying 30, some 60, some 100 times."

Then Jesus said, "Whoever has ears to hear, let them hear."

Weeks later, I was back in the crowd again. All we talk about in the Temple is this Jesus. From one end of the country to the other everyone is only talking about Jesus. What new thing has He said now? Whom has He healed? The stories are everywhere, and to be honest, I didn't really have to be in the crowd. I could

collect these stories right from the Temple. Everyone had gone
crazy! And you know what? I have ears, good ears. I heard every
word He said to the crowd, but a lot of good it did me. I didn't
understand a single thing the man said. I had no idea why people
took everything He said to be so important.

During one of our rare times of visiting, I told John I never
understood a word the Nazarene said. By calling Him the Nazarene, I was actually hoping to get a rise out of my cousin, but
he only smiled. I asked him about the story where the person is
sowing. He smiled shyly. "Well, don't think you are alone. None
of us understood it either! When He was alone, we Twelve and
some others around Him asked Him about the parables. He told
us, 'God has given to you the secret of the Kingdom of God, but
to everyone on the outside, I will only speak in parables.' Then
He, quoting from the prophet Isaiah, said:

> '...They may be ever seeing but never perceiving, and
> ever hearing but never understanding; otherwise they
> might turn and be forgiven!' "

I felt the hot sun on my face and squinting my eyes against
the glare off the lake I sighed. "John, I guess I am way on the outside, because I hear, but I surely have never understood a word
the man has said. Not sure what I need forgiveness for, though.
Oh, I was going to ask you. I heard Him tell Nicodemus that if
you don't believe, you are condemned already. Come on, John,
do you think I am condemned?" I tried to act nonchalant as I
asked John but I was afraid he could see how nervous this talk
made me.

John smiled, "Malchus, instead of hearing the negative about being condemned, why didn't you hear what He said about God loving the world so much that HE gave HIS only Son. That whoever believes on Him will have eternal life. Why can't you hear those words?"

I had to change the subject. "Well, okay, but what did He tell you about the man sowing his field? How did Jesus explain that?"

I could tell from John's look that he knew I had changed the subject on purpose, but he let it go. He nodded and picked up the story where he had left it before I interrupted him.

"So then Jesus said to us, 'Don't you understand this parable? How then will you understand any parable? The farmer sows the Word. Some people are like seed along the path, where the word is sown. As soon as they hear it, Satan comes and takes away the word that was sown in them. Others, like seed sown on rocky places, hear the word and at once receive it with joy. But since they have no root, they last only a short time. When trouble or persecution comes because of the word, they quickly fall away. Still others, like seed sown among thorns, hear the word; but the worries of this life, the deceitfulness of wealth and the desires for other things come in and choke the word, making it unfruitful. Others, like seed sown on good soil, hear the word, accept it, and produce a crop—some 30, some 60, some 100 times what was sown.' "

"To be honest, John, I don't think I understand it any better now after the explanation." I shrugged helplessly.

John grinned. "Don't worry, there are plenty more stories. Listen to this one.

"On the same day He told us that parable about the sower, that evening, He said to us, 'Let's go over to the other side of the lake.' He had been teaching from the boat all day and was really tired, so since He was already in the boat, we shoved out. Leaving the crowds still on the shore, we headed over to the other side. A furious storm came up, I have never seen such a storm! The waves breaking over the boat; I was literally afraid the boat was going to break apart. We were nearly swamped! We panicked.

"Jesus was in the stern, sleeping on a cushion. We woke Him and were screaming at Him, 'Teacher, don't You care if we drown?' " John interrupted his own story. "Malchus, you know James, Andrew, Peter, and I have fished on that lake for years. We fish it during the day, during the night, and have watched storms blow up all the time. None of us have ever seen a storm like this one. It was somehow different."

"So Jesus got up, rebuked the wind, and said to the waves, 'Quiet! Be still!' You should have seen the calm! I mean, it was very obvious the wind and the waves obeyed Him. He said to us, 'Why are you so afraid? Do you still have no faith?' I'll tell you, we were terrified and asked each other, 'Who is this? Even the wind and the waves obey Him!' " John shook his head at the memory of that time. Then went on, "After Jesus calmed the storm, I got the feeling from listening to Him that somehow this storm was demonic, like the whole evil world was arrayed against Jesus, trying to stop Him.

"Our boat was heavy with all the water we had taken on during the storm, and we slowly bailed it, each of us deep in our own thoughts. I kept looking at Peter, Andrew, and James, I mean, we were the ones with experience on the water. Poor Peter kept shaking his head like he still could not believe we were alive. We finally landed our boat in the region of the Gerasenes, which is across the lake from Galilee.

"When Jesus stepped ashore, a demon-possessed man rushed at Him. This man was totally naked and lived there in the nearby tombs. We all thought he was going to attack Jesus, and I still think that had been his original intent, but as he got near Jesus he began to shake uncontrollably and fell at Jesus' feet. He was shouting at the top of his lungs. 'Jesus, Son of the Most High God, what do you want with me? Don't torture me I beg you!' Looking at him I could see the chains still tied around his ankles and wrists where people had tried to bind him, but they hung from his limbs broken and rusty.

" 'What is your name?' Jesus asked him.It was clear the man did not want to obey Him, but it was also obvious that he had no choice.

" 'Legion,' he replied. His voice changed when he said his name; it rumbled out of the man as the sound of many voices. 'Don't send us into the abyss,' they begged Jesus. 'Let us go into those pigs,' they said, with the man pointing at a large herd of swine feeding on a nearby hillside. At a nod from Jesus they left the man and entered into the herd of pigs.

"The men in charge of the pigs stood helplessly by as their herd thundered into the lake and with a loud splash disappeared from sight. It was not long before their lifeless bodies were floating on the surface of the water. Their keepers ran off to the village to report what had happened.

"Hearing the news, everyone from the town rushed back out to see what the pig herders were talking about. Almost as far as the eye could see, there were dead pigs floating on the water. But the man who had been demon-possessed was sitting at Jesus' feet, clothed, and in his right mind. Those who had seen it all told how Jesus had commanded the demons to leave the man and how Jesus had cured him. The people were in shock! They begged Jesus to leave their region as they were terrified of all that had happened

"The man was still sitting at Jesus' feet. His face was now calm instead of tortured like we had first seen him. 'Master, let me go with You. I will serve You for the rest of my life,' he begged. But Jesus smiled at him. 'No, you need to return to your home and tell how much God has done for you.' "

Now that I had John speaking, I could not get him to stop. He told story after story. It was obvious that Jesus was his passion. He could not stop talking about Him. As John told his next story, I was disappointed to hear that some of our religious leaders were coming under the Nazarene's spell. I knew we had lost Nicodemus, but I was hoping maybe it was only because he was old and perhaps senile; but Jairus was not that old and was a very respected leader! So like I said, I was disappointed to hear this next story, but John went right into it assuming, I guess, that I was as excited to hear it as he was to tell it. I did not know how to make him stop.

Well, that was what I kept telling myself, but you know, I did like hearing the stories without understanding why. There was just something about them that was hard to explain. I remember when my master was sending me out to listen to John the Baptizer and then to Jesus, thinking that this job might get to be dangerous and or very difficult for me in ways that I, back then, did not understand. I still didn't understand it, to be honest.

Anyway, John went right on into the next story. "When we got back over to the other side, there was already a crowd on the shore to welcome Him. From the hills surrounding the lake, they had known for awhile He was on His way so they were waiting for Him. Before He was hardly settled back on shore, a syna-gogue leader named Jairus pushed through the crowd. He finally made it to Jesus and fell at His feet, saying, 'My only daughter is dying! She is 12 years old. Could you come to my house please? Right now?'

"Jesus agreed, and we started following Jairus. It was hard to even walk, the crowds were pressing us so hard, but Jairus was like a madman, pushing his way through in his desperation.

"Meanwhile, a woman had come up wanting to see Jesus, but she was afraid to be seen close to Him. She wormed her way through the crowd until she was close enough to touch the edge of His cloak. She grasped the hem, and immediately she felt she was healed. She tried to melt away into the crowd, but Jesus stopped.

" 'Who touched Me'? Jesus asked.

"Everyone looked surprised and puzzled and denied any-thing. Finally Peter said. 'Master, the crowds! Everyone is pressing against everyone else and against You as well.'

"But Jesus said, 'Someone touched Me; I felt My power go out from Me.'

"Finally, the woman realizing that if Jesus knew power had gone out from Him, He probably knew who she was, knew she could not go unnoticed. She came trembling and fell at His feet, and with everyone listening, she started crying. Through her tears her story came out. 'Master, I have been subject to bleed-ing for 12 years. I have been to many doctors, but now, I have no more resources to spend on doctors. I am broke, too poor to pay for any more care, and the doctors have never helped me anyway. In my desperation I thought if I could only touch Your clothes I would be healed. I was healed!' she whispered.

Jesus gently said to her, 'Daughter, your faith has healed you. Go in peace.'

"While Jesus was still speaking, we saw a man pushing through the crowd. From the look on his face, I knew the news was not going to be good. Jairus must have known the same thing, as I saw tears well up in his eyes. Finally getting close enough, the man said to him, 'I am sorry Jairus. Your daughter is dead. Don't bother the teacher anymore.'

"Hearing this, Jesus said to Jairus, 'Don't be afraid; just believe, and she will be healed.'

"When we arrived at Jairus' house, Jesus did not let anyone go in with Him except Peter, James, and myself, and the child's father and mother. Meanwhile, all the people were wailing and mourning for her. 'Stop wailing,' Jesus said. 'She is only asleep.'

"They laughed at Him, knowing that she was dead. We followed Him into an inner room where the dead girl still lay on her bed. Jesus took her by the hand and gently whispered, 'Talitha Koum — Little girl, get up!'

"Malchus, I saw that little girl start breathing and a flush came on her pale little face. Life returned to her body and Jesus, taking her hand, helped her to her feet and gave her back to her mother. 'Give her something to eat,' Jesus told the astonished parents and then He added, 'Don't tell anyone what happened in here.' "

"How in the world could you keep a secret like that?" I asked, surprised that anyone would even ask someone to try and keep that kind of a secret.

John smiled. "Yes, you are right. No one keeps His secrets. Before we were even out of town again, the word was everywhere. Jairus was so overjoyed at what Jesus had done for him I think he personally told everyone in that entire region.

"Speaking of telling people, you won't believe the response the next time we were over across the lake where Jesus healed the man in the tombs. We arrived there one day, and Jesus was swarmed. It seems the man Jesus had healed had told everyone, and this time they wanted to make sure they listened to Him and were healed by Jesus. We were totally swamped with people.

"You will like this story, too, Malchus," John went on. "Unless you have already heard it. It is about Simon, a Pharisee from Capernaum." At the negative shake of my head, he told me the story.

Simon the Pharisee had invited Jesus to eat at his house."He went to the Pharisee's house and reclined at the table. A woman in that town who lived a sinful life," John said delicately, "learned that Jesus was eating at the Pharisee's house, so she came there with an alabaster jar of perfume. As she stood behind Him at His feet weeping, she began to wet His feet with her tears. Then she wiped them with her hair, kissed them, and poured perfume on them.

"I happened to glance over at Simon, and from his face I could tell what he was thinking. He might as well have been shouting his displeasure. If this man were a prophet, He would know who is touching him and what kind of woman she is. She is a prostitute! A sinner, his face said.

"Jesus must have also seen his face and asked him, 'Simon, may I tell you something?'

" 'Tell me, teacher,' he said.

" 'Two people owed money to a moneylender. One owed him 500 denarii, and the other 50. Neither of them had the money to pay him back, so he forgave the debts of both. Now which of them will love him more?'

"Simon replied, 'I suppose the one who had the bigger debt forgiven.'

" 'You have judged correctly,' Jesus said.

"Then He turned toward the woman and said to Simon, 'You see this woman? All you see is what you think about her. But I came into your house, you did not give Me any water for My feet, but she wet My feet with her tears and wiped them with her hair. You did not give Me a kiss, but this woman, from the time I entered, has not stopped kissing My feet. You did not put oil on My head, but she has poured perfume on My feet. She shows her great love for Me because her many sins have been forgiven. But whoever has been forgiven little, loves little.'

"You should have heard the ripple of disapproval around the table when Jesus said to her, 'Your sins are forgiven.' I could hear shocked whispers from the guests seated near me as they began to say to each other, 'Who is this who even forgives sins?'

"Jesus ignored them and said to the woman, 'Your faith has saved you. Go in peace.' "

V

I was once again on my way to Capernaum. At first, I really disliked getting away from my comforts and my duties attending my master. But the Temple was in such turmoil and everyone was so short and angry with each other that, to be honest, I was happy to get a chance to get away. This time, my master heard a story about the rabbi giving His disciples the same power over sicknesses and death that up till now, only Jesus had, so he sent me to verify this. My master feared that if this charlatan could multiply and duplicate Himself, all would be lost. He was almost frantic, so afraid that if the Temple leaders couldn't control and stop this madman from Nazareth that Rome would step in and take control, and they wouldn't stop there. So here I was again, hurrying to the small seaside town of Capernaum, to see what I can find out for him.

I arrived there and, once again, I only had to follow the crowd to get to where Jesus was. I saw my friend Levi. He seemed happy to see me, although our last time talking had not gone that well. It just hurt me to see my friend so brainwashed, but it was still good to see him.

After we greeted each other, I asked him what was going on with his Nazarene. Had Jesus really given His disciples some kind of strange power? Although he knew I was mocking him, his face lit up.

"Malchus, you would be astonished. It is official. I am one of the chosen twelve! I still can't believe it. I mean, who am I that the Messiah would chose me as one of His close friends and helpers? It is amazing to be able to listen and learn from Him. After He chose us, He called us apart — and yes, He gave us power over unclean spirits, to cast them out, and to heal all kinds of sickness and all kinds of disease."

"Who are the rest of the twelve?" I asked him. Part of me felt guilty for taking advantage of my friend and using his friendship to flesh out my reports to my master, but what could I do? I knew my master would want to know all who were in this inner circle.

Levi started counting off on his fingers. "Well, there is Simon, who is called Peter, and Andrew his brother; James the son of Zebedee, and John his brother; Philip and Nathanael who used to be called Bartholomew; Thomas and James the son of Alphaeus, and Lebbaeus, whose surname was Thaddaeus; Simon the Canaanite, and Judas Iscariot." Levi stopped with a grin. "Do you want to know what He calls me now?" I frowned but nodded. Levi's face split in a huge grin.

"My new name is Matthew! Can you believe my Master calls me 'gift of YAHWEH'? Me, the tax collector, He calls a gift of YAHWEH! I love the name, and I love that He would single me out in this way."

"So what do you mean He gave you power over stuff? Levi,

are you ok?"

"Well, after He gave us this power, He sent us out two by two
to all the different towns and villages. These were His words to
us. 'Don't go to the Gentiles, but I am only sending you to the
house of Israel. This is what you are to say. "The kingdom of
God is at hand!" You are to heal the sick, cleanse people with
skin diseases, cast out demons, and raise the dead. Don't take
anything to pay your way, not even an extra tunic, sandals, or
staff, because a workman is worthy of his food.' "

Levi droned on and on about houses being worthy, shaking
dust off their feet, and making the judgement day of Sodom
and Gomorrah easier than it would be for the cities who did
not receive them. According to Levi, Jesus said they were sheep
among wolves; they were to be wise as serpents and as harmless
as doves. They were going to be delivered up to scourging and
death. Brother raising against brother, father against his child,
and the children against the parents. They would be compared
to demons and the master of demons. According to Levi, Jesus
did not come to bring peace, but a sword. In other words, who in
the world could handle this?

"Stop, stop, Levi! I can't take any more!" I told him. "You are
sounding deranged!"

"No, Malchus, you haven't heard what He said at the end,
about us needing to take up our cross and follow Him, how by
giving up our lives we would save them. Jesus went on to remind
us that two sparrows are worth a penny and not one of them
is killed without His Father in Heaven knowing about it. Then
He said we were worth much more than a sparrow. He told us
the very hairs of our heads are numbered and that we are more
valuable than many sparrows."

"I don't want to hear any more, Levi!" I raged to him. "I can't believe you are even parroting this nonsense to me. What am I supposed to do with this?"

"That is up to you, Malchus. Jesus said he who receives you receives Me, and he who receives Me, receives Him who sent Me. He told us that if we welcome a prophet in the name of a prophet we would get a prophet's reward. And welcoming a righteous man in the name of a righteous man, we would receive a righteous man's reward. Then pointing to some little children playing there alongside of where Jesus was talking to us, He said, 'If anyone only gives one of these little ones just a cup of cold water in the name of a disciple, I promise you, he will certainly get his reward.' " Levi finished practically panting. In his excitement, he had almost forgotten to breathe. I was almost speechless that he could recite the whole thing.

"Well, did you try it?" At Levi's blank look, I said, "The power? Did you try the power over sicknesses and over death?"

Levi nodded his head sheepishly, like he knew I was not going to believe him. At my stare, he nodded vigorously. "Yes, Malchus, His power does work. We did heal people, we preached and taught in all the towns. After we finished, we all met back up with Him and could not wait to let Him know how excited we were to be working for His kingdom."

At my raised eyebrow, Levi said, "Well, it is a heavenly kingdom. But yes, His power is real; He gave us the same power, and it works. I personally have touched and healed many people. It is incredible!"But you know what was almost the most amazing about the entire experience?"

I shook my head. He went on. "The most amazing thing was when we returned to Him all excited and happy, saying, 'Lord,

even the demons are subject to us in Your n'
'I saw Satan fall from heaven like lightning.'
authority to over serpents and scorpions,
of the enemy and nothing shall by any means ɦu.
ten to Me, don't rejoice over the fact that the spirits are sᴜ
to you, but rather rejoice because I have written your names in
heaven.' "

"How come He is so fixated on names?" I mumbled. I turned
to go. I could only take so much before getting antsy and needing to put some distance between myself and hearing about this
Man.

But before I could leave him, Levi took my arm. "Malchus,
wait. You met the Baptizer, and I know you were secretly impressed but also bothered by him, so listen to this. Before Jesus
sent us out alone, he took us over to a place near Aenon. There,
Jesus had us baptize people who came to hear Him. I did not
know until later that John and his disciples were also baptizing in
that area as there is a lot of water over there. I heard later that
some important men went to question John about his baptism.
For some reason, they seemed to think the baptism was just another one of the cleansing rituals that we Jews like to argue over
so much. While talking with John, they were eager to point out
that Jesus was now also baptizing. I think they were trying to
make John jealous as they told him that the crowds following
Jesus were much larger than his own crowds."

I had heard that John had been killed, so I wondered where
Levi was going with this. Maybe he had not heard about his
death yet?

"But John was unfazed," continued Levi. "He responded to
them, 'I have always been clear that I was not the Messiah and

nly sent ahead of Him. He must increase and my role is
ng. Remember: the bridegroom's friend guards and protects
e bride for the groom. When the groom comes, his friend re-
joices. My joy is now complete.'

"John went on to say that the One who comes from heaven
is over all and that God sent Him and He gives the Spirit limit-
lessly. He talked of God loving the Son and they who believe on
Him will have life, but they who refuses to believe will not see life.
They will only know the wrath of God."

Levi must have seen me getting nervous, because he rushed
on to say, "Wait, I need to tell you this. After we returned from
our preaching and healing trips, two of John's disciples came to
us. I am sure you know that John was in prison, so when John
heard in prison about the works of Christ, he sent them to ask
Jesus, 'Are You the Coming One, or do we look for another?'
Jesus listened quietly to their question. When they were finished,
He beckoned them to follow Him.

"He moved through the crowd calmly touching this person
and that. Each one He touched was healed instantly of his or
her ailment. There were blind people, deaf people, there were
people with plagues of every kind, even some lepers sit off a distance from the crowd clamoring for His attention. Even people
with evil spirits. Jesus healed them all. John's disciples looked on
in awe. Finally turning to them with a smile, Jesus said. 'Go and
tell John the things which you have heard and seen: The blind
see and the lame walk; the lepers are cleansed and the deaf hear;
the dead are raised up and the poor have the gospel preached
to them. And blessed is he who is not offended because of Me.'

"As they were leaving, Jesus started talking to the crowds
about John: 'When you went out into the wilderness to see John,

what did you expect him to be like? Grass blowing in the wind? Were you looking for a man dressed in soft, beautiful clothes? Indeed, those who wear soft clothing are in kings' houses. But did you go out to see a prophet? Yes, and he is more than just a prophet. For John is the man foretold in the Scriptures—a messenger to precede Me, to announce My coming, and prepare people to receive Me:

"Behold, I send My messenger before Your face,
Who will prepare Your way before You."

" 'Assuredly, I say to you, among those born of women there has not risen one greater than John the Baptist; but he who is least in the kingdom of heaven is greater than he. And from the days of John the Baptist until now the kingdom of heaven suffers violence, and the violent take it by force. For all the prophets and the law prophesied until John. And if you are willing to receive him, he is Elijah who is to come. He who has ears to hear, let him hear! Anyone with ears to hear should listen and understand!' "

"All the time I hear Him say, 'He who has ears to hear, let him hear!' but I never understand it. I do have ears, and I listen. I heard John say, 'Behold the Lamb of God which takes away the sin of the world!' I also heard John say, 'He must increase and I must decrease.' Well, it does not sound like John himself is very convinced does it? I remember hearing Nicodemus say that John, while still in his mother's womb, recognized that Mary was carrying the Messiah in her womb. Well, if that was the case, how come John is doubting?" I was almost sneering at Levi. "You would think if John was as important as Elijah and Jesus is 'God's Son,' surely Jesus could get him out of prison. If I were

John, I would have doubted too!"

Levi looked at me, sadly shaking his head. He seemed at a loss for words. Finally he picked up his narration again.

"I know you are confused, Malchus, but I wish you could really hear Him. Because Jesus kept on talking about John. 'But to what shall I liken this generation? It is like children sitting in the marketplaces and calling to their companions,

"We played the flute for you,
And you did not dance;
We mourned to you,
And you did not lament."

" 'For John came neither eating nor drinking, and they say, "He has a demon." The Son of Man came eating and drinking, and they say, "Look, a glutton and a winebibber, a friend of tax collectors and sinners!" But wisdom is justified by her children.'"

"I just wish I could understand what He says!" I said, looking down. "I never understand what He means ...'wisdom is justified by her children'? Do you understand that?"

Levi nodded his head. "I know what you mean. So much goes over my head, too. Later on, when we are alone, just the other disciples and Jesus, we always ask Him. He is very patient to make sure we understand."

Shifting gears, Levi's eyes turned sad as he remembered something. "What I really wanted to tell you was this. Did you know that Herod had John killed a few days ago?"

I nodded. "Yes, I was surprised you talked like he was still alive. I wondered if you knew he had been killed. I heard about it on the way over here, but what happened? I thought Herod respected and was almost afraid of John and would call him in to question him and listen to him. Why then, did he have him killed so quickly and quietly?"

"Well, as you know, King Herod himself had given orders to have John arrested, and he had him bound and put in prison. He did this because of Herodias, his brother Philip's wife, whom he had married. John had been saying to Herod, 'It is wrong for you to have your brother's wife.' So Herodias nursed a grudge against John and wanted to kill him. But she was not able to, because Herod feared John and protected him, knowing him to be a righteous and holy man. When Herod heard John, he was greatly puzzled yet he liked to listen to him."

Levi lowered his voice. "Finally she got her chance. For his birthday, Herod gave a banquet for his high officials, military commanders, and leading men of Galilee. When his step-daughter who was also his niece, the daughter of Herodias, came in and danced, she pleased Herod and his dinner guests. The king jumped up and applauded the girl. calling her over to him, he swore an oath saying, 'Ask me for anything you want, and I'll give it to you, up to half my kingdom.' Begging the king's permission, she ran out and said to her mother, 'What shall I ask for?'

" 'The head of John the Baptist,' her mother answered. At once the girl hurried in to the king with the request: 'I want you to give me, right now, the head of John the Baptist on a platter.'

"The king was shocked and saddened, but because of his oaths and his dinner guests, he was afraid to refuse her. So he immediately sent an executioner with orders to bring John's head. The man went, beheaded John in the prison, and brought back his head on a platter. He presented it to the girl, and she gave it to her mother. Then John's disciples came and took away the body and buried it, and went and told Jesus.

"When Jesus heard it, He called us saying, 'Let's go over to a quiet place so we can get some rest.' We knew John was His cousin, and we could tell He took his death hard, although I got the feeling it did not take Him by surprise but still bothered Him. Also, I could understand why He would want to get away after awhile; even if He would not have been grieving for His cousin, the crowds just overwhelmed us, especially Jesus. There were so many people coming and going that we did not even have a chance to eat. So we went away by ourselves in a boat to a solitary place. But as you know, from any of the hills surrounding the lake, you can see a boat and where it is headed. Many who saw us leaving recognized us and ran on foot from all the towns and got there ahead of us.

"When we got to the other side, instead of the deserted place there was a huge crowd waiting for us. I looked at Jesus, knowing He was not going to get any rest here. I wondered if we could just push back out and try somewhere else. But it was obvious Jesus felt sorry for them, because, according to Him, they were like milling sheep with no one to guide them. So Jesus waded ashore, with a smile of welcome on His face, and went right into teaching them. No one could tell by looking at Him that He was exhausted and grieving over His cousin.

"Finally, late in the day, we went to Jesus. 'Master,' said Peter, 'this is a deserted place and it's already very late. We need to send the people away so that they can go to the surrounding countryside and villages and buy themselves something to eat.' Jesus had that grin on His face like He was enjoying a secret joke. 'Why don't you give them something to eat?' Then, He turned to Phillip and asked him, 'Where can we buy bread so that these people can eat?'

"First I thought He was asking Phillip because he was from Bethsaida, the nearest town to us, but looking at Jesus' face and the twinkle in His eye, I knew now He was just testing us. But Phillip bravely answered, 'Two hundred denarii worth of bread wouldn't be enough for each of them to even have a little.' "

Levi laughed softly. I realized he was laughing at himself.

He went on, "I said to him, 'Two hundred denarii is more than half a year's wages! Are we to go and spend that much on bread and give it to them to eat?' Judas was already shaking his head as if to say, 'We don't have that kind of money!' Then Jesus said, 'Go and see how many loaves you can find here.' Before too long, Andrew, Peter's brother, came back leading a boy with his lunch.

"I looked at the kid," continued Levi, "and his face was beaming. He was so happy to have something to share with Jesus. Andrew looked as happy as the kid, although I sure did not see much to be happy over. We still had an enormous crowd of hungry people that Jesus seemed to expect us to feed and take care of. 'My friend here has five barley loaves and two fish that he would like to give you,' Andrew told Jesus."

I interrupted Levi's story. "Barley loaves? Man, that kid must have been poor. Who eats barley? I thought barley was only for beasts or Roman solders! And what in the world can he do with five barley loaves and two small fish? That would barely be enough for Jesus, let alone you twelve, which would still leave the huge crowd with nothing!"

"I am sure the kid was thinking that he was giving his lunch to Jesus and that at least Jesus would have something to eat," Levi answered. Then he went on. "But you'll see about the crowd!

"Jesus told us to have everyone sit down in groups on the green grass," continued Levi, "so we had them sit down in groups of hundreds and fifties. Taking the five loaves and the two fish and looking up to heaven, He gave thanks and broke the loaves. Then He gave them to us to distribute to the people. He also divided the two fish among us. They all ate and were satisfied, and we picked up twelve small basketfuls of broken pieces of bread and fish."

"Wait, wait," I interrupted Levi, "where did He get all the bread and fish? What happened?"

Levi smiled. "Malchus, you won't believe me since you are always saying He is a charlatan ... but I will tell you anyway. He gave thanks and broke the bread and handed us the fish, and it just would not stop! He gave until all twelve of us had some and, as we gave it, we never ran out. We just always had some more in our hands. It was a powerful but quiet miracle! I doubt if anyone in the crowd even realized what was happening. It was so amazing to see all those people eat until they were satisfied. It was a huge crowd, too. There were at least 5,000 men, and most of them had their families with them. Jesus is amazing! I wish you would come with me and meet Him."

I shook my head. I could picture my master's face if he heard I had gone to meet the Nazarene. It was not a pretty sight. "Then what happened?" I asked Levi.

"Well, Jesus told us to gather the leftovers. We gathered everything up and, again, you won't believe this. We gathered up exactly twelve small baskets of leftovers. One for each of us twelve men. We could not believe it. Not only did He make a meal for upwards of 15,000 people, but He made just enough to give each of us, His disciples, a lunch to go. As soon as we were finished gathering up everything, Jesus made us get into the boat and go on ahead of Him to Bethsaida, while He dismissed the crowd."

"What did Jesus do? Why did He stay and send you all away with your little lunch baskets? Was He angry?" In spite of myself, I had to try and goad Levi.

"No, after a stressful day, He likes getting off by Himself. He tells us that He talks to His Father." At my raised eyebrow, Levi clarified that Jesus liked to go off by Himself and pray.

"We missed Him that night, I'll tell you," Levi explained with raised eyebrows. "The wind was terrible and we could not make any headway at all! Seems most of the night, we were losing ground. Finally, probably around three in the morning, we were about beat and were still less than halfway across the lake. Suddenly, someone happened to look behind us and screamed! We all looked. In the almost continuous flashes of lightning we could clearly see something was walking on the water. We thought He was a ghost. I am not sure why, but it looked like He was about to pass by us. But at our screams of fright, He looked over at us. We all saw Him and were terrified. Immediately He spoke to us and said, 'Don't be afraid. I AM.'

"Malchus, If I would not already have believed that He was the Son of God, seeing Him walking on the water and then hearing Him use the name of God for Himself ... wow!

"Then Peter — you would really like Peter, Malchus — Peter jumps up and says, 'Master, if You are really You, command me to come to You on the water.' And Jesus said, 'Come.'

Well, Peter climbed out of that boat and actually started walking on the water toward Jesus!

"Then, I am not sure what happened, but he stopped looking at Jesus and looked down at his feet on the water and his cloak billowing around him in the wind, and he started to sink. You should have heard his scream! 'Lord, save me!' Well, Jesus reached out His hand and lifted him back up. They moved to the side of the boat, and Jesus helped Peter back into the boat. Looking closely at Peter, Jesus asked, 'Why did you doubt? Do you still have such little faith?' Then He climbed into the boat with us, and the wind died down.

"We were completely amazed. We in the boat worshiped Him, saying, 'Truly You are the Son of God!'

"Malchus, you have got to come meet Jesus!"

I looked at my friend. He actually had tears in his eyes as he pleaded with me. I turned my head. Mumbling my goodbyes, I started on my long trip back to Jerusalem.

VI

After a few days back in the temple, I found myself almost bored with my everyday duties. I could not get the Rabbi's words out of my head. I also felt badly that I had offended my friend Levi, and I wondered if Levi had figured out I was really only asking him questions and listening to his stories because I was a spy for my master. They were so protective of Jesus, I didn't want to contemplate what they might do to me if they ever did figure it out.

Hearing my master's call, I quickly made my way to where he was sitting with a large group of men. Bowing, I waited for him to tell me to approach. Seeing me standing there, he motioned me over and told me there was a delegation of Pharisees and other legal experts heading over to Capernaum to question Jesus. "You will accompany them," my master ordered. I nodded and, bowing, left the room to get ready for this trip.

It is a long, hard road to Capernaum straight north from Jerusalem, but we finally arrived, and the men I was with wasted no time in confronting Jesus. "Why do your disciples not respect the elders? Our traditions go back all the way to Moses. So why don't they respect the tradition and wash their hands before they eat bread?"

Jesus looked at them sadly. "Why do you allow your traditions to stop you from obeying God's commandments? For God commanded that a man should honor his parents. But you say to your parents, 'I would help you, but all my wealth has been set aside as holy to the Lord.' So in your minds, since it has been consecrated as holy to the Lord, you don't have to help your parents although you still have everything to use for yourselves. You are hypocrites! This is what Isaiah meant when he prophesied about you saying.

'People draw near to Me with their mouth,
And honor Me with their lips,
But their heart is far from Me.
In vain they worship Me,
Teaching as doctrines the commandments of men.' "

I was watching the faces of the men as the Nazarene responded. When Jesus called them hypocrites, I thought they were going to have some kind of an attack or something. Their eyes bugged out, and their faces were red, then starkly white. They moved away, to lick their wounds I guess, but Jesus was not finished with them.

He had called the crowd of people closer to Himself, and said to them, "Come here and listen. You have to understand Me. It is not what a person eats that makes a man unclean, but rather what comes out of his mouth. This is what defiles a man!"

I watched His disciples come and start talking to Him. From where I was standing, I could barely hear them, but I did catch the words, "Do You know the Pharisees were offended when they heard what You said to them?"

Boy, I thought to myself, that is an understatement! But Jesus calmly answered and said, "Every plant which My heavenly Father has not planted will be uprooted. Let them alone. They are blind leaders of the blind. And if the blind leads the blind, both will fall into a ditch."

Then Peter asked Him, "Explain this parable to us."

So Jesus said, "I can't believe you don't understand this! How can this be hard to understand? Here is what I meant. Our bodies are not defiled by what you eat. What you eat goes into your stomach and is then thrown away. But our bodies are defiled by our words that come out of our mouth, because these words come from a man's thoughts, which start in the heart. For out of a man's heart comes evil thoughts, murders, adulteries, fornications thefts, lyings, and blasphemies. These are the things which make a man defiled. But to eat without washing your hands does not defile a man."

Well, after that verbal beating, my Pharisee friends could not wait to leave that backwater town and head back to Jerusalem. As usual, the road was crowded with people returning to the capital city. As I passed this one or that one passed me, I could not help but look at their faces and wonder which of these fellow travelers had also been to see the Rabbi. Funny, you can really see a lot in people's faces. More than I ever realized. I saw people hurrying up the road with their faces set as if running from something; others' faces reflected a love and peace that I couldn't explain. It made me wonder what my face looked like to those who looked at me. I didn't feel like I was running ...

Even now, take for instance a woman walking just ahead of me. I could tell from her dress she was not a Jewish woman. From her attire, I placed her as someone from the coastal area, probably a Canaanite. At one of the last places many of us paused for a drink from a clear brook, I saw such a look of peace and joy on her face. I would have loved to ask her what happened, but someone in my position would never be seen publicly speaking with a woman.

Traveling anywhere in the region of Galilee, rules of interaction with Gentiles and other unclean peoples are almost non-existent in comparison to how they are observed in Judea and especially Jerusalem, which is why there is so much division between we who keep all the laws and the people from Nazareth. I mean, they even talk to Samaritans!

But I found it so much easier not to make a big issue of our laws while in this area, so I didn't stand out so much. It helped my fact-gathering for my master to be able to blend in more, which is why, on our second day of travel (actually on the evening of our second day of travel), a bunch of us stopped at a tiny inn in some little backwater town. The Pharisees would have rather stayed at a more refined place, but we intended to stay with the crowds. While sitting in the large common room, I noticed the woman whom I had seen on the road the day before. She was speaking with some other women. While not trying to listen to their conversations, from where I was sitting I could clearly hear every word.

"I was able to see the Rabbi," the lady was saying. "First, I did not think I was going to be able to talk with Him. His disciples tried to keep me away from Him. They kept saying He was tired and needed to rest, but I kept on until I finally got into the same room with Him. 'Have mercy on me!' I cried, but He ignored me. His disciples again tried to make me leave and even told their Master to make me leave.

" 'Send her away,' they begged Him, 'she is embarrassing us.'

"The fact that I was a Gentile was what was really bothering them, not so much that I was begging for help. I mean, everyone was begging for His help.

"But I cried louder, 'Have mercy on me, O Lord, Son of David! My daughter is possessed by a powerful spirit.' Again, it seemed He just ignored me. In my desperation I cried, 'Lord help me!' Finally it seemed I had His attention, but His words did not give me much hope.

" 'I was not sent except to the lost sheep of the house of Israel,' He said.

"I took a deep breath, fell at His feet and whispered, 'Lord help me!'

"His next words almost made me lose all hope. 'It is not good to take the children's bread and throw it to the dogs,' He said.

"Keeping my face toward the ground, I whispered, 'Yes, Lord, yet, even the little dogs eat the crumbs which fall from their masters' table.' I was still looking down, but I swear I think I heard Him chuckle. 'O woman, great is your faith! Let it be to you as you desire.' I looked up at His face. I have never seen such love on anyone's face. I knew He cared about me and my daughter. I also knew in my heart that my daughter was healed. I hurried home, and she was well! I can't stop thanking Him and thanking God. I am not Jewish, but somehow, from His look, I don't think it mattered to Him. I truly believe He is the Messiah the Jews have been waiting for— but somehow, I don't think He is just for the Jews. I think, even I, a Gentile have a place at the table with Him."

See! This is what bothers me about this man, this charlatan! I thought to myself. Why would she think that she would have a place at the table with Him, why would she even want a place anywhere near Him? He was beyond rude. I mean, He called her a dog—well, to be honest, the word He used for dog means little puppy and I know the Gentiles have dogs as pets—but I mean, a dog? Then she said He showed love? I was happy to hear one of the women with her ask her the very question I was wishing I could yell out, even though I was only eavesdropping on their conversation.

But she said, "Why do you think you might have a place at the Rabbi's table? He is Jewish. Even if He is the Christos, the Messiah, He is not for us but for the Jews."

"I know that, but in my heart, I believe He is for all peoples. I am not sure exactly why I believe this, but everything I have heard about Him makes me think He is for all peoples. Did you hear what He said to a Samaritan woman?"

The ladies with whom she was speaking shook their heads. The woman continued, "Well, I have a friend in Samaria, in the town of Sychar. She was really a mess, but we share family, so I always visit her when having to travel through. The last time I went through there, I could not believe her. She is a totally different person. I can't even explain the change I saw in her. I mean, she has married the man she had been living with, and her entire outlook has changed. It was such a remarkable change that I asked her what had happened, and she told me her story.

"According to her, she had gotten up late after an all-night party and, realizing she needed water, she got her water jar and headed for the well. She told me it was about the sixth hour. I mean, whoever goes to the well at noon? But she said when she got there, there was a man resting in the shade of a tree near the well. When she approached the well, He asked her for a drink.

"She told me, 'Looking over at Him, realizing He was just another stuck up Jewish rabbi, I was really surprised that He would even talk to me. I mean, I am a Samaritan, and since when has a self-respecting Jew ever associated with a Samaritan? Especially since I am a woman. So, I cringed and retorted, "How can You, being a Jew, ask for a drink from me, a Samaritan woman?"

" 'But He answered me and said, "If you knew who it was that is asking for a drink, you would ask Him and He would give you living water." '

" 'You know me, I am ever the practical thing,' my friend went on, 'so I told Him, "Sir, You don't even have a bucket, and when our father Jacob dug this well, he dug it deep. He drank from this well himself and so did his sons and livestock, so how are you going to get this living water? Do you think you are greater than our father Jacob?" '

" 'The man told me, "Everyone who drinks from this water will get thirsty again, but whoever drinks from the water that I will give him will never get thirsty again, ever! In fact, the water I will give him will become a well of water springing up within him for eternal life." '

" 'Now, I am not a fool!' my friend looked at me and laughed, 'so I told Him, "Sir, give me some of this water so I won't get thirsty again and have to keep coming here to draw water." '

" ' "Go call your husband," the man told me. "Call him and then come back with him." I looked down at the ground. "I don't have a husband," I whispered.'

" ' "You are right, you don't have a husband. You have had five husbands, and the man you have now is not your husband. You answered correctly," the man said gently.

" 'I looked at him expecting to see condemnation in his eyes, but saw only compassion. "Sir, I see that You are a prophet. Our fathers worshiped on this mountain, yet you Jews say we can only worship God in Jerusalem." I just did not know what to say. I mean, He knew all about me!

" 'Then the man told me, "The time is coming when you will worship the Father in spirit and in truth, and it does not have to be on this mountain or in Jerusalem, but you Samaritans worship what you do not know. We worship what we know, because salvation is from the Jews. But true worship has to be in spirit and truth, because God is spirit, and those who worship HIM must worship in spirit and truth."

" 'His gentle words cut through my ritualistic excuse for worship. I stared at Him and said, "I know that the Taheb, the Messiah, is coming. He is called Christos; when He comes He will reveal everything to us."

" 'His next words floored me. "I Am He, the One speaking to you."

" 'Just then, all these men came back from town. I assume they were His disciples since He was a Rabbi. His words were still burning in my ears: "I AM." But when His disciples noticed that He was talking to me, a Samaritan, and worse yet, a woman, they looked shocked but did not say anything. I just left my water jar and hurried back to town.

" 'I ran to the marketplace and up to the first large group of men standing there talking. "Come see! There is a man over by our well and He told me everything I have ever done! Could He be the Revealer, our Taheb?" '

"She led the large delegation of people from her village back to the well to talk to the man. She explained, 'After listening to Him for awhile, they invited Him into our village to stay with us. To be honest, I don't think any of us thought a Jewish rabbi would ever set foot in one of our villages, but He sure surprised us. By the time He was ready to leave our village, most of the village believed on Him. It was funny, they told me, "Well, you told us about Him, but we believed on Him after we listened to Him ourselves." Oh, I found out His name was Jesus. And I am convinced He really is our Messiah!' my friend told me.

"It was her testimony of Him that caused me to seek Him out in the first place when my daughter was so tormented by that evil spirit. It is one of the reasons why I am convinced we Gentiles are going to have a place with Him, too. Also, do you remember hearing a few years ago that Jesus took a whip and made everyone buying and selling leave the Temple? These were the merchants who had taken over the Court of the Gentiles. Jesus totally cleared them out, leaving the space once again for the Gentiles who were God-fearers to have a place to quietly pray. Why would He give us and allow us a place to pray if we were not going to have a place with HIM?" The wide-eyed women all looked deep in thought.

VII

I always love the Feast days! Of course, they are the busiest days for the Temple, but the crowds come in from all over the land and across the world! Wherever there are Jews living, many of them try to come to the different Feasts. This year's Feast days had been especially busy and hectic as my master insisted I keep up with what the Nazarene was doing and the latest gossip on Him. My master, for some reason, appeared terrified that He would declare Himself king and, thus, bring down the full weight and might of Rome on us. I had heard Him probably as much as anyone except His closest disciples, and I had never heard Him sound like He wanted to be crowned king, but what did I know?

The Feast we were preparing for was Tabernacles or Succoth. It is the festival that reminds us of our forefathers wondering in the desert. Since it happens during our harvest time, it is a time of real celebration, with many people going out and living in little booths to commemorate the wanderings. Because of the harvest, it is a good time to spend out in our fields.

Since the Rabbi almost always came to the Feasts, I had been told to keep an eye out for Him and to report anything I saw. Everywhere I looked, I saw groups of men standing around talking, and it seemed the name on everyone's lips was Jesus. Everyone expected Him to be there, and no one quite knew what He might do this year. The year before, He cleaned out the court of the Gentiles! No one had gotten brave enough to reopen the Temple market again, although I expected them to do so at any time. It was a huge moneymaker for my master. He still had not forgiven or forgotten what the Nazarene had done.

I kept looking out for someone I knew. I would have loved to find out if Jesus was planning on coming. From the Temple courtyard, I would for sure see anyone who arrived, as everyone coming to the Feast stopped first to leave their mandated offering.

I could hardly believe the first people I spotted there. Not that I really knew them, but I had seen them and knew who they were. I still remembered how embarrassed they looked when the Pharisees were calling their brother demon-possessed. Yes, it was Jesus' brothers: James, Joseph, Simon, and Jude. I wondered if they knew when their brother would arrive. I sure would have loved to get their take on the whole thing. They looked so embarrassed and seemed to hate that their brother was so much in the public eye, but was that how they thought all the time or only during that difficult time?

I walked up to them. Smiling, I introduced myself and explained that I had family in the Galilee area and was wondering if they might know them and if they were planning on making it to the Feast this year.

"Who is your family?" James asked.

"Oh, it is James and John. They are the sons of Zebedee, a fisherman on the lake," I answered.

"Yes, we know them." James seemed to hesitate. "We don't know if they are coming this year."

"Might I ask when you last saw them?" I did not wish to appear rude, but I was hoping to get the conversation around to Jesus.

Simon spoke up just then. "We saw them just a day before we came up here. They were with our brother. We asked our brother if He was coming, and it did not sound like He was planning on it."

"I was hoping to hear the Rabbi," I said, wondering how they would respond to this.

"Yes, seems like everyone wants to hear and see the Rabbi. Everyone we see is always asking about Him." Simon shrugged and almost sneered. "We even told Him that He should not be hiding in Galilee but should come to Jerusalem and into Judea. We figured if He was going to be doing so many miracles, He should do them where it would be a big enough and important enough crowd to make a difference. I mean, if He is trying to seek public recognition, He might as well be here in Jerusalem. Right?"

"What did your brother the Rabbi say?" I asked. I was a little surprised at the bitterness I heard in his voice.

"I don't know. So much of what He says, I don't even understand," Simon continued. "But it was something about His time not having come yet. He went on to say that the world doesn't hate us but the world hates Him, because He testifies that its deeds are evil. Then He told us to go on up by ourselves--that

He was not coming up yet as His time had not yet fully come. Anyway," Simon shrugged again, "like I said, I never understand Him." His brothers nodded.

"I thought the people were going to stone Him in Capernaum," Jude told me. "This was right after He had supposedly fed 5,000 men with five little barley loaves and two fish! It was a miracle, they say. The next day or so, everyone wanted to be fed again."

"Well," I said, "I heard about the feeding with the barley loaves. I still can't believe anyone eats barley, but the story, while sounding fantastic, is true. One of your brother's close disciples is a really good friend of mine. His name is Levi — well, it was Levi, until your brother changed his name to Matthew. But anyway, he told me the whole story, and he was right there helping give out the food. He claimed it just would not quit. And that even after everyone was finished eating, he and the other disciples gathered up 12 small baskets, so they got to eat, too."

They all nodded. Jude rolled his eyes and complained, "Yes, we have heard the stories about Him until we are tired to death of the tales. But what happened the other day is the worst I have ever seen people with Him. He basically told them they were only looking and waiting for Him because they wanted to eat again. He scolded them for always thinking about the food that perishes and yet not caring about the food that gives eternal life, which, according to Him, 'the Son of Man will give you.' They came right back with, 'What can we do to perform the works of God?' and He said, 'This is the work of God, that you believe in the one He has sent.' So then they asked for a sign. Not that I agree with my brother, but my goodness, after He fed almost 20,000 people with just five little loaves and two fish, they still want a sign?

"Yet, according to what I heard, they kept demanding He give them manna like Moses did. My brother told them, 'I assure you Moses didn't give you the bread from heaven, but My Father gives you the real bread from heaven. For the bread of God is the One who comes down from heaven and gives life to the world.' Then they said, 'Sir, give us this bread always!' "

"What did your brother say then?" I asked, interested in spite of myself.

"Well, it was not what they wanted to hear, I can tell you that," put in Joseph, the quiet one. "Because He said, 'I am the bread of life. No one who comes to Me will ever be hungry, and no one who believes in Me will ever be thirsty again.' After He said that, you should have heard them! They were furious. From what I heard, they kept saying, 'Isn't this Jesus the son of Joseph, whose father and mother we know? How can He now say, "I have come down from heaven"?' "

Jude shrugged his thin shoulders. "He makes it so hard on Himself! If that was not bad enough, then He went on, 'I assure you: Anyone who believes has eternal life. I am the bread of life. Your fathers ate the manna in the wilderness, and they died. This is the bread that comes down from heaven so that anyone may eat of it and not die. I am the living bread that came down from heaven. If anyone eats of this bread he will live forever. The bread that I will give for the life of the world is My flesh.'

"Then those very strict Jews, sitting there in the synagogue in Capernaum, thought Jesus was telling them they had to be cannibals and eat His flesh. They were shocked and horrified," Jude went on. "It was just terrible."

James shook his head. "As if the crowd were not shocked

enough, my brother said, 'I assure you, unless you eat the flesh of the Son of Man and drink His blood, you do not have life in yourselves. Anyone who eats My flesh and drinks My blood has eternal life, and I will raise him up on the last day, because My flesh is real food and My blood is real drink. The one who eats My flesh and drinks My blood lives in Me, and I in him. Just as the living Father sent Me and I live because of the Father, so the one who feeds on Me will live because of Me. This is the bread that came down from heaven; it is not like the manna your fathers ate—and they died. The one who eats this bread will live forever.'

"That was too much! At His words the crowd turned away in disgust, and even many of His disciples who had been following Him almost since He had started teaching, left Him. His closest disciples said, 'This teaching is hard! Who can accept it?' " James was obviously hurt by the people rejecting his brother.

"I have to tell you, from what I heard," added Simon, "my brother was very hurt by this rejection. He even asked His closest disciples, 'You don't want to go away too, do you?' One of the disciples who has been with Him the longest, a man by the name of Peter, answered, 'Lord, who will we go to? You alone have the words of eternal life. We have come to believe and know that You are the Holy One of God!'

"His reply seemed to cheer my brother up a bit, and He said, 'Didn't I choose you, the Twelve?' But then, He said, frowning, 'Yet one of you is the devil!' " Simon shook his head and scowled, murmuring, "I wish I knew what He meant by 'one of you is the devil.' "

I looked at the four brothers. It was easy to see that they loved their brother and were hurt by the people's response to

Him, but at the same time they were also a bit embarrassed by their own criticisms of Him.

Toward the middle of the week, I was still on duty in the outer court of the Temple. It was almost funny, the longer people were waiting to see and hear Jesus, the more they were talking about Him. In every crowd there were people saying He was a good man and people disagreeing with them, saying He was just deceiving people. Still, it was all very hush-hush, because people were afraid of my master and the other priests. The Temple authority had ordered that no one was to talk about the Rabbi, and the priests and Pharisees were to be notified as soon as He showed up.

Then, when the festival was half over Jesus walked into the Temple. He walked right by me. I happened to turn around and looked straight at Him. His return look pierced me as He walked past me into the Temple complex, and I could not help myself. I should have immediately went and notified my master, but I found myself following Him inside. I listened to Him teach and was once again captivated by His voice. It had such a magical quality about it that made me hang on His every word, but I could not understand a thing He said. I was frustrated when everyone started saying, "He has never been taught the Scriptures, how does He know them so well that He can teach them?"

But Jesus answered, "I am not speaking on My own, everything I teach is from the One who sent Me. If you want to obey God, you need to understand whether My teaching is from God, or if I am only speaking on My own. If I were seeking My own glory I would speak for Myself, but since I seek only the Glory of Him who sent Me, I speak truth and there is no unrighteousness in Me. You are so proud of the fact that Moses gave you the Law, yet none of you bother to keep the Law! Why do you want to kill Me?"

From there it went from bad to worse. The crowd became more and more divided, with many of them saying, "I thought the High Priest and Temple authorities wanted to kill this man and yet, here He is openly teaching in the Temple and they're saying nothing to Him. Can it be true that the authorities know He is the Messiah?" There was so much confusion.

"He can't be the Messiah," others shouted. "We know where this man is from. When the Messiah comes, no one will know where He is from!"

Then Jesus, trying to be heard over the confusion, yelled above the noise of the crowd, "Yes, you think you know Me and where I am from, but you don't really know Me. I did not come on My own, but I was sent here by the True One. You don't know HIM but I know Him, because I was sent here by Him."

Boy, when He said they did not know HIM, they knew exactly Whom He was talking about and they became even more furious. They tried to seize Him, but for some reason they were all afraid to lay a hand on Him. By this time, the confusion had gotten the attention of the Temple priests. The Chief Priest and the Pharisees called the Temple guards and ordered us to arrest Jesus.

VIII

The next morning, before dawn, I was back at my post in the Temple. After the turmoil of the day before, I wondered what would come today. Thankfully, this was the last day of the festival, and I was ready for the tension and turmoil of the Feast days to be behind us. As I was pondering these things, I glimpsed my cousin James come in and look around. He saw me and made his way over.

"Shalom! Boker Tov, James. Good morning," I greeted him. In a lower voice I asked, "Where is your Master?"

"We spent the night on the Mount of Olives," he told me. "Jesus likes to go off by Himself, away from the crowds. I came a little early to make sure there was not a trap set for Him here. Everyone will be here shortly." I had not had a chance to talk with James much for a while, so it was good to be able to catch up on things without worrying too much about many people being around. I knew it was only a matter of time before this courtyard began filling up again. James seemed nervous as well.

Right at first light, I saw Jesus coming in with His disciples, and, just as I knew they would, here came the crowds behind Him. There were many people from the day before who had listened and liked and believed on Him; but I also knew there was a huge crowd who wanted to catch Him and put Him to death if they could get away with it. The Romans had very strict laws against us Jews being able to put anyone to death. My master and the rest of the Sanhedrin would have to be very careful if they did not want to get in trouble with Pontious Pilate, the governor of this region.

The crowd who hated Him had not arrived yet. The masses that swarmed around Him were calm and respectful, and I was fascinated to see how attentive back to them Jesus was. I was still not sure who He was, although I no longer believed He was just a charlatan. To be honest, I no longer knew what I believed about Him. I loved listening to Him talk, but I still didn't understand a single thing He said.

Jesus took a seat not too far from where I was standing. James had left my side and was standing with the group of Jesus' disciples, and the throng of people was both standing and seated around Jesus. Suddenly, there was a commotion near one of the entrances. A big group of men thrust into the area, and they were dragging a young woman. Pushing into the circle of people trying to listen to Jesus, they rudely threw her to the ground at Jesus' feet. He looked up, waiting. I got the impression He knew what was coming.

"Teacher," they said to Him, "this woman was caught in the act of committing adultery. The law of Moses commanded us to stone such women. So what do You say?"

I studied Jesus' face. He glanced at the woman, now standing with her head hanging in shame, tears running down her face. Briefly taking in the men's angry faces, He did not say anything, but stooped down and began writing on the ground with His finger.

I knew what they were doing. It was a trap! Made all the more obvious by the fact they had only brought the woman in. Moses' law actually specified that both parties were to be put to death. If Jesus said to stone her as our Law instructed, He would be in trouble with the Romans, as they had taken away our ability to administer the death penalty. But if He said to let her go, He would be in harsh violation of our Jewish Law. It seemed to me it was a lose-lose situation for the Nazarene. I could not figure out how He could possibly get out of the trap.

While they kept insisting Jesus give an answer, He ignored them. Finally, He stood up and said to them, "The one without sin among you should be the first to throw a stone at her." Then He stooped down again and continued writing on the ground. When they heard this, they left one by one, starting with the older men. Soon only Jesus was left, with the woman in the center. He looked up at the woman standing alone and stood up. He said to her, "Woman, where are they? Has no one condemned you?"

"No one, Lord," she answered.

"Neither do I condemn you," said Jesus. "Go, and from now on, do not sin anymore."

I would have loved to see what He had written there on the ground, but I noticed that Jesus took His sandaled foot and wiped out whatever He had written. Looking at the departing backs of all the men who thought they had a foolproof plan, I could not help but think of a passage from one of our old prophets.

"O Lord, the hope of Israel,
all that forsake thee shall be ashamed,
and they that depart from me shall be written in the dust,
because they have forsaken the Lord, the fountain of
living waters."

So interesting that Jesus had just said He could give an eternal fountain of living waters. Might He be connecting Himself to this verse?

I also thought of the sentence right after this passage and wondered how it might apply to me— but who was I? I had no place with the Rabbi.

"Heal me, O Lord, and I shall be healed;
save me, and I shall be saved: for You are my praise."

Besides, what did I need to be healed from? I was in good health, I had the security of a good job, and I enjoyed my work. My master gave me much responsibility. In comparison to other possible jobs, my job was safe and rewarding. No, I did not need to be healed or saved from anything. Not even sure why this passage came to my mind.

I had thought after the incident with the woman, Jesus would either head out of the Temple complex or at least tone everything down. But since this was the last day and greatest day of the Feast, I guess Jesus did not want to miss it. The tension in the air was palatable, and I knew everyone else was wondering how much longer the Temple authorities were going to put up with Him. No sooner had I thought this when I noticed a crowd gathering by the treasury. I walked over and stood there, listening to Him and waiting for the inevitable clash between Him and the Pharisees and other Jews.

Standing near the place where the offerings were put in, Jesus said, "I am the Light of the world. Anyone who follows Me will never walk in darkness but will have the light of life." I could not help but notice the four large candelabra behind Him as He made this statement. These candelabra are always lit for the last day of Tabernacles, and they stood there with their brilliant light illuminating Jesus. What a perfect stage for this discourse! I thought.

But the Pharisees said to Him, "Enough of Your bragging! Since You are only speaking of Yourself, Your testimony is not admissible!"

Jesus' words back to them were calm. "The Truth is the Truth, and so My testimony is valid since I know where I am from and where I am going, but you don't know anything about Me. You are always judging by your human standards, while I judge no one ..."

For a minute, I thought back to the woman standing there in the courtyard alone, all her accusers leaving in humiliation, and Jesus calmly writing there in the dust at His feet. I don't think I could ever forget the look on His face as He stood to His feet and asked the woman, "Woman, where are they? Has no one condemned you?"

"From now on, do not sin anymore," He had said.

Who is this man? I thought to myself, Who can stand here

and tell the world He judges no one and then tell the woman to go and sin no more? Am I hearing Him right? It almost sounded like He was telling her that He forgave her sins and not to sin anymore. Does He think He has the right to forgive even that kind of sin?

I was jerked back to the present by the crowd's growing restlessness against Jesus. They were almost shouting when they asked Him, "Where is Your Father?"

"You don't know Me or My Father," Jesus answered. "If you really knew Me, you would know My Father."

"Well then, tell us plainly who You are!" they shouted in growing frustration.

"I Am Who I have said I was from the beginning," Jesus told them. "There are many things to say and much to judge against you. I tell the world the things I have heard from the One who sent Me and it is Truth. You won't understand these things until you lift up the Son of Man, then you will know that I am He and that I do nothing on My own. As the Father teaches Me, these are the things I say. The One who sent Me is with Me and He has not left Me alone because I do what pleases Him."

Again, I remembered this man's midnight words to Nicodemus about Moses lifting up the serpent in the wilderness and so would the Son of Man be lifted up. But what did this code mean? Who would do it, and why would they lift Him up? The most common use of the word is to say someone is being crucified. Surely, He was not saying He would be crucified, was He? Maybe He was saying they were going to crown Him king? I couldn't see the Temple authorities, especially my master, ever allowing Him to be crowned king; but on the other hand, only the Romans can crucify someone, and I have never heard Him say anything against Rome.

I watched the crowd as He spoke. It was obvious from their faces that many believed in Him. So Jesus said to these Jews, "If you listen to my words and do the things I say, you really are My disciples. You will know the Truth, and the Truth will set you free."

Boy, this got the Pharisees and other leaders of the Temple furious! One voice raged, "What do You mean, set us free? Our father is Abraham, and we have never been slaves to anyone!"

I had to shake my head at that statement, for surely they knew our history better than I did, and even I knew our fathers served in Egypt for over 400 years. Then we were taken captive by Babylon, just to name another one, and our history is full of times we were taken captive and held as slaves. For the most glaring example, one only had to look up the hill and see the Roman garrison. Not slaves?

But Jesus sadly responded, "Anyone who has ever sinned is a slave to sin. Everyone knows that a slave does not inherit like a son does. But if the Son sets you free you will really be free. You claim to be Abraham's children, but you are trying to kill Me. Abraham never did that, so I say, if you were really Abraham's children you would do what he did, but you don't. You are acting like your real father!"

"We weren't born of sexual immorality! Our father is Abraham!" they shouted. "We have one father! God!"

Uh oh, I thought, here it comes. I remembered Nicodemus had talked of the scandal when Jesus was born. How His mother was pregnant out of wedlock and yet, Mary, His mother, had said the baby was supernaturally conceived and she was still a virgin. I recalled how they were shocked that Joseph still married her. I also remembered Zechariah thinking and believing it was the fulfillment of an old prophecy that a virgin would conceive. After talking to Nicodemus, I was sure he believed in Jesus' supernatural conception as well. But I wondered how Jesus would answer this accusation.

Jesus said to them, "If God were really your Father, you would love Me, because I am not here on My own but because He sent me. You really don't hear what I say nor understand Me, because you are of your father the devil, and you want to do what he wants you to do. That is why you want to kill Me. Your father the devil was a murderer and a liar from the beginning. He kills and lies because it is his nature to do so. I tell the truth, and you refuse to believe Me, which proves to Me you don't know or listen to God. If you knew God, you would believe Me. So who among you can convict Me of sin?"

Things were really getting tense. I did not know which way it would go right then, but the best the Jews could come up with was name calling. "You're just a Samaritan and have a demon," they yelled. Looking around, I could tell from the faces of most of the people watching that Jesus was getting the best of them.

"No, I do not have a demon. But rather, everything I do, I do to honor My Father and give all glory to Him. I seek His glory, and He is the One who judges. But let Me tell you, if anyone keeps My word, he will never die. Never!"

"Ha!" the Jews sneered. "Now we are sure You are demon-possessed! Abraham died and so did all the prophets, and You are going to try and tell us that if anyone keeps Your word they will never die? Ever? Do You think You are greater than our father Abraham and the prophets who all died? Who do you think You are?"

"You say God is your God. I say He is My Father. If I tried to glorify Myself, it would be nothing. He is the One who glorifies Me. If you knew Him, you would know Me, but you have never known God. I know Him and keep His word, and your father Abraham was overjoyed to see My day. He saw it and was glad."

They all laughed raucously. "Ha! You are not even 50 years old and you've seen Abraham?"

"I assure you," Jesus said to them, "before Abraham was, I AM!"

Everything got confusing. People began looking for rocks to use to stone Jesus, because He dared to use the sacred name of God for Himself. There was no doubt He was declaring He Himself was God, not just God's representative. The crowd was furious.

I did not know what to think. I remembered when, two years ago, I had joined in a different attempt to kill Him. How was it different now? I heard Him say God's name, but I could not work up any anger. I knew my master would just as soon have a mob kill him as anything. It would sure make it easier on him and the rest of the Temple authorities, but could I stand here and allow the mob to stone him? Could I even stop them? My mind raced frantically.

All of a sudden, I realized Jesus was gone! Where had He gone? The mob also noticed He had disappeared into the crowd. They milled around, everyone asking his neighbor where He had gone. But Jesus was hidden somewhere, and went out of the temple complex.

I was standing there thinking about all that had just happened and wondering how I was going to word my report to my master, when suddenly Jesus' words came back to me and hit me between the eyes. I was shocked to realize He could have said those exact words to me. I went back over them in my mind.

"You really don't hear what I say nor understand Me because you are of your father the devil, and you want to do what he wants you to do. That is why you want to kill Me." I took a deep breath and went off to give my report. This job was getting harder and harder. I wondered where it would end.

My master was frantic with anger and frustration over the Nazarene escaping. He listened in silence, but I could tell from his face that my report did not please him.

"Why was He not arrested? How could all you guards allow Him to escape?" he finally demanded. I did not know what to say.

"Master," I began but stopped. "Master," I said again, "The Temple complex is so jammed with people that somehow He was just gone. I was right there, but He disappeared into the crowd and was somehow able to leave the Temple."

Later on, by myself, I thought about what I had heard the Nazarene say. I knew I always misunderstood Him. It was like I didn't even hear Him, according to my cousins and Levi. But this time, I think I was listening. He first called Himself the Light of the world, then He gave a promise that those who followed Him would never walk in darkness. Then He said the Truth would set them free. And the way He worded it, it was as if He personally was Truth, and He would set them free. Then He said they would never die. How could any sane person say someone will never die, when one of the unalterable facts of life is that we all die? I guess I still did not hear Him correctly.

We were ordered to arrest Jesus, but we decided we could not do it during my master's most important day for this Feast week. I don't know when this ritual started, but as far as I know it has been going on, for hundreds of years. On the last day of the Feast of Tabernacles, my master, the High Priest, leads a procession from the Temple down to the pool of Siloam. With the crowd softly singing a psalm, he dipped a purified golden pitcher into the pool, filling it with water, and he will slowly raise it high. Then, with the crowd chanting from our book of Songs, the psalm that says, "Save now, we beseech Thee, O Jehovah," the High Priest leads the procession back up the mountain to the Temple.

Accompanied by blasts of trumpets, they enter through the water gate, into the Court of the Priests. Even though initially it is cool, as it is the fall season, while climbing back up that ridge to the Temple it gets hot. When the crowd finally makes it back to the Temple, footsore, tired, sweating, and thirsty from the long, hard climb, the High Priest holds his golden pitcher high and pours out the water on the ground. This reminds us of Moses hitting the rock in the wilderness and God providing water for His people. As the High Priest pours out the water, he will proclaim a passage as a blessing, from our prophet Isaiah, "With joy you will draw water from the well of salvation."

So today, on this last day (sometimes called the Great day) of the Festival, with the water droplets still splashing on the pavement, from the back of the crowd Jesus stood up on something so everyone could see Him. He cried out, "If anyone is thirsty, he should come to Me and drink! The one who believes in Me, as the Scripture has said, will have streams of living water flow from deep within him."

The crowd went crazy! Many were saying He was "the Prophet" and others proclaimed, "This is the Messiah!" But still others said, "He can't be the Messiah, because the Messiah does not come from Galilee, but from Bethlehem. Doesn't the Scripture say that the Messiah comes from David's offspring and from the town of Bethlehem, where David once lived?" The priests were trying to get the crowd to seize Him, but no one laid a hand on Him.

Finally the Temple authorities called for us to give a report. "Why have you not arrested Him?" they demanded.

I was on duty and leading the detachment, and all I could say was the first thing that came into my head. "We have never heard anyone speak like He does!"

The Pharisees in charge were furious. "Are you fooled, too? You don't see any of us believing on Him do you? You should know better than to be deceived; you can't follow this accursed crowd. Of course they are going to be misled; they don't know the Law!"

I was surprised to hear Nicodemus, my old friend and mentor, take up for us and the Nazarene. "Our Law doesn't judge a man before it hears from him and knows what he's doing, does it?" he asked softly.

I felt badly for Nicodemus, because he was my friend and had taken up for us guards and because he took all the pent-up fury of the chief priests and other temple authorities.

"You aren't from Galilee, too, are you?" they shouted. "Investigate and you will see that no prophet arises from Galilee." But thankfully Nicodemus was such a figure in the Sanhedrin that no one really wanted to oppose him, so each one went to his house.

Later on, while walking with Nicodemus to his home, I could not help but ask him about what I had heard the Nazarene say. "Master," I said, "what did He mean when He said 'If anyone is thirsty, he should come to Me and drink! The one who believes in Me, as the Scripture has said, will have streams of living water flow from deep within him.' What can He mean by this? Streams of living water? Never thirsting again?" Nicodemus stopped and peered at my confused face.

"Oh, I have to tell you," I added, "I overheard a conversation where a lady was saying that Jesus said basically the same thing about never thirsting again to a Samaritan woman. I have been wondering about it ever since I heard that. I honestly never understand a thing that man says. And I try. I do have ears. I do listen, but I don't understand Him."

Nicodemus was silent for a minute as we walked down the crowed street. Finally he said, "Well, remember, we are celebrating the Feast of Tabernacles, which commemorates the children of Israel's wandering in the desert. Remember Moses struck the rock to give them water. I think He is saying that as Moses struck the stone in the desert and gave the people water to drink, He is going to provide everlasting water. If I am reading the old prophets right, I am afraid He is going to be struck, like Moses struck the rock, but I don't really know how yet. I get a picture in my mind, and He did say as Moses lifted up the serpent in the wilderness ..." his voice trailed off. "Anyway," Nicodemus went on, "I am pretty sure this is what many of them were thinking—about Moses providing water in the desert—when they were calling Him 'the Prophet.' "

"Master, I hesitate to bother you with more questions, but something I hear Him say bothers me because I don't understand what the term means," I went on in a hurry while I had the old man's ear." I mean, I hear Jesus call Himself the 'Son of Man' all the time. It almost seems like it is His favorite name for Himself. But aren't we all sons of men? What can He possibly mean by using this term for Himself?"

Nicodemus was quiet for a bit as he pondered his reply. I was starting to worry that Nicodemus might think he couldn't trust me. I knew he knew whom I worked for, but I had always tried to show him that our conversations were confidential. My master and the other priests at the Temple had made such an issue of the Nazarene, and people had already been thrown out of the Temple and synagogues because of Him, so everyone was nervous about being too openly in favor of Him. I was almost ready to mention our confidentiality to him when he started to talk. I was glad to hear he had just been thinking of my question and not whether or not I could be trusted.

But Nicodemus cleared his throat. "That is a great question, Malchus! I was trying to recall a passage I read after a conversation I had with Him. Remember, we went to visit Him that night a while back. During that visit, He referred to Himself as the 'Son of Man.' I knew I had read this term in different passages from our prophets, so I searched until I found one of them. It is from our prophet Daniel. In his scroll, he wrote this:.

'I saw in the night, visions.
And behold, One like the Son of Man,
Coming with the clouds of heaven!
He came to the Ancient of Days,
And they brought Him near before Him.
Then to Him was given dominion and glory and a

kingdom,
That all peoples, nations, and languages should serve
Him.
His dominion is an everlasting dominion,
Which shall not pass away,
And His kingdom the one
Which shall not be destroyed.'

"So in this passage, a passage we ascribe to our Messiah, clearly the term 'Son of Man' is showing Jesus' divinity. I don't see how you can take it any other way. And you are right. Jesus uses this term for Himself more than any other. He is asserting His divinity when He does so, and your master and everyone else knows it. They refuse to accept His claims."

"Who do you think He is, master?" I asked quietly.

Nicodemus turned to look at me. "I am convinced in my heart He is the Messiah. The Christ. Our long-awaited Promise!"

"Malchus, my boy, I am glad you were there today," Nicodemus went on. "I am saddened by the blindness of our High Priest and the rest there in the Temple. By the way, I don't know if you know it, but their comment about no prophet coming from Galilee is not true. The old-time prophets did say He was going to be called a Nazarene, although we know He was born in Bethlehem. Beth lehem, the house of bread. Interesting that Jesus refers to Himself as the Bread of Life. But about Galilee, the prophet Isaiah spoke of Him long ago in a passage that we all know to be describing our Messiah. He said:

'The land of Zebulun and the land of Naphtali,
By the way of the sea, beyond the Jordan,

Galilee of the Gentiles:
The people who sat in darkness have seen a great light,
And upon those who sat in the region and shadow of
    death
Light has dawned.'

"Never get so blinded, my boy, that you think you know it all. My esteemed colleagues study so hard, and yet they are blind. They were wrong about another prophet, too. The prophet Jonah was from Galilee. They only show their own ignorance when they are so blind."

We walked on in silence. I was thinking about all I had seen and heard that day, and then I thought of Nicodemus standing up for the Nazarene. I did not know the old man had that much spunk. From what I saw, he had really taken the fire out of everyone else, probably saving me and the other Temple guards. If left unchecked, my master had a terrible temper!

Then I thought of something else. Ever since I had heard someone refer to Jesus as the Nazarene, I had used it as a term of derision. But now, according to Nicodemus, our old prophets had said He would be called a Nazarene. I shook my head and grinned in spite of myself. Funny, I thought I was making fun of Him, but I was fulfilling prophecy!

IX

Nothing seemed real anymore! I had heard so much of and studied and reported on the Nazarene's miracles, but I had never personally seen one. All my information was second-hand up to this point. I just had no idea of how the man really worked.

So the day after the Feast was really something. I was still trying to process all I saw and heard. Here is what happened: after the feast of Tabernacles was over, the Temple authorities, especially the Sadducees (the sect of which my master is Chief Priest of the Temple), basically decided that the Nazarene had to go. They were not sure how yet, but He had to disappear. There was no turning back. Because of this decision, I had been sent to shadow the Nazarene and keep track of everything He did, who He saw, who He talked to, and anything else I could add. As I said earlier, this particular day was unreal!

I was in the crowd trying to not be noticed by His disciples who knew me—my cousins James and John, my good friend

Levi, and Nathanael, who was in the crowd most of the time. As Jesus was walking along, we saw a man blind from birth. His disciples questioned Him: "Rabbi, why was this man born blind? Was it because of some sin committed by his parents, or was it possibly for some sin he himself was going to do?"

I was surprised at Jesus' answer, as I knew for a fact what my master and any of the other Pharisees or teachers of the Law would have said. They would have declared the parents guilty and probably the blind man as well. But Jesus stared at the man, deep in thought, and said, "No, it was not him or his parents who sinned. This happened to him so that God's power and might would be displayed in him. This is one of the works My Father sent us to do. We must work while it is day. Night is coming when no one can work. As long as I am here, it is light, as I am the Light of the world."

But what shocked me the most was Jesus then spit on the ground. Mixing a little mud out of the dust in the road with His spittle, He took the mud and spread it on the blind man's eyes.

Watching the man's face was such an experience. First, when he heard the commotion around him, I am sure he thought they were going to give him some kind of alms. He had his hand stretched out to receive it. Then, when he felt the wet slimy mud on his eyes, a look of fright crossed his face. Jesus was speaking gently to him, and I could not hear what He said, but the man calmed down. Then, Jesus said louder, "Go wash in the pool of Siloam."

The man stumbled off with the hesitant steps of the blind, and I missed the next part, as I continued walking on with Jesus. But I heard he did as he was directed. He washed, and from what I was told, came back seeing. Everyone who had formerly seen him as a beggar and others who knew him were shocked to see him not blind. They said, "Isn't this the man who sat begging?" Some said, "He's the one." But others kept insisting, "No, he only looks like the blind man. You can see for yourself this man is not blind! He just looks like him."

The once blind man kept saying, "I'm the one! It is really me."

So they asked him, "Then how were your eyes opened?"

He answered, "The man called Jesus made mud, spread it on my eyes, and told me, 'Go to Siloam and wash.' So when I went and washed I received my sight."

"Where is He?" they asked.

"I don't know," he said.

I had seen someone I knew from the Temple standing with a group of Pharisees talking and had briefly left the crowd following Jesus to visit them. While I was there, they brought the once-blind man to the Pharisees. Oh boy, I thought, because from my knowledge of the Pharisees, I knew what this was going to be about. They would be much more interested in the fact that Jesus had the nerve to spit on the Sabbath than that He had healed a man. I was not disappointed. One of the oral laws for the Sabbath forbids the act of spitting, since, if you spit, your spit might roll in the dust and make mud, thus doing work. Which we all knew was forbidden. So the Pharisees asked him how he received his sight.

"He put mud on my eyes," the man explained. "I washed, and I can see."

Hearing that, some of the Pharisees immediately said, "This man is not from God, for He doesn't keep the Sabbath!" But others were saying, "How can a sinful man perform such signs?"

And there was a division among them.

Again they asked the blind man, "What do you say about Him, since He opened your eyes?"

"He's a prophet," he said.

The Jews, figuring the whole thing was an elaborate hoax, refused to believe that he had even been blind, so they summoned the parents of the one who had received his sight.

They asked them, "Is this your son, the one you say was born blind? If he was born blind, how was he healed?"

"We know this is our son and that he was born blind," his parents answered. "But we don't know how he was healed, and we don't know who opened his eyes. Ask him; he's of age. He will speak for himself." They were obviously afraid to say anything else, afraid of the Jews, since the Jews had already agreed if anyone confessed Him as Messiah, they would be banned from the synagogue. So the only thing his parents could safely say was, "He's of age; ask him."

A second time they summoned the man who had been blind and told him, "Give glory to God by telling the truth. We know that this man is a sinner!"

He answered, "Whether or not He's a sinner, I don't know. One thing I do know: I was blind, and now I can see!"

Then they asked him, "What did He do to you? How did He open your eyes?"

The poor guy rolled his now-cured eyes in frustration, and I also caught the glint of amusement in them as he sarcastically answered, "I have repeatedly told you, and you didn't listen. I am not going to change my story. Why do you want to hear it again? You don't want to become His disciples too, do you?"

Then they ridiculed him. "You're that man's disciple, but

we're Moses' disciples. We know that God has spoken to Moses. But this man—we don't know where He's from!"

"This is an amazing thing," the man told them. "You don't know where He is from, yet He opened my eyes! We know that God doesn't listen to sinners, but if anyone is God-fearing and does His will, He listens to him. Throughout history no one has ever heard of someone opening the eyes of a person born blind. If this man were not from God, He wouldn't be able to do anything."

"You were born entirely in sin and now, you would teach us?" they screamed. Then they threw him out of the Temple.

Well, that did not take long! I thought to myself. I knew they would say he was blind because of his parents' sin! Still shaking my head at their stubbornness, I walked on up the road to rejoin the crowd following Jesus. Someone had already told Him the man had been kicked out of the synagogue by the time I returned. As we slowly walked along, Jesus kept glancing up each alley and byway that we passed. Finally, He spotted the person He was obviously looking for and changed direction to walk up to the man He had healed. I was glad the man was healed, don't get me wrong, but getting kicked out of the synagogue and Temple really meant you were excluded from every facet of our Jewish life. This man would be a social outcast for the rest of his life. Well, he didn't have much of a social life anyway, I consoled myself.

Jesus asked him, "Do you believe in the Son of Man?"

"Who is He, Sir, that I may believe in Him?" he asked.

Jesus answered, "You have seen Him; in fact, He is the One speaking with you."

"I believe, Lord!" he said, and he worshiped Him.

Jesus said, "I came into this world for judgment, in order that those who do not see will see and those who do see will become blind."

For me, as I was listening to Jesus, I thought He was contradicting Himself at first. In the last couple of days, I'd heard Him say a number of times, "I have not come to judge the world." So now, when I heard, "I came into this world for judgment," it confused me. But then, I reflected on all He had said about being the Light, and they that walk in the light won't stumble and then healing the blind man, which was in essence giving him light. For the first time, I might have understood the Nazarene. He was using the word judgment in the sense of being a revealer. So, He, as the light, revealed all things.

When the Pharisees who were with Him heard Him say all who do see will become blind, they bristled with anger. "We aren't 'blind' too, are we?" they demanded.

"If you were blind," Jesus told them, "you wouldn't have sin. But now that you say, 'We see'—your sin remains."

Well, maybe I spoke too soon about understanding Him. Because, as much as I thought about what He answered to the Pharisees, I had no idea what He was talking about.

One thing did come to me later on while I was thinking about the blind guy Jesus had healed. I remembered the man who had lain by the pool for 38 years. While I am not positive how old the blind guy was, by his looks I would say he was between the age of 35 and 40 years old. He might be about 38 years old, and he was blind from birth. I pictured both men of about the same age, invalid from birth, then healed by Jesus. Both men were healed on the Sabbath, and both men were scolded (or worse) by the Pharisees. Both were later found by Jesus and talked to. I consid-

ered each man. The lame man: Jesus found him and introduced
Himself. The lame man rushed off to tell the Pharisees Jesus'
name. The man who was born blind fell down and worshiped Jesus as soon as he learned His name. The difference was striking.

———————————

The days were so hectic with reports and rumors coming
into the Temple at all hours. My master and the rest of the Temple authority were practically beside themselves not knowing
how to handle the Nazarene. The only ones who seemed to have
settled the matter were Nicodemus and Joseph of Arimathea. I
hadn't had time to talk with either of them lately, but it seemed
like they had a totally different view of the man Jesus and His
role in Scripture. Now, I'm not saying that I believed them, but
I knew one thing: of the two different sections, they sure seemed
calmer and at peace with the whole thing. Not that they are not
worried. The last time I talked with Nicodemus, he told me he
had a report from one of the many disciples that Jesus sat down
and talked to them at length about what was coming. According
to Nicodemus, Jesus told His group of men that He was going to
be arrested and killed, but would rise again. Nicodemus seemed
to think this was what Jesus meant by saying He was going to be
lifted up. But I didn't understand how someone could predict
his own death and why He would want to anyway? All I knew
was my master was in a terrible mood all the time, and all the
priests did was plan one trap after another to try and take out
the Nazarene.

It had been a couple of months since they tried to trap Him
with the woman in adultery, and I didn't think any of the high-

er-ups had gotten over the anger and humiliation they suffered at Jesus' hands. They had been waiting with anticipation for this Festival of Dedication that was starting. I was on my way over to the part of the Temple known as Solomon's Colonnade because my master was told Jesus was over there. Sure enough, I could already see the crowd that gathered as soon as He arrived anywhere.

Just as I walked up, one of the Pharisees asked Him, "How long are You going to keep us in suspense? If You are the Messiah, tell us plainly."

"I did tell you, and you refuse to believe me," Jesus answered them. "Everything I do, I do in My Father's name, and My works testify about Him. But you refuse to believe because you are not one of My sheep."

My mind went back to a conversation I had had with James, my cousin. He was telling me all the things Jesus said He was. Let's see, according to James, Jesus said HE was the Way, Life, Truth, the Door, Bread from Heaven, and I forget what else. It just seemed funny to me that these men who followed every little thing the Nazarene did to break it down, tear it apart, and then ask for more signs demanded that Jesus tell them "plainly" if He was the Messiah. Come on, I had not seen or heard of all His miracles, but my goodness, turning the water to wine, feeding all those people more than once, walking on the water and healing the lame, the blind, the ones sick with leprosy, the demon-possessed, even bringing back to life Jairus' daughter and the widow's son on the way to Nain ... Surely if they wanted to believe, He had more than demonstrated enough to go on.

Right along with what I was thinking, Jesus said, "My sheep hear My voice. They obey Me and follow Me. My Father has given them to Me, and no one will ever be able to take them out of My hands. I give them eternal life, and they are Mine forever. My Father and I are one."

But when He said, "My Father and I are one," that is all they needed to hear. They picked up stones to stone Him.

Jesus asked them, "I have shown you many good works from the Father. Which of these works are you stoning Me for?"

"We aren't stoning You for a good work," the Jews answered, "but for blasphemy, because You—being a man—make Yourself God."

Jesus answered them, "Do you say, 'You are blaspheming' to the One the Father set apart and sent into the world, because I said I am the Son of God? If I am not doing My Father's works, don't believe Me. But if I am doing them and you don't believe Me, believe the works. This way you will know and understand that the Father is in Me and I in the Father."

It was actually quite amazing how Jesus could push a crowd until they were just frantic enough to kill Him; then, He knew exactly when to cut it short and melt into the crowd. I was watching Him closer this time as He pushed them to the point of blind rage. They rushed around picking up stones, then turned around and He was gone.

I heard later He left Jerusalem and went across the Jordan. Seemed He was not even welcome anymore in Galilee. I heard they tried to kill Him there as well. So He went across the Jordan, interestingly enough, back to the area where I had first seen Him when John baptized Him. I heard He stayed there for a while. Someone told me that many people went to Him there and were saying, "Listen, we heard the prophet John, and while he never did any miracles, everything he said about Jesus is true." The guy telling me said, "Many people believed on Him over there." I just didn't have the heart to tell my master this. I had never seen him so upset.

X

Once again, I was chasing Jesus. My master had a delegation in from Bethany, just a few miles up the road. There was some wild story that a man there had been dead for over four days when the Nazarene raised him back to life.

Now my master was swearing he would have Jesus killed. As a matter of fact, he was so angry that even if Jesus did raise the man from the dead, my master was liable to kill him again to get rid of the bother of answering questions. But man, was he ever angry! He wanted me to go find out what really happened, if anything. There were so many stories running around about healings, feeding people, calming storms—I couldn't keep anything straight anymore. What was really concerning my master were the rumors the people were going to make Him king! My master was afraid the Romans would get wind of this, and the Temple and its priests would be the ones to take the blame and fall.

Someone mentioned that the Nazarene was in a small village

called "Bethany beyond the Jordan," about 20 miles away (not to be confused with the Bethany right here close to Jerusalem), so I was heading there to see if I could find James, John, or Levi to help me with this story. I would have loved to find Nathanael. We really hit it off well, and I did not have any background with him, so he was so easy to talk with. I never felt I had to worry about offending him because I did not, as they would say it, "believe on Him."

By this time, I was almost to the outskirts of the closer Bethany, and I couldn't believe it! Here came Nathanael toward me on the road from Galilee! I could not contain my excitement at seeing him and was happy to see he also recognized me. We again fell into step, and I waited to see if he would volunteer the information about what he was doing way up here, away from his normal stomping grounds.

"I am surprised to see you, my friend," he began. "Where are you headed this fine spring morning? I figured this close to Passover your master would have you so busy you would not come out into the sunlight for a few more weeks yet!"

"I am heading over to Bethany over the Jordan," I told him. "Let's walk together, I have some things to ask you." My friend nodded, and we continued on together.

"What would you ask? I hope I can answer your question," he said with a smile.

I kept walking, trying to think of the best way to word my question. "I am assuming you still believe the Nazarene is the Messiah," I started. He flashed a smile and nodded. "Well, I heard a few days ago—in this very town, as a matter of fact—people are saying he brought a dead man back to life. Not just a dead man either: a man who had already been in his tomb for four days!"

"Yes! That is true! You are talking about Lazarus!" Nathanael exclaimed. "You won't believe this, but I am on my way to the house of Simon the Leper. He is hosting a party for Jesus and Lazarus. He lives next door to Lazarus and his sisters, so I am assuming he volunteered his house; it is so much bigger and can serve more people. Plus, I think he is related to Lazarus and his sisters somehow, I forget the details. Anyway, his sisters are giving a party for Lazarus and Jesus and all his close friends have been invited." I just stared at him. "Come walk on with me until we get there, and I will tell you all about it."

"Why would you go to the house of a leper?" I asked, shocked.

Nathanael smiled. "Jesus healed him. He is not sick now! Getting back to Lazarus, he is from this town. He was so very sick and his sisters, Mary and Martha, sent messengers to Jesus, saying, 'Lord, Your best friend is sick, and we are really worried.' According to what John told me, when Jesus heard that, He said, 'This sickness is not serious. This is for God's glory and to bring glory to Me.'

"Everyone was shocked at Jesus' lack of concern, because they all knew how much Jesus loved Lazarus and his two sisters. He always enjoyed spending time with them in their house, and they always made Him feel welcome. But He stayed two more days in the place He and His disciples were staying, actually in Bethany over the Jordan, where you are headed now.

"But then, after two days, He said to His disciples, 'Let's go back across into Judea.'

"When His disciples heard Him say that, they reminded Him, 'Master, don't You remember the Jews tried to stone You the last time we were over there?'

"Jesus answered, 'We have 12 hours in each day. If you walk during the daylight hours you won't trip and fall, because you can see where you are going. If you try to walk at night, it is easy to trip and fall, because you can't see where you are going.' They looked at Him blankly and then Jesus said, 'Our friend Lazarus is sleeping. I need to go and awake him.'

"So then His disciples said, 'Lord, if he is asleep, it must mean he is getting better.' By this time, they knew Him well enough not to question how He might know that Lazarus was asleep," Nathanael grinned at me.

"They misunderstood Jesus. They thought when He said Lazarus was sleeping that he was resting, but then Jesus spoke to them plainly. 'Lazarus is dead. And, to be honest, I am glad for your sakes that I was not there, so that you can really believe; but now, let us go to him.' Then Thomas said to the other disciples, 'Well, let's go with Him, at least He won't have to die by Himself.'

"When Jesus was still on the outskirts of Bethany, He got word that Lazarus had already died and been buried four days earlier. Bethany is so close to Jerusalem, and Lazarus was so well-known, that many people came for his funeral and were still there mourning with Mary and Martha. Not wanting to deal with a crowd right then, Jesus stopped and asked someone to run ahead and tell Martha and Mary that we would be there soon. When Martha heard that Jesus was close, she hurried down the road to meet Him. I am sure her words had to hurt Jesus, because the first thing she said to Him was, 'Lord, if You would have been here, my brother would not have died.' She had a hard time keeping the bitterness out of her voice. But she quickly added,

'But I know, that even now, whatever You ask of God, God will give it to You.'

"Jesus looking deep into her eyes and said, 'Your brother will rise again, Martha.' Martha, possibly realizing she had hurt Jesus, lowered her eyes and said, 'I know that he will rise again in the resurrection at the last day.'

"I got my story from John. Hey, he is your cousin right?" I nodded, eager for Nathanael to go on with his story.

"John told me that Jesus' next words sent goosebumps all over him. He said they were some of the most powerful words he had ever heard Jesus utter." Nathanael stopped, a glint of a laugh in his eyes.

"Okay, okay, what did He say? Come on, Nathanael!"

Nathanael smiled, "Wait, I want to make sure I get it exactly like John told me. Here is what Jesus said. 'I am the Resurrection and the Life: he that believes in Me, even though he were dead, yet shall he live: And who ever lives and believes in Me shall never die. Do you believe this?'

"Martha nodded with tears running down her cheeks, 'Yes, Lord: I believe that You are the Christ, the Son of God, which should come into the world!'

"After saying this, she sent someone to call Mary, her sister, secretly, saying, 'The Master is come and is asking for you.' As soon as Mary heard that, she got up quickly and ran out of the house.

"Jesus had not actually gotten into town yet, but was still where Martha had talked with Him. When the mourners in the house with Mary saw her get up and hurriedly leave the house, they followed her, saying, 'She is going to the tomb to mourn. Come, let's go with her to comfort her.' When Mary saw Jesus, she ran and fell at His feet sobbing, and said. 'Lord, if You would have been here, my brother would not have died.' When Jesus saw her weeping and the Jews who had come with her wailing, He was overcome with grief Himself and asked, 'Where have you laid him?'

" 'Lord, come and see,' someone answered, and the crowd started heading over to where their family tomb was located.

"John told me that he was watching Jesus, because he knew He was going to do something. By this time, they had seen Him do so much that John had no doubt Jesus was going to do something big. But he could not figure out why Jesus was so sad. He told me he actually watched a tear slide down Jesus' face," Nathanael continued. "John said he heard different ones in the crowd of mourners with Mary and Martha say, 'Look, He really must have loved him, the Rabbi is crying.' But others said, 'You would have thought anyone who could open the eyes of the blind could have kept His friend alive.'

"They brought Jesus to the tomb. It was a cave, and a stone blocked the entrance. Jesus was visibly shaken, according to John and the other disciples who told me the story," Nathanael went on. "Jesus said, 'Take away the stone.' Mary and Martha were standing beside Him and were trying to comfort Him, but Martha said to Him, 'Lord, it has been four days, the smell is going to be terrible.' But Jesus said to her, 'Didn't I tell you that if you believed you would see the glory of God?'

"At a motion from the sisters, some guys ran up and began pushing the stone away from the mouth of the cave. People started moving back a little, not sure what was going to happen. Jesus looked up to heaven and said, 'Father, I thank You that You hear Me. And I know that You always hear Me: but because of everyone standing here, I said it, that they may believe that You have sent Me.'

Nathanael paused for effect. "What?" I demanded.

"According to all the disciples, it was incredible! They said Jesus yelled out at the top of His voice, 'Lazarus, come here!'" Nathanael lowered his voice. "You will not believe this, but the dead man came out of the tomb. He was bound hand and foot with grave clothes and his face was bound about with a napkin. Jesus said to Mary and Martha, who were standing there wide-eyed and speechless, 'Loose him and take him home.'

"Malchus, it was literally amazing! John told me that even they who had watched Jesus do so many miracles were speechless. He also said that a lot of the Jews who had gone to the gravesite with them believed on Jesus as the Messiah after that. But you know ..." he trailed off, his face saddened. "In spite of watching someone being dead for four days be brought back to life, some people still did not believe. But they could not wait to run to the Pharisees and tell them what had happened."

I could have clued Nathanael in on that, because the only reason I was on my fact-finding mission was because after the Jews had brought the report to my master, he summoned the whole council of chief priests and the Pharisees. I was not in the meeting, but they were so loud, it was not hard to hear what they were saying. I decided to tell Nathanael a bit. I figured I owed him that much. I also thought maybe he could warn Jesus. I still did not trust the Nazarene, but as far as I could see, I had not seen Him do anything deserving a death sentence.

"Nathanael?" I spoke slowly. "I could not help but overhear my master and the council debating what to do about this Nazarene. Things have reached the boiling point. If you have any input at all with Him, you had better tell Him to stay away from Jerusalem. They are plotting to kill Him."

Nathanael's eyes opened in alarm, but then he slowly shook his head indicating he had no input on what Jesus did. "Malchus, Jesus is going to Jerusalem. I don't think anyone can stop Him. I don't think he would even listen to Peter or John."

I went on, "I wish He would listen to someone. They are frantic because He does so many miracles and everyone is believing on Him. They have even received reports that people want to make Him king. When that happens, they know the Romans will come and take away their places of power and the Temple. I even heard my master say it was better that one man die instead of taking down the entire nation. I have to tell you, Nathanael. He almost sounded prophetic. If I were you, I would take this very seriously. They are planning to kill Him!"

We had stopped before a nice house. Nathanael looked at me. "Malchus, come on in. This is the house of Simon the leper. As I mentioned, Jesus healed him, and now he is allowing Martha and Mary to use his house to give a banquet in honor of both Jesus and Lazarus. You are John and James' cousin and good friends with Levi—I mean, Matthew. So come on in. There are going to be so many people here no one will even notice one more."

To be polite, I acted like I had to go on; but at my friend's insistence, I followed him into the yard and then on into the house, figuring I could hang in the back and no one would notice me.

I could not believe the spread. The meal was almost ready to be served and the guests were, for the most part, already reclining around the table. Nathanael and I took places and set down. I found myself staring at Jesus. I had seen Him many times, but

I had never had an opportunity just to study Him. He appeared relaxed and happy in this quiet home. I assumed the man reclining next to Him must be Lazarus. Hey, I thought, it is not often one has a "raising from the dead" party!

My cousin John sat on the other side of Jesus, and he looked like he was enjoying the party. Neither James nor John had seen me yet, and I was hoping to stay in the background. I inferred the lady serving the meal must be a sister, and Nathanael leaned over and confirmed that it was the older sister, Martha, who was serving.

I wondered where the younger sister, Mary, was, but did not have to speculate too long. A young, beautiful woman came into the room and walked directly to Jesus. From the look on everyone's faces, it was clear that no one knew what she was going to do. She took a bottle of fragrant oil (it looked to be about a one pound bottle), broke the beautiful bottle, and poured it first on Jesus's head. And then she poured the rest of that expensive perfume on His feet. She let down her long, dark hair and wiped His feet dry with her hair. The entire house was filled with the fragrance of the oil. From the fragrance, it was obvious to all that it was a pure and very expensive nard. I looked at the beautiful broken bottle. She had broken it on purpose, signifying that after this she would never want to use it for any other purpose. The woman had tears in her eyes.

Then, just up the table from me, a man spoke up with a whining voice that seemed totally out of place in this loving atmosphere. "Why wasn't this fragrant oil sold for 300 denarii, and that money given to the poor?" he grumbled.

Nathanael leaned over and whispered, "That is Judas Iscariot. He is always worried about money."

Jesus answered, "Leave her alone; she has kept it for the day of My burial. You always have the poor with you, but you do not always have Me. She has done what she could; she has anointed My body in advance for burial. I assure you: Wherever the gospel is proclaimed in the whole world, what this woman has done will also be told in memory of her."

Everyone was staring, and all talk at the tables died down as everyone thought about what Jesus had said. The quiet, joyful mood at the table was gone. Judas looked down, obviously embarrassed at the rebuke he had received from Jesus. Not wanting to stare, I turned my face away, but not before I had seen Judas' face burn red with embarrassment. I was sure I had also caught the glint of anger in his eyes. I thought to myself that this man would bear watching.

Suddenly, Levi noticed me. He rushed over and hugged me. He was so exuberant it was easy to forget I was a party crasher. He sat down beside Nathanael and me. He was so happy, but I knew he was also wondering what I was doing here at the party. Well, I thought, I am wondering too.

"What do you think about all this? Malchus? Have you ever had a party for a man who was dead for four days?"

I shook my head. Levi, as usual, had a hard time stopping his mouth once he started to speak. But Nathanael interrupted his nonstop talking to fill him in on my warning about my master's decision — that it would be better for one man to die rather than take out the entire nation. Levi frowned.

"You know," he said, "seeing Lazarus there by Jesus reminds me of a story Jesus told us all about a rich man and a different man named Lazarus. In Jesus' story, there was a rich man, attired in beautiful clothes, eating whatever and whenever he wanted.

There was also an extremely poor, invalid beggar by the name of Lazarus. He was brought and laid outside the rich man's house, and he longed to eat the crumbs that fell off the rich man's table; but the only relief he had was when the dogs would come and lick his sores. Finally, Lazarus died and the angels came and carried him to Abraham's side in paradise. Then the rich man died.

"The rich man opened his eyes in hell, and he was tormented by the flames. A long way off, he saw Abraham, and he also recognized the poor man, Lazarus, who used to lay beside his house. 'Father Abraham!' he called. 'Please send Lazarus to dip his finger in some water and come touch my lips with his wet finger to give me some relief.'

"But Abraham replied, 'Son, remember that in your lifetime you received your good things, while Lazarus received bad things; but now he is comforted here, and you are in agony. And besides all this, between us and you a great chasm has been set in place, so that those who want to go from here to you cannot, nor can anyone cross over from there to us.'

"The rich man answered, 'Then I beg you, father, send Lazarus to my family, for I have five brothers. Let him warn them, so that they will not also come to this place of torment.'

"Abraham replied, 'They have Moses and the Prophets; let them listen to them.'

" 'No, Father Abraham,' he said, 'but if someone from the dead goes to them, they will repent.'

"Abraham said to him, 'If they do not listen to Moses and the Prophets, they will not be convinced even if someone rises from the dead.'

"You know," Levi continued, "with our Lazarus here, it is proof positive of what the Rabbi was telling the crowd. If you won't accept who Jesus is by faith, nothing you see, nothing you hear, no miracle, no sign will convince you. So sad, that so many people, like the rich man, find out too late."

I looked down. Here is where I always got nervous around Levi. He was continually trying to make me feel guilty that I was not, as he would put it, "a believer." I mean, I heard what Jesus said. He was always saying, "He who has ears let him hear." Well, I had two ears as good as the next man, but nothing the man said had ever made any sense to me.

Suddenly, everyone got quiet as Lazarus stood to his feet. He looked around, and finally his gaze settled on Jesus, reclining at the table beside him. Lazarus spoke. "Thank you all for coming; it is a real honor for us to have you all here. I especially want to thank Jesus, because if it were not for Him, you all know, I would not be here." Laughter filled the room. Jesus smiled. The man's face really lit up when He smiled.

Lazarus went on. "Everyone is always asking what it is like on the other side. Well, my memory is a bit vague on some details, but I do remember having a conversation with a large group of people, and they were so excited to hear that Jesus was here and that I knew Him. I had never thought about this, but people in Paradise are as eager for the Messiah as we are, possibly even more so. You see, from Paradise you can see the flames of hell, and it is a good reminder that we need a Savior and what we have been saved from. They understand the sacrifice that has yet to be made to ensure their permanent salvation, but they don't know exactly what that means. They had so many questions about Jesus. I tried to answer everyone the best I could, but by sheer volume of questions and people asking questions and talking over one another, I kept getting interrupted. But finally, this blond-haired, blue-eyed little girl tugged on my hand to get my attention. I looked down at her and smiled. She asked me, 'Lazarus, what was your favorite thing about Jesus? What did you like the most?'

"That was easy …" Lazarus responded as he looked down at Jesus. "I told her — and the whole crowd quieted down to hear my answer. With everyone hanging onto my every word, it was hard not to feel nervous." He laughed. "I know. Who is going to be nervous in Paradise, right?

"But I told them, 'I loved the way He made me feel special. I loved that when He was talking with me, I was the most important thing to Him. But the thing I loved the most was hearing Him say my name. Such a magical quality to His voice. I can't explain it, but when He spoke my name, I almost wanted to act like I was ignoring Him so He would have to call me again. I loved hearing Him call my name!' " Here Lazarus got an almost sad look on his face. "They were hanging on to my every word when all of a sudden, I heard Jesus call my name! 'I'm sorry to have to leave you all,' I stammered, 'but I hear Him calling my name right now! I have to go!' And you all know the rest of the story. Here I am!" His face was beaming as Jesus stood up and gave him a big bear hug.

Then, sad to say, our party was over. A large crowd learned Jesus was there so they came to see Him, and also to see Lazarus, the one He had raised from the dead.

Now, it was almost time for the Passover. People from all over the Jewish nation were heading up early to Jerusalem so they could find lodging and also fulfill the purification rites. I too made my way back to Jerusalem, deep in thought because of all I had heard and seen there in Bethany. I had enjoyed, more than I cared to admit, the party the night before.

After making my report to my master, I was leaving his quarters, and I was puzzled to see the man from Simon the Leper's party being led into the same room I had just left. He must have left Bethany about the same time I had. I was surprised I had not seen him on the road; but then, remembering the crowds on their way to the Passover Feast, decided it would have been easy to miss someone on that hectic road. Wondering what in the world he could possibly be doing here, I busied myself in a position where the doorway to the room they had entered was visible. The man did not stay long, but leaving the room, looked futilely around and hurriedly exited the compound. Now, I was really curious. I remember what Nathanael had told me about him the night before. "That is Judas Iscariot. He is always worried about money." Well, unless I missed my guess, he was not worried about money now. It looked like a pretty hefty, heavy, little bag he stuffed into his robe as he left.

Everywhere I looked, there were groups of men standing around talking, and the question on everyone's lips was whether Jesus would be brave enough to come to this Passover. I knew He had not missed one yet in the three years since He came on the scene; but knowing the anger of my master, I truly feared for Him. Because I knew there had already been orders given that when He was spotted in the area to let both the chief priests and the Pharisees know, so that they could have Him arrested.

Just days before Passover week started, I was once again heading over the Jordan to where I had heard Jesus was. I was happy to be away from Jerusalem, the Temple, and especially from my master. Things were not going well in the Temple. They had forbidden anyone to even speak Jesus' name, and yet, my master continually wanted me to let him know what was happening. I also had a message for Jesus from Nicodemus and Joseph. Of course, I was not going to give it to Jesus myself, but I encountered my cousin John on the road, and he could deliver it for me.

Since I had not seen John for a while, I was happy to have this chance to talk with him. I was curious to know what he thought about what I had heard Jesus say in the Temple. John knew I did not believe, but he also knew that I tried to be fair. While my master was the High Priest and sent me out on fact-finding missions, John knew I tried to tell my master everything without a bias. John had never treated me like a spy; I assumed he knew I was reporting back to my master.

John was full of enthusiasm this morning as we walked along. He was telling me of this long trip up north from which they'd just returned. I asked him about opposition to Jesus' ministry up there, and he explained while there was always someone against Jesus, it was not anywhere near as bad up there as it was in Jerusalem and areas close to the city.

"Oh," he said as he got a pensive look on his face. "It is getting worse up there through. When we were first starting the northern trip, a group of Pharisees and Sadducees came to see Jesus. As soon as they started talking, it was easy to see they were just trying to trap Him in something."

"What happened?" I asked. "What did they do?"

"Well, they seemed to think the Messiah should be able to

show them proof by causing a great demonstration in the skies."

"So what did Jesus do?" I asked.

He frowned. "It was kind of sad, actually. Jesus looked at the sky and then looked back at the waiting men. 'You are great at being able to tell what the weather is going to be, by looking at the sky. You say, if it is red at night it is going to be a good day tomorrow, and if the sky is red in the morning, you say it is going to be bad weather all day. So you can see the obvious in the sky, but yet, you are so blind when it comes to reading the obvious signs of the times we are living in. But I have to tell you. You are an evil, unbelieving generation, always wanting another sign and now, one in the heavens? No more signs for you! The only proof of who I am will be the same miracle that happened to Jonah!' "

"Why is that so sad?" I asked, smiling, picturing that group of pious, stuck-up men's discomfort at Jesus' answer.

"Well, the sad part was after Jesus told them about not getting another sign except the one of Jonah, whatever that is, then without another word to them, Jesus walked out."

"I was going to ask you about the miracle of Jonah, but it doesn't sound like you know what that is either," I said. "Hearing that, reminds me of something the Temple authorities yelled at Nicodemus one day when he gently took up for Jesus. The authorities were furious. They challenged Nicodemus because they told him he did not know the Scriptures. They smugly told him that no prophet had ever come from Galilee. Nicodemus did not respond to their outburst, but later on while walking to his house, he sadly remarked it was a shame the religious authorities were so blind. They were wrong about Jesus, because He was born in Bethlehem, and they were also wrong about no prophet ever coming from Galilee, because the prophet Jonah was from

Nazareth in Galilee."

We walked in silence for a few minutes until I remembered a question that had kept me awake at night. I had asked James this question, but I felt his answers only gave me more questions, so I decided to get John's take as well.

"John," I said. "I heard Jesus say, 'Before Abraham, I Am.' Nicodemus tells me this is Jesus calling Himself God. He also used almost the same name when you told me He walked on the water. You said He said, 'I AM; no fear!' I have heard Him say, 'I AM the Way, I AM the Resurrection, I AM the Truth, I AM the Door, I AM the Gate, I AM the Bread from heaven, and I AM the Good Shepherd. I also heard Him call Himself the Son of Man and the Son of God. Who is this Son of Man, John?"

John looked at me intently. "You really don't know, Malchus?" I shook my head. "Well, let me answer you by telling you about something that happened a few days ago.

"The other disciples and I were going with Jesus to the villages around Caesarea Philippi and were approaching the city proper," John went on. "In all our traveling this great land, this is the furtherest north Jesus took us and His ministry. The city is located on the southwestern slope of Mount Hermon. Legends abound about this highest mountain in all the land of Israel, one of which states that it was to this mountain that when the sons of God rebelled and took human wives—this was before the great flood—they descended from heaven to the top of Mount Hermon. But in more recent history, this mountain has always been associated with the demigod Baal and his worship. As a matter of fact," John frowned, "in this small area, there is a concentration of pagan religious worship like nowhere I have ever seen. Temple after temple to all these gods, and even a great white marble temple for Caesar worship, which is why the city was renamed Caesarea."

John looked at me. "Among them is a temple to the Greek god Pan, god of the shepherds and the wild. Also in this temple area, there is the cave of Pan where there is, supposedly, a bottomless pit. The Greeks believed inside this pit were the 'gates of hades.' "

John stopped walking and faced me. I stopped with him. He lowered his voice. "As we were nearing this pagan temple, with Mount Hermon soaring up as a backdrop, Jesus turned to us and asked, 'Who do people say I Am?' We all told Him what people were saying. Some say John the Baptist come back to life, others say Elijah, and others Jeremiah or one of the prophets. Looking at us intently, Jesus asked us, 'But you, who do you say I AM?' Simon answered and said, 'You are the Christ, the Son of the living God!' And Jesus said to him, 'You are blessed, Simon, son of John: because you did not learn this from any man, but My Father who is in heaven has shown you this truth. I will tell you again, from now on, your name is Peter, and upon this Rock I will build My church, and the gates of hell will not stand against it.'

"Malchus, I get goosebumps just telling you about it. As I think back on the setting and Jesus' words, I realize Jesus was drawing a line in the sand, so to speak. He wanted us to know that He was the only Way. With Him for us, we do not have to fear all these other powers. All other religions are false. Only Him. I know you don't believe us, and I know you don't believe that Jesus is the Messiah, the Christ, but if you would have been there ... With that pagan temple to the fake god of the shepherds as His backdrop, and Jesus, who said the other day that He is the good Shepherd ... well, like I said, I wish you could really hear Him, Malchus. I know I am repeating myself, but I can't tell you how much His words, that scene, everything so impressed me. Remember, this happened in the midst of all these pagan temples. So the Good Shepard stands in this thriving temple of the god of shepherds, the god Pan, and asks, 'Who do you say I AM?' Peter said, 'You are the Christ, the Son of the Living God!' It almost took my breath away! I'm sorry I am talking too much." John sheepishly grinned, but then he quickly rushed to finish his story anyway.

"You know, Malchus, I think something dramatically changed for Peter at that time. His name had been changed before, but it was as if he had finally grown into it. It seemed like at that time, he almost became our band's leader. It is hard to describe exactly what happened. Like I said, you would have had to have been there," John finished quietly.

"So Peter really believes this man is the Son of God? Well, I can believe that about Peter, but you, John, do you really believe He is the Son of God?"

"Malchus, yes, I really do believe. I have heard Him speak, and I have seen Him do things that are humanly impossible. The only thing that makes any sense is that He truly is the Son of God. Our long-promised Messiah! I believe this with all my heart."

"Okay, I accept that you believe Him to be the Messiah, and to be honest, I don't know what I believe. I too have listened to Him, but I have told you before, I hardly understand a word He says. But Jesus has a few friends among the Pharisees, and they have asked me to pass this message to Jesus. They told me to tell Him, 'Go, get out of here! Herod wants to kill You!' "

John looked at me. He nodded his head. "Malchus, I have to tell you, this last number of days, when we are alone, the only thing He talks about is that He is going to be killed. We know He is the Messiah, God's Son, so how can He die? We don't understand. You know I was telling you that Jesus blessed Peter for saying He was the Christ, and Jesus told him that God had revealed it to him? Well, just a bit further up the road, He starts telling us that He has to go to Jerusalem, and He is going to be turned over to the authorities, and He is going to be killed. Peter rebuked Him …" John shook his head sadly as he thought of it.

I waited for him to tell me what had happened, but John changed the subject, protecting his close friend.

John continued, "Then Jesus turned to all of us and said, 'If anyone wants to come with Me, he has to deny himself, take up his cross, and follow Me. For whoever wants to save his life will lose it, but whoever loses his life because of Me will find it. What will it benefit a man if he gains the whole world yet loses his life? Or what will a man give in exchange for his life? For the Son of Man is going to come with His angels in the glory of His Father, and then He will reward each according to what he has done. I assure you: There are some standing here who will not taste death until they see the Son of Man in His glory.' "

"See John, this is what I mean! Who can understand that? Take up your cross? What does that mean? What did He mean by 'finding his life'? This is why I say I don't understand a thing the man says. I just don't hear Him. But more importantly for you all, exactly which of you are not going to taste death?"

"We did not have any idea either, to be honest," John told me, frowning. "But you won't believe what happened about a week after He had told us this. We were still camping on one of the gentle slopes of Mount Hermon, when one morning, early, while the rest of the guys were still asleep, Jesus called Peter, James, and me to go up with Him to the top of the mountain. We know He goes off by Himself and talks to His Father, but this was the first time He had ever called anyone to go with Him. After a long, hard climb, we finally reached the summit. The three of us basically collapsed there, but Jesus left us and walked on a short distance. We were tired. We have criss-crossed this country from end to end and are dealing with crowds, and now we have the stress of not knowing what Jesus is talking about when He keeps talking about His coming death. We don't know if it is figurative or if He is really going to die. Then, if that were not enough, we had that difficult climb, and — no excuses I guess — we just started dozing off.

"Suddenly, we jerked awake! I don't know what caused us to wake up, but I can't even describe what happened. You are the first person I have told this to. Jesus was transfigured in front of us! His face shone like the sun. Even His clothes became as white as light. I think for the first time, we saw Him as He really is. Suddenly, Moses and Elijah appeared with Him. We knew exactly who they were, don't ask me how, but we knew. We strained to hear what they were talking about and though it was difficult, we did understand they were talking to Jesus about what was going to happen to Him in Jerusalem. From what I heard, they were even talking about His coming death. They actually called it 'His exodus'! I know it sounds hard to believe, and I even struggle with what I am sure I heard, but they were encouraging Him to stay the course!

"I knew we were looking at the face of God, and I was terrified! Speechless! But Peter — Peter shakily asked Jesus, 'Rabbi, is it good for us to be here?' I think he knew we were seeing something we should not be seeing. At that point, I think we all thought we were going to die, because we were looking on the glory of the Lord! Peter rushed to say, 'Let us make three shelters: one for You, one for Moses, and one for Elijah.' I know what he was thinking. He wanted them behind shelters so they would be hidden from us. Like I said, we were terrified. But then, it was as if God Himself covered them, because the shekinah glory of God as a cloud appeared, totally covering them up, and we heard a voice come from the cloud saying:

'This is My Son, the Chosen One. Listen to Him!'

"We fell on the ground, trembling in fear. I don't know how long we lay there, but all of a sudden, I felt Jesus beside me. His light touch on my shoulder gave me a peace I can't explain. I bolted up. Peter and James were also getting to their feet. We looked around. I don't know about the other guys, but I was surprised to still be alive! I mean, we had seen the face of God! Not only that, we had been covered by God's own shining cloud, like our ancestors in the wilderness, God's shekinah cloud! We were alive, but the cloud was gone, and Moses and Elijah were gone, and Jesus looked like He has always looked. But Malchus, to see the face of God and live to tell about it! I can't stop thinking about it. You know how in our sacred Scriptures we are told that when Moses was up on the mountain with God, in a moment of quiet intimacy, Moses said. 'Lord, show me Your face'?

"But God told him, 'I will make all my goodness pass before you, and I will tell you My name. I will have mercy and compassion on anyone I choose, but Moses, for your own sake, I cannot allow you to see My face, because for you to look on My face would kill you. But because I do love you and desire to grant your request, you stand here in this cleft of this rock wall. While My glory passes by, I will cover you with My hand; but once I have gone by, I will withdraw My hand so you can see Me from behind, but you can't see My face.'

"Here is the part I keep thinking about," John said. "I think this shows again how much God really does love us. He truly does desire to do things we ask of Him, because of all the people He could have chosen to encourage His Son there on the top of the mountain, one of the ones He sends is Moses, a man we know longed to see God's face. Well on top of that mountain that morning, Moses was finally able to see the face of God that before he had to hide from! We saw the face of God and lived! It is still so very difficult to even talk about this ..." his voice trailed off.

"That entire day was filled with so much! But then, early the next day, we were almost back to the others. I kind of hated to get back to the crowds and wished we could just stay with Jesus alone. Because as we walked up to the other disciples, we could hear they were in some kind of big debate with scribes of the Law. Jesus asked them what they were arguing about.

"Before the disciples could even answer, a man spoke up. 'Sir, I brought my son to You. You were not here so I asked Your disciples to help me, but they could not. He has a demon and it does not allow him to speak. He foams at the mouth and the demon throws him violently around. Your disciples could not help me. Please help me!' The father had tears in his eyes in his desperation.

"Jesus looked around at the crowd, then directly at us, His disciples. Malchus, I have never seen Jesus so frustrated with us. I had seen Him frustrated and yes, even angry with your Temple authorities and the Pharisees, but never at us, His chosen. With a sense of urgency in His voice He finished with, 'How long must I put up with you?' He said this to us, not the other people. We all looked at each other in disbelief.

"While some men were bringing the boy to Jesus, the demon convulsed him again, throwing him to the ground with such violence that many people in the crowd said he was dead. 'How long has this been going on?' Jesus asked the father. 'Since he was a baby. He even throws him into the fire in his attempts to destroy my son. I am afraid it is going to kill him. If You can do anything for us, please help us.' The man's eyes glistened with tears.

"Jesus, looking at the father intently said, 'If You can? Everything is possible to anyone who believes.'

"The father took a deep breath and cried out, 'I do believe! Help my unbelief!'

"Jesus, seeming to notice the rapidly growing crowd, looked back down at the boy laying as one dead. He said, 'You mute and deaf spirit, I command you: come out of him and never enter him again!' The spirit came out, shrieking and convulsing him violently. I thought the boy was dead, and so did many of the people who had gathered. He might really have been dead for all I know," added John. "But Jesus took him by the hand and raised him up and led him to his father. You should have seen that father's face as he slowly sank to his knees in front of Jesus.

"The other disciples, who could not make the demon leave the boy, were ashamed that they had not been able to heal him. They were embarrassed that Jesus was disappointed with them, so later on, when we were by ourselves with Jesus, they asked Him, 'Why could we not drive it out?' Jesus told them that this kind of demon only comes out by prayer."

John paused. "I have thought about His answer, and it is true. If we pray and give our problems to God, we are allowing His power to work through us. I think when we had gone out when Jesus gave us the power to go preaching about His coming Kingdom, we became over-confident and thought somehow that the power was ours. So when the other disciples tried to make the demon come out of the boy, they were trying in their own power instead of relying on God's power. Thinking about this reminded me of all the times I have heard Jesus say, 'I only do My Father's will.' Which probably explains why He spends so much time alone, talking with His Father."

At my raised eyebrows, John clarified. "He prays a lot. Sometimes all night long."

As we got to the outskirts of Jericho, we could hear a crowd coming. Figuring it was Jesus, John and I decided to wait in the shade of a large sycamore tree by the side of the road until they came up to us. We were both tired and hot from the long walk. Hearing a small sound above me, I glanced up into the tree and was surprised to see a man there in the branches. He was peering up the road from where the sounds of the crowd were growing closer, approaching the city from the north. I did a double take. I knew that man! He was Zacchaeus. He was extremely rich, and as one of the head tax collectors of the entire area, he was not very well-liked. I could not figure out what he was doing up there above me. He did not look very dignified up there, I can tell you that. I had to hide a smile. I don't know why, but seeing that pudgy, short, little man hiding in a tree just struck me as funny. I nudged John. He glanced up, but then we both looked at Jesus, who was walking right toward us. I was surprised to have

Him stop beside me and look right up into the tree, like He was expecting someone to be up there.

I don't know why I was always surprised by what Jesus did. You would think I would have been used to His ways by now, but He surprised me this time again! I saw a smile playing across His face, and He cleared his throat. Zacchaeus looked down sheepishly.

Jesus waved His hand and said, "Come on down. What are you doing up there? I am going to your house today." I thought ol' Zacchaeus would fall out of that sycamore tree in his haste to get down, and he rushed to Jesus' side. I saw frowns and sneers from the people as Zacchaeus grabbed Jesus by the arm and led Him into the city to his house. Since I was still with John, I decided to walk along and see what would happen.

One thing is for certain: the crowd was not happy. I heard many different people muttering about Jesus having gone too far this time! Zacchaeus was a sinner and a thief! There just was nothing else to say about him. If Jesus wanted credibility, He needed to stay away from people like this short guy. I mean, Zacchaeus was not only a tax collector but also in charge of all the tax collectors of this entire region. He had made himself very rich by overcharging everyone and making all who worked for him do the same so he could get a bigger cut. I still could not figure out why he had been up in the tree, but then I overheard someone telling his friend that Zacchaeus climbed the tree because he was too short to see above the crowd. He had actually been down in the crowd earlier, but could not see over anyone's head, so he ran ahead to get to the tree in his desperation to see Jesus. The man sneered, "A lot of good it will do him! Sure don't see what the Rabbi was thinking to go with him, though." He finished with a frown.

Well, he got his wish! I thought to myself, but I doubted it would do him much good. What could someone like Jesus possibly do with a sinner like Zacchaeus? I thought back to what Jesus' face had looked like as He peered up at the tax collector. I never saw any contempt or disrespect; I only saw a look of genuine love and something else. Might this be what Levi had called compassion?

The usual group of Pharisees and scribes were in the crowd. "This man spends way to much time with sinners! He seems to enjoy their company," I heard one of them say loudly to his neighbor. It was obvious he was speaking for Jesus' benefit. Their contempt was overt and was echoed in the nods of agreement by a large portion of the watching crowd.

Jesus stopped and looked sadly at the frowning men. Moving closer, He addressed them. Right about then, the crowd surged forward, and I was momentarily blocked from seeing Jesus. I could barely catch a word He said. I did hear Him mention a lost sheep, but I could not follow His story. I fought to get closer, and I heard Him say there was joy in the "presence of God's angels over one sinner who repents." But I could not hear Him enough to hazard a guess about what He was talking about.

The crowd was going crazy. Finally, I fought my way in close enough to hear Him clearly. But His subject had changed. Now He was talking about a man with two sons. Thankfully, the crowd quieted, and I could hear His every word. Here is His story.

"A man had two sons. The youngest son came and told his father, 'Father, I don't want to wait until you die for me to get my inheritance; give me my inheritance now.' So the father split his possessions and gave his sons their inheritance. As soon as the youngest son had received his, he packed it all up and went to live in a far-off country. There, he wasted his wealth in raucous living and partying. Soon he was out of money. About that same time, a famine hit that land, and the young man was destitute and hungry. He finally found a job feeding pigs. He was so hungry many times he wished he could share the pig's food.

"Finally he came to his senses and said to himself, 'Here I am feeding pigs and wishing I could eat with them. My father's hired servants have more than enough to eat, and I am starving. I need to go back home. But I will tell my father, "Father, I sinned against you and against heaven. I am not worthy to be called your son. Let me just be one of your servants."'" After rehearsing what he would say to his father, he set off on the long road home. He kept rehearsing as he walked. But when he was still a long way off, his father saw him coming. With compassion, he ran down the road to meet his son. He hugged his son and kissed him. Pushing the father off a bit, the son, with bowed head, mumbled the words he had practiced. 'Father, I have sinned against heaven and against you. I am not worthy to be called your son …'

"But the father interrupted him and called to his servants, 'Quickly, bring me our best robe and a ring and sandals! Put them on my son. Then bring the fatted calf and kill it. Prepare us a feast because we are going to celebrate. My son was dead and is now alive. He was lost and now is found!' So they began to have a party.

"Now the older son had been out in the field working. When he got near the house, he heard music and partying. He called one of the servants to find out what was going on. 'Your brother has come home, and your father has killed the fatted calf and is giving a party because he has him back safe!' explained the servant.

"The older brother became angry and refused to go in. So his father finally came out and pleaded with him to come in. But the angry son refused and told his father, 'I have been slaving many years for you. I obey everything you tell me. But not once did you ever give me even as much as a young goat so I could have a party with my friends. Now this son of yours who wasted your fortune on prostitutes comes home and you have the fatted calf killed for him!'

" 'My son,' said the father, 'you are always with me, and everything I have is yours. But we have to be happy and celebrate because your brother was dead and is alive again; he was lost and is now found.' "

As I was listening to the story, I thought the whole intent of the tale was the boy who had squandered the father's inheritance. But when I heard the part of the older brother, I knew the story was aimed right at the critical Pharisees. Looking at their angry faces, some outwardly sneering, it was easy to see they had also grasped that they were the story's intended audience. Then, remembering my own contempt of Zacchaeus, I wondered where I fit in the story.

By this time, we were approaching a beautiful home. John needed to rejoin Jesus and the rest of the disciples, and I needed to find lodging. It was getting late, and I figured I would get an early start in the morning to head back to Jerusalem. Before leaving John, we agreed to meet in the morning in the town square. "Don't forget the warning!" I whispered. He nodded and disappeared into the crowd toward Jesus.

The next morning, I was waiting for John. I knew Jesus was on His way to Jerusalem, but I actually preferred to walk by myself, away from the crowd that always followed Jesus. I didn't know how He could stand the constant, noisy crowds! I was thankful to see John coming toward me. He looked flushed and excited.

"Well, how was your meal with the tax collector?" I chided him.

He grinned. "It is amazing the impact that Jesus has on people. You should have heard Zacchaeus last night! After he had fed us an absolutely amazing meal, he stood up and addressed Jesus. 'Master,' he said, 'I am going to give one half of all I have to the poor, and anyone whom I have cheated on their taxes, I am going to give back to that person four times what I stole from him.' "

"What did Jesus say?" I asked.

John smiled. "He was happy for him! I remember how sad he was when, a few days ago, another rich, young ruler came to Him and asked Him what he needed to do to inherit eternal life. Jesus looked at him intently and finally asked him, 'Why do you call me good? No one is good but God! But you know what the commandments say.

"Do not commit adultery;
do not murder;
do not steal;
do not bear false witness;
honor your father and mother.'"

"The young man nodded his head. Looking Jesus right in the eyes he assured Him, 'I have kept every one of these commandments since I was young!' He beamed; I assumed he thought

Jesus was going to be happy with his answer and would commend him. But Jesus gently told him, 'You still lack one thing. Go, sell what you have, and give the money to the poor. Then, come and follow Me.' I was watching the young man's face," John continued. "His face fell and without another word, he turned and walked away. I watched him disappear into the crowd. I remember Jesus sadly looking after him as he walked away, and Jesus made a comment about how hard it was for the wealthy to give up their riches and be saved. It actually impressed us all deeply. I remember Peter saying, 'Lord, we have given up everything to follow You.' We all nodded because, Malchus, we have given up everything, but none of the rest of us were brave enough to say it."

I knew my cousins had given up a successful fishing business, and I assumed the other disciples had given up things as well, so I was curious about how Jesus answered Peter. "What did Jesus say?" I asked John.

"Jesus put His arm around Peter," said John. " 'Peter,' Jesus said, 'any one who leaves anything down here for Me or for My kingdom,' — and he listed off a bunch of things: houses, lands, parents, brothers, even children — 'will receive even more in this life, although persecution, too; and in the next, he will have eternal life!' "

I always got nervous when John or Levi started in on me about eternal life, so I quickly interrupted him. "So Jesus was a lot happier with Zacchaeus then with the other guy, right?"

John nodded. "Yes," he agreed. "Jesus was positively beaming! Smiling from ear to ear. 'Today salvation has come to this house. This is why I have come!' He looked at us. 'After all, he is a son of Abraham, too. The Son of Man came to find and restore the lost!' "

By this time, we had started walking toward the gate. I knew
John was going to wait for Jesus, but I had to start my long trek
back. "Did you give Him the message?" I asked him.

John nodded. Frowning, he gave me the message from Jesus.
I have to say, I was no closer to being able to understand Jesus
than when He first started speaking. Here, in its entirety, is Jesus'
message to me to give to Nicodemus so it could be sent back to
Herod.

"Go tell that Fox, 'Look! I'm driving out demons and performing healings today and tomorrow, and on the third day I will
complete My work. Yet I must travel today, tomorrow, and the
next day, because it is not possible for a prophet to perish outside
of Jerusalem!'"

"Seems awfully dark to me," I prodded. "I can understand
the part about driving out demons and performing healings,
as this is what Jesus has done consistently since He started His
ministry. But what does He mean about 'it is not possible for a
prophet to perish outside of Jerusalem'?" I asked, my brows knit
together.

Then John added the last part, and it was even sadder yet.
He said, "Jesus, with a look of deep sorrow on His face, with
tears in His eyes, lamented, 'Jerusalem, Jerusalem! The city who
kills the prophets and stones those who are sent to her. How often I wanted to gather your children together, as a hen gathers
her chicks under her wings, but you were not willing!' "

XI

After delivering Jesus' message for Nicodemus to give to Herod, Nicodemus asked me if I could try and meet Jesus on His way to Jerusalem. This sent me hurrying back down the long, dusty road toward Jericho. I was pretty sure I would meet them before having to go all the way into the actual city of Jericho, as John had told me they would be heading up to Jerusalem this day. The warning I was carrying, along with the verbal warning to give to a disciple, was a letter to Jesus; it was sealed, because Nicodemus wanted to make sure He personally received the warning. I had to get it down there and return to start my own post that evening. During the Passover weeks, Jerusalem rarely slept, so we pretty much had to man our posts in continuous shifts.

Shortly after passing the small town of Bethpage, near Bethany, I saw a mass of people coming in the distance. Figuring it would be Jesus' crowd, I stopped under the limbs of a leafy fig tree to enjoy the shade and wait for them to draw closer. I figured if it was Jesus' entourage, I would either find one of my cousins or Levi and talk with them as we headed back to Jerusalem. I was glad I had not had to go very far; I would get back into Jerusalem well before the time I had to be there for work.

Sure enough, it was Jesus' crowd, but just before they got near where I was, I saw two figures split off of the main group and start coming my way much faster. I was pleasantly surprised that the two were disciples, and not only that, but one of them was my cousin John, alongside Peter. After greeting the men, I fell into step with them. They were deep in thought and appeared to be preoccupied.

"Where are you going in such a hurry?" I asked.

"We have to hurry ahead to get a donkey for Jesus," answered John. "Jesus told us right where to find it."

"Do you mind if I walk along?" I asked. "I have a message for your master." At John's nod I continued with them. "What is wrong, John? You look like you are ready to cry." I spoke half in jest, but, to be honest, he really did look distraught.

John shook his head and tried to smile, but it turned to a frown. "While we were coming up to Jerusalem, Jesus took us 12 disciples aside privately and said to us, 'Listen! We are going up to Jerusalem. The Son of Man will be handed over to the chief priests and scribes, and they will condemn Him to death. Then they will hand Him over to the Gentiles to be mocked, flogged, and crucified, and He will be resurrected on the third day.' This is not the first time He has told us this either. Lately, His death is about all He talks about. We see the crowds and hear them adore Him, and we know people want to crown Him King. So why does He think He is going to be killed? I just don't understand Him."

"Now you sound like me, John," I teased, but then I turned serious. "John, this is exactly what my message to your master is about. He can't continue on into Jerusalem. They are ready for Him." John and Peter both nodded, frowning, but did not say anything more. I could sympathize with them. They could not stop Jesus; all they could do was hope He was only talking figuratively about coming to Jerusalem to be killed. Thinking about the graphic details they'd heard of His upcoming death, they had a hard time really believing that.

But I needed to convince them to heed the message. "Listen, don't take this lightly," I begged. "My master has moved the Temple marketplace back into the Court of the Gentiles. He knows this infuriated Jesus before, and he reopened it to dare Jesus to do something about it. He is ready for Him this time. Please, you must tell Jesus." I turned to John. "John, you remember that old man I came with to Jesus that night?" John nodded. "Well, he sent me out to warn Jesus that my master Caiaphas is really serious. Ever since Jesus raised Lazarus from the dead, they have looked for a way to not only kill Jesus but also to kill Lazarus."

We continued on into the village. Suddenly, Peter and John stopped. I looked around. Peter was untying a young donkey from a post where it was tied with its mother. A man standing nearby moved over to us.

"What are you doing?" he asked.

John did not miss a beat. "The master needs him," he said. The man nodded and, stepping aside, waved us on. Peter lead off the small animal.

"But the colt has never been ridden," the owner added as we walked away. I looked behind us; the mother donkey was walking right behind us, afraid of straying from her colt. John looked back as well and said, "Oh, let it come on. It won't hurt anything." Peter and I both nodded and hurried on down the road.

We left the town and joined the main road. By this time, the crowd had grown in size, and I noticed many of them were carrying palm branches and waving them ecstatically in the air. Many of them spread their clothes on the road, and others spread the palm branches on the road in front of Jesus. By this time, Peter had led the little donkey up to Jesus. His disciples took off their coats and draped them over the animal as a saddle. Jesus sat on the little beast, and, with Peter still leading it, as one would lead a great man through the streets, started walking up the back side of the Mount of Olives toward the city.

I heard a nameless man in the crowd exclaiming to his neighbors, "I knew this day was going to come when I saw Jesus raise Lazarus from the dead." He shook his head. "Four days he had been dead, too!" Everyone hearing him chimed in with their own versions of the story and affirmed this was the reason they were out here on the mountain to welcome their king. This is really serious, I thought. What would my master do now?

As we crested the Mount, everyone began yelling at the top of their lungs. "Hosanna! 'Blessed is He who comes in the name of the Lord!' The King of Israel!" I could not help but remember a passage from our ancient Scriptures where it says, "Fear no more, Daughter of Zion. Look, your King is coming, sitting on a donkey's colt."

Upon hearing the commotion, many people rushed out of Jerusalem to see what was going on. The people were so ready for Jesus to do something that it had not taken long for this additional crowd to be absorbed by the original one. I noticed many

Pharisees and other leaders of the Jews rushing up the hill from the city to meet us. From their clenched teeth and hands balled into fists, it was easy to see this was not a welcoming party. I quickly assumed a place near them, to make it look like I had only now come out from the city with them.

They were beside themselves with anger at the people's shouting. "Tell them to stop!" they screamed at Jesus. Jesus' calm, deep voice projected so well, I was able to hear Him in spite of the noise of the crowd. "If these people were not praising God at this time on this day, the stones themselves would cry out," Jesus said.

We had crested the Mount of Olives and were now descending toward the city. Jesus stopped, looking down at the city sprawled out in all its glory before us, with the Temple bright and dazzling in the morning sun. Our Temple complex was the largest sacred enclosure in the Roman world, five times the area of the Acropolis in Athens. We were proud of the fact that some of its foundation stones were larger than the blocks of the pyramids in Egypt. With the Temple itself gleaming of white marble and pure gold, I knew why Jesus, or anyone for that matter, would stop here and feast their eyes on the panorama laid out below them. I looked over at Jesus. What was this? Was I seeing tears?

Yes! Since I was walking just on the outside of the disciples, close enough to see and hear Jesus, I was surprised to see tears running down His face. He began to weep. Realizing something was going on, the crowd near us became silent. I could clearly hear Jesus' words through His tears.

"Eternal peace was right in your grasp today, and you rejected Me," He wept, "and now it is too late. Your enemies will make earthen ramps against your walls and surround you and close in on you, and crush you to the ground, and your children within you; your enemies will not leave one stone upon another—for you have rejected the opportunity God offered you." With a visible effort, Jesus composed Himself. Behind us the crowd was still cheering. With a small jerk, Peter got the little donkey walking on down the hill to, what I was afraid, was going to be a fateful day.

Because of the Passover, the city's population was huge with all the people who had come for the mandated feast days. So when He entered Jerusalem, the entire city was in an uproar! Everyone was asking, "Who is this?" And the crowds of people who had come in with Him kept answering, "This is the prophet Jesus from Nazareth in Galilee!"

I was worried what might happen when Jesus saw my master had moved the market back into the Court of the Gentiles. I also knew my master would expect me to be there protecting his interests. Jesus wasted no time. He marched into the Temple, but then He surprised me and probably everyone who had laid the trap. Because, looking around, He quietly turned and walked out. He and His disciples left the city and headed on back to Bethany.

But the next day, early, He was back. No one, not even me, dared stop Him. He was a one-man whirlwind as He drove out all those buying and selling in the temple. He overturned the moneychangers' tables and chairs, let down the bars and rushed the animals out, and opened the cages of doves. Again, mass confusion! All of those white doves rising into the early-morning sunlight were quite a sight! There were animals mooing and bleating, jumping and running everywhere. What a riot! I just stood and watched. I mean, what could I do to stop this confusion? A large crowd of Pharisees and priests had come rushing up at the first sounds of the disturbance, but they, like me, stood in silent awe at the fury of His rampage. Finally, He stopped. I saw the sweat beaded on His forehead. Turning to the group of furious Temple authorities, He said to them, "It is written, 'My house will be called a house of prayer.' But you are making it a den of thieves!'"

Looking around at all the people watching, I became aware of a man standing not too far away from me with his hands in the air, his face lifted to God, his lips moving, but he was only whispering his praise. I took a second glance, as he looked familiar. I could not place where I had seen him at first, but suddenly it struck me. He was the blind beggar I passed every time I went down to Jericho. He always set at the gate begging. I moved over for a closer look and stood there quietly while he continued to praise the Lord. As if suddenly becoming aware that I was standing there, he looked over at me and smiled.

"Are you Bartimaeus? From Jericho?" I asked.

He smiled from ear to ear. "Yes! I am Bartimaeus. I was the blind beggar, but now I can see! Yesterday morning, I was sitting by the gate in my usual place when I heard a crowd coming. First, I just figured it was people on their way to Jerusalem for the Feast days, but then someone told me it was Jesus. I fumbled in the dirt for my cane. Finding it, I used it to help me get to my feet. 'Son of David, Jesus, have mercy on me!' I shouted. People around me began to yell at me to shut up, but I refused to be silenced. I knew this was my only chance. I had heard of Him healing so many other people, I needed my chance; and if this was it, I was going to give my best shot to get it. 'Jesus! Son of David! Jesus, have mercy on me!' I shouted louder. Suddenly the crowd was silent. In the silence, I heard a man's voice say, 'Call him.'

" 'He is calling you,' someone said as they grabbed my arm. 'Be brave!' Throwing off my cloak, I tapped with my staff and hurried as fast as I could to where I had heard the voice.

" 'What do you want Me to do for you?' a deep, kind voice asked me. Taking a deep breath so my voice would not tremble, I answered. 'Rabbouni,' my voice faltered in spite of my resolve. I was so desperate. 'I want to see!' It came out as a whisper at the end.

" 'Go your way,' Jesus told me. 'Your faith has made you well.'

"I have not been able to stop praising God and our Messiah since He healed me."

I looked at the man and wished things could be that clear for me. The more I saw, the more I heard, the more I was confused by everything. I moved away into the crowd.

Later on, I saw the blind and the lame come to Jesus in the Temple complex, and He healed them. Funny, of all that had happened in our complex that morning, I think the two things that aggravated my master and the other priests and Pharisees the most was the fact that Jesus not only allowed the blind and the lame to come into the Temple complex (which our oral law forbade), but he also encouraged them and healed them there. The straw that broke the camel's back, so to speak, was when the chief priests and the scribes heard the children singing in the temple complex,

"Save now, I pray, O Lord.
O Lord, I pray, send now prosperity.
Blessed is He who comes in the name of the Lord!

We have blessed You from the house of the Lord.
Hosanna to the Son of David!"

The priests and other authorities were furious and said to
Him, "Do You hear what these children are singing?"

"Yes," Jesus told them. "Have you never read:

'You have prepared praise
from the mouths of children and nursing infants'?"

At His words, I realized the children were singing from Israel's songbook, our ancient book of the Psalms.

The next morning, Jesus was back teaching in the now-
cleared Court of the Gentiles. For some reason—and I have to
be honest, I can't even tell you why—I cannot stay away from
where the Nazarene is teaching. While there, I overheard some
men, obviously foreigners, talking about how great it was to have
a quiet place to pray again. It was clear they had come up to Jerusalem for the Feast. We call foreigners like them "God-fearers."

While I was standing there in thought, they moved over to
one of Jesus' disciples, the one called Phillip. I heard them ask
him if he thought they could see Jesus. Philip went and called
Andrew, another disciple. Andrew listened to their request, then
he took the men to Jesus. After talking with them for a bit, Jesus
made the cryptic comment that now His hour had come. All the
times I had listened to Him, I had heard Him say, "My hour has
not come," but with these Greeks, it almost seemed to be a sign
He was looking for. But His next words were so sad they were
almost scary.

He said, "I assure you: Unless a grain of wheat falls to the ground and dies, it remains by itself. But if it dies, it produces a large crop. The one who loves his life will lose it, and the one who hates his life in this world will keep it for eternal life. If anyone serves Me, he must follow Me. Where I am, there My servant also will be. If anyone serves Me, the Father will honor him."

Jesus continued teaching and preaching the Good News in the Temple, and the authorities, my master included, seemed powerless to stop Him. Finally my master decided His flaunting of Temple authority had to be stopped. He had to be stopped. I was in close attendance as my master, along with other chief priests, religious leaders, and councilmen, moved in to confront Him. He politely stopped talking as we approached Him. Without even the most meager of greetings, they harshly demanded to know by what authority He had driven the merchants from the Temple.

What was interesting to me listening to them was that they never said He was wrong to clear out the Temple complex, they only wanted to know by what authority He had done so. But in true rabbinic fashion, before answering their question, Jesus asked one of His own first.

"I'll ask you a question before I answer," He replied. "Was John's authority from God, or was he merely acting under his own authority?"

I could hear the desperation and confusion in their voices as they debated back and forth. "If we say his message was from heaven, then we are trapped because He will ask, 'Then why didn't you believe him?' But if we say John was not sent from God, the people will mob us, for they are convinced that he was a prophet." Finally they replied with words I never thought I would ever hear these self-righteous, pious men use: "We don't know!" they muttered, not even looking at Him.

And Jesus responded, "Then I won't answer your question either."

Now He turned to the people again and told them this story: "A man planted a vineyard and rented it out to some farmers, and went away to a distant land to live for several years. When harvest time came, he sent one of his men to the farm to collect his share of the crops. But the tenants beat him up and sent him back empty-handed. Then he sent another, but the same thing happened; he was beaten up and insulted and sent away without collecting. A third man was sent and the same thing happened. He, too, was wounded and chased away.

" 'What shall I do?' the owner asked himself. 'I know! I'll send my cherished son. Surely they will show respect for him.'

"But when the tenants saw his son, they said, 'This is our chance! This fellow will inherit all the land when his father dies. Come on. Let's kill him, and then it will be ours.' So they dragged him out of the vineyard and killed him.

"What do you think the owner will do? I'll tell you—he will come and kill them and rent the vineyard to others."

"But they would never do a thing like that," his listeners protested.

Jesus looked at them and said, "Then what does the Scripture mean where it says, 'The Stone rejected by the builders was made the cornerstone'?" And He added, "Whoever stumbles over that Stone shall be broken; and those on whom it falls will be crushed to dust."

When the chief priests and religious leaders heard this story He had told, they wanted Him arrested immediately, for they realized that He was talking about them. They were the wicked tenants in His illustration. But they were afraid that if they themselves arrested Him, there would be a riot. So they tried to get Him to say something that could be reported to the Roman governor as reason to arrest Him.

Watching their opportunity, they sent secret agents pretending to be honest men. These spies said to Jesus, "Sir, we know what an honest teacher You are. You always tell the truth and don't budge an inch in the face of what others think, but teach the ways of God. Now tell us—is it right to pay taxes to the Roman government or not?"

I was watching Jesus' face as He listened to their question. I swear He saw through their trickery, because He said, "Show me a coin. Whose portrait is this on it? And whose name?"

They replied, "Caesar's—the Roman emperor's."

I was almost positive I saw a glint of humor in His eyes as He said, "Then give the emperor all that is his—and give to God all that is His!"

Because I was on duty and the day was still young, I knew I was going to watch this same scene play out over and over today as my master had decided Jesus had to be stopped for good this time. But at least this time, their attempt to outwit Him before the people failed. Marveling at His answer, they were silent.

Then, just as I had figured, some Sadducees (this is a sect of men who believe that death is the end of existence, that there is no resurrection) came to Jesus with this: "The laws of Moses state that if a man dies without children, the man's brother shall marry the widow, and their children will legally belong to the dead man, to carry on his name. We know of a family of seven brothers. The oldest married and then died without any children. His brother married the widow and he, too, died. Still no children. And so it went, one after the other, until each of the seven had married her and died, leaving no children. Finally the woman died also. Now here is our question: Whose wife will she be in the resurrection? For all of them were married to her!"

Jesus replied, "Marriage is for people here on earth, but when those who are counted worthy of being raised from the dead get to heaven, they do not marry. And they never die again; in these respects they are like angels, and are sons of God, for they are raised up in new life from the dead.

"But as to your real question—whether or not there is a resurrection—why, even the writings of Moses himself prove this. For when he describes how God appeared to him in the burning bush, he speaks of God as 'the God of Abraham, the God of Isaac, and the God of Jacob.' To say that the Lord is some person's God means that person is alive, not dead! So from God's point of view, all men are living."

"Well said, sir!" I looked over and saw Joseph of Aramathea and Nicodemus standing with some other experts in the Jewish Law. Of all the Temple authorities in the complex that day listening to Jesus, they were the only ones who appeared to be enjoying themselves. And that ended the questions, for they dared ask no more!

Then Jesus presented them with a question. "Why is it," He asked, "that Christ, the Messiah, is said to be a descendant of King David? For David himself wrote in the book of Psalms: 'God said to my Lord, the Messiah, "Sit at my right hand until I place your enemies beneath your feet." ' How can the Messiah be both David's son and David's God at the same time?"

I was happy to get a chance to talk with Nicodemus. He and Joseph had been in deep conversations this week and had been interested observers in all the different traps and points of law their colleagues had brought up with Jesus. From their manner, it was pretty obvious they were not in agreement at all with the majority of the Temple authorities. As Nicodemus was leaving this evening to walk to his home, he informed me that my master had granted permission for me to walk with him. The streets were not safe with so many people in the city for the Feast. As we walked, he appeared deep in thought. I hesitated to disturb him, but I had been waiting for a chance to ask him some questions about the Nazarene.

"Master," I began, "I heard the Nazarene tell the rulers and other Pharisees up on the Mount of Olives the other day that if the people were silent on that specific day, the rocks of the mountain would cry out for Him. What did He mean, Master? I still never understand a word the man says, but I really do listen. I am intrigued by His words."

"Truly a good question, my young friend, a good question," Nicodemus assented. "Joseph and I have been discussing just this question and others that line of thought brings up. I hesitate to explain our interpretation, and I would not even mention it if you were not asking the exact same question Joseph and I have been wrestling with. So here is the conclusion we have come to.

"Our line of questioning, as usual, took us to our Holy Scriptures. The scroll of Daniel, to be exact. Daniel tells us that he understood from his reading the prophecies of Jeremiah that the 70 years of captivity of his people was just about to come to an end. He was praying for his people when the angel Gabriel appeared to him, interrupting his prayer. His message to the aging prophet had to have really shaken Daniel. Gabriel said to him, 'Seventy weeks are determined upon thy people and upon thy holy city, to finish the transgression, and to make an end of sins, and to make reconciliation for iniquity, and to bring in everlasting righteousness, and to seal up the vision and prophecy, and to anoint the most Holy Place.'

"My young friend, it was a common practice to refer to time when it applied to the land of Israel as 'weeks of years,' since God told Moses that our land was to lie fallow every seventh year as a 'sabbath to the land.' One of the main reasons for the Babylonian captivity was because the nation had refused to honor the land's sabbath. I only bring this out to help you understand the 70 weeks Gabriel refers to. So according to the angel Gabriel, 70 weeks of years are determined for our nation of Israel. So 70 times 7 is 490 years. But wait, you say, it has already been longer than that since the prophet Daniel, and you are correct— but Gabriel was not finished. He went on with his declaration by telling Daniel when the nation's timepiece was going to start counting. Here are his exact words: 'Know therefore and understand, that from the going forth of the commandment to restore and to build Jerusalem unto the Messiah the Prince, shall be seven weeks, and threescore and two weeks: the street shall be built again, and the wall, even in troublous times. And after the sixty-two weeks Messiah shall be cut off, but not for Himself.'

"So according to the angel Gabriel, the calendar starts counting when the commandment is given to rebuild Jerusalem, and Gabriel wanted to make sure they got the right commandment down. It was going to be when the order was given to restore the city, including its streets and its wall. The emphasis on 'the street' and 'the wall' was to make sure there would be no confusion with other earlier degrees, which specified rebuilding the Temple. So we have a very specific time frame. That only happened when King Artaxerxes made a decree giving Nehemiah permission, safe passage, and supplies to return to Jerusalem to rebuild the city and the wall.

"Now, I have followed Messiah's story since I heard the magi from the East had come asking where the King of the Jews was going to be born. I have searched the Holy Scriptures diligently for every reference of our Messiah. I am convinced the reason Jesus told the angry Pharisees that the rocks would cry out if the people stopped praising Him was last Sunday was the day foretold by the Prophet Daniel that the Messiah would be presented to our nation. This was the only day He could be presented.

"Remember how you always came and told me He would say, 'My hour is not come'? Well, this was the reason. He was waiting for the exact day foretold by Daniel. My friend Joseph and I have spent months working on just this question, and we determined, based on when the degree was given by King Artaxerxes, that counting off the 69 weeks of years gives us a total of 483 years, 483 times 360 days a year gives us 173,880 days. My young friend, two days ago, when Jesus, the Nazarene, came into Jerusalem riding on a young donkey, He rode into the city on the 173,880th day—to the day! Can you believe the accuracy in our Scriptures?!

"That is not all, either! We all know there were many times the people tried to make Jesus king, but He avoided any mention of it. He, in fact, would always tell people not to tell when He had done a miracle. But two days ago was different! You told me yourself how Jesus set the entire day up. He meticulously arranged the entire day, including having a young donkey waiting for Him. And do you know why, my young friend? Well, another one of our prophets told that the future King of Israel, our Messiah, would present Himself to the nation in just this way. Jesus deliberately fulfilled Zechariah's prophecy. Zechariah's exact words were:

Rejoice greatly, O daughter of Zion; shout, O daughter of Jerusalem: behold, thy King cometh unto thee: He is just, and having salvation; lowly, and riding upon an ass, and upon a colt the foal of an ass.

"It was no mistake the Pharisees were furious. They felt the exuberant crowd was blaspheming. They knew the crowd was proclaiming Jesus, Messiah, the King! I think they were shocked when Jesus endorsed it by telling them, 'I tell you that, if these people should hold their peace, the stones would immediately cry out.' " Nicodemus paused. "I believe this was the day King David talked about in his Psalms when he wrote so long ago, 'This is the day which the Lord has made; we will rejoice and be glad in it.' "

I frowned. I felt like I was missing something. Suddenly I realized the part of the passage I had heard that had not been explained. "Master, you said the Scriptures say, 'And after the sixty-two weeks Messiah shall be cut off, but not for Himself.' Master, what does this mean?"

Nicodemus nodded. Frowning he said, "Do you remember the night you went with me to visit Jesus? You stood outside the door and waited for me. I am not sure if you could overhear the conversation, but one thing Jesus said I have pondered. To be honest, it goes along with other passages from our ancient writings from the Prophet Isaiah. Here are a few highlights from the prophet's writings: '…He is despised and rejected by men, a

Man of sorrows and acquainted with grief … He was led as a lamb to the slaughter, and as a sheep before its shearers is silent, so He opened not His mouth…'

"These and many other passages have long been ascribed as referring to our Messiah. But since these passages do not sound like what we think our Messiah should be, we chose to ignore these Scriptures. But if you put these prophecies of our Messiah with the prophecies of Daniel that you are asking about, where Daniel says, 'Messiah shall be cut off, but not for Himself,' and, if you add what Jesus told me that night, 'And as Moses lifted up the serpent in the wilderness, even so must the Son of Man be lifted up,' I am afraid they are foretelling the death of our Messiah."

Suddenly something John had told me came back to my mind. "Master, on the day the Nazarene came into the city in triumph, I had gone to take Him your warning. Remember? Right outside of Bethpage I ran into John and Peter on an errand for Jesus. He had sent them to bring the donkey for Him to ride. While we were walking, noticing their dark and sad faces, I asked John about it. He told me Jesus had taken the 12 disciples aside and told them that the Son of Man will be handed over to the chief priests and scribes, and they will condemn Him to death. Then they will hand Him over to the Gentiles to be mocked, flogged, and crucified. Master, could He really be lifted up and cut off like the prophecies say?"

At Nicodemus' dark nod, my heart sank. The Son of Man handed over to the chief priests and scribes, and they would condemn Him to death? My master would condemn Him to death? Then they would hand Him over to the Gentiles to be mocked, flogged, and crucified? Crucified? Only the Romans could crucify. All I could think was, I hope it will not be on my watch. While I did not know what I believed or didn't believe about Him, and while I did not understand a word the man said, as a person, I found myself drawn to Him.

XII

I did not have a good night last night. I tossed and turned on my mat all night long. I kept thinking about Nicodemus' prediction that Jesus would be killed soon, fulfilling Daniel's prophecy given so many centuries ago. But today, as I listened to Jesus, He did not act worried at all as He continued berating the Temple and religious authorities.

For instance, with the crowds hanging on His every word, He turned to His disciples and said, "Don't be impressed with these experts in religion. Beware of them! You've seen them, how they love to parade in robes fit for a king and to be adored by everyone as they walk along the street. And they love the best seats in the synagogue and at religious festivals! With great outward piety, they pray long prayers, but even while they are praying, they are planning schemes to cheat widows out of their property. I tell you, God's heaviest judgement is against these men."

I could not help but look over at a group of priests listening and took note of their dark expressions. The priests were, for the most part, Sadducees—the most wealthy and aristocratic—of which my master was Chief Priest. The Sadducees, along with the leading scribes and Pharisees, had brokered a truce with Rome. This deal permitted them to form their joint ruling body called the Sanhedrin and allowed them to retain some semblance of authority over Israel in religious matters. They could not be happy with Jesus criticizing them in front of the very people they held in such disdain.

Jesus went on to say, "These are the men who put on great shows when they come by the treasury to put in their offerings. They made sure they always have a crowd to applaud their generosity." He had no sooner outlined their schemes to cheat widows when there was a commotion. One of the very people Jesus was talking about walked by solemnly, with great fanfare. Making sure everyone was watching, he poured his offering into the temple treasury, the coins clattering noisily as they spiraled down into the horn-shaped vault. Jesus didn't say a word, just stood there watching with a sad face. But then a poor widow slipped by, trying to be as inconspicuous as possible. She quietly dropped in two tiny coins.

"I tell you the truth," Jesus said. "This poor widow has put in more than everyone has. Everyone else put in gifts out of their abundance, but she has given all she had to live on."

While standing there trying to blend into the crowd, I could not help but notice a man looking at Jesus with tears in his eyes. I wondered what his story would be. He must have felt me watching him, because he looked at me and gave a shaky smile. Wiping his eyes, he motioned a greeting to me. I walked closer and acknowledged him, welcoming him to the Temple. He nodded. His eyes stayed on Jesus.

"You would not believe it!" he told me. "Two days ago I was an outcast, a leper. Nine other lepers and myself had banded together for our own protection and, I guess, so we would not have to be alone. Our lives as lepers were worse than I can even convey. It was so bad, I can't even believe that is what my life was, just two days ago."

"What happened, friend?" I asked.

"Our band of 10 men lived on the outskirts of a small village between Samaria and Galilee," he answered. "Three days ago, early, a crowd came toward us, and we heard people shouting that it was the prophet Jesus from Nazareth. We started scream-ing and crying for help, 'Jesus, Master, have mercy on us!'

"We had to shout, because the Law forbids us to get close to other people and possibly infect them. Jesus stopped and looked at us. His face was so kind and full of compassion for our sad state. I am not sure what I expected Him to do, but all He did was look at us. I saw Him nod His head at our request for mercy. He said, 'Go and show yourselves to the priests.' Without anoth-er word, He resumed his journey, which I know now was here to Jerusalem.

"We were all struck with the excitement of the moment. Turning, we hurried toward the nearest synagogue to find a priest. It was not until we were already a distance away from Him that I thought of something. 'Wait a minute," I said to the other guys, 'what are we doing? The Law states that one only shows himself to the priest after he has been healed. What are we doing?' Suddenly I stared at my companions; they all had the same look of amazement on their faces that I am sure was on my own. Before our very eyes, we were all healed! With heightened excitement, we hurried on to find a priest like the prophet had told us. It was not until later I realized there were only nine of us on the road. I wondered where the tenth man, the Samaritan of our group, had gotten off to, but I was too excited to worry about him.

"I found out later he had turned around and gone back to Jesus. I was told that he ran up to Jesus and fell at His feet, and, with his face down, gave glory to God and thanked Jesus for his recovered life. The part that makes me feel so badly and the reason I came on to Jerusalem as fast as I could was that some-one said Jesus looked around and finally asked, 'Were there not 10 lepers healed? How is it that only one has come back to say "Thank You"? Why is it that the only one to come back and give glory to God is this foreigner?' Then, I was told Jesus instructed him, 'Get up and go on to your home, your faith has made you well.'

"I realized I had not said thank you to Jesus, so I have come to find Him and thank Him for my new life. If you could have only seen me just a few days ago…," his voice trailed off.

I stood there with him for a while, but finally had to head over to another section of the Temple complex. I don't know if he was ever able to get to Jesus or not. It seemed I was always left listening to people telling me what they wished they would have told Jesus.

Passover week, of all the Feast weeks, is the hardest week of my year, due to all that is required of us Temple workers and especially us who work directly for the High Priest. I was happy this week was almost half over; perhaps we would get through the last half with no problems. But we who are trained in fight-ing and being prepared, well, sometimes it seems we have a sixth sense—and mine was sending up all kinds of red flags. I just knew something was going to happen, which is why Nicodemus' prophecy still gave me chills.

As I was walking down a long hallway, I saw a man come out of a door that led to a large room used for informal meetings of the Temple authority. I thought I knew this man, and he looked guilty as he exited the door. Figuring he would come out and head across the courtyard for the nearest main gate, I took a shortcut. I waited to see who would cut across the courtyard, and I did not have to wait long. I could not believe it. It was Judas, the disciple that Nathanael had pointed out to me. Judas Iscariot. I watched him cross the courtyard and head on out the gate. I hoped John and the rest of them were watching him. If I didn't know better, I would bet that Judas was cooking up something. I remembered that bag of coins.

Finally, the long day was over. I watched Jesus and His disciples head out the main gate on the road leading to Bethany. I noticed that Peter and John were not with the group and wondered where they could have gone. It had been hours since I last saw John. I had not been keeping track of Peter, but I assumed they probably left together. Might they be out preparing their Passover meal? Where Jesus would eat it? I wondered, but I was too tired to care. All I wanted to do was get to my room and sit down for a change. During Passover we just lived on our feet, and I was exhausted. My feet were sore.

When I arrived at my quarters, though, a guard awaited me. "You are required to report to Caiaphas' quarters," he said. I considered Judas' visit to the High Priest and wondered if this call was related. I hurried over to report to my master, but I was pretty sure I would not like the orders I was going to get tonight.

As I was walking to my meeting, the words I had heard Jesus

tell the Greeks came back to me for some reason.

> "I assure you: Unless a grain of wheat falls to the ground
> and dies,
>> it remains by itself. But if it dies, it produces a large
>> crop.
> The one who loves his life will lose it,
>> and the one who hates his life in this world will keep it
>> for eternal life.
> If anyone serves Me, he must follow Me. Where I am,
> there My servant also will be.
> If anyone serves Me, the Father will honor him."

While His words still sounded sad and almost prophetic, and I was almost sure tonight was going to be the night, His last words came to me much clearer than when I had actually heard Him say them. "If anyone serves Me, the Father will honor him." These words of His caused me to pause, that was for sure ... If He was the Son of God, what would His Father do to someone who killed His Son? Would God really allow someone to kill His Son? I remembered Jesus telling Nicodemus that He was God's only Son. A lot to think about this night!

XIII

My band moved quietly through the trees. We had torches, although we had not lit them yet, as we did not want to give away our approach too soon. The Passover full moon made it so we did not need the torches, anyway. I led the band, but I was not comfortable leading them on this night going after this particular person. While we were a heavily armed group of Temple guards along with some Roman solders to make us legal, we had a full contingent of priests and Pharisees along with us, making me feel on edge. I mentioned earlier that my master is of the sect of the Sadducees, as are most of the chief priests, but the largest group represented this night were of the sect of the Pharisees. These two groups of Temple authorities were normally bitter enemies, but due to their hatred of the Nazarene they joined forces in their determination to rid themselves of Him.

Judas walked right behind me, directing me where to go. By this time, we had crossed the Kidron Valley and were in the garden of Gethsemane itself. Judas took the lead, pretty sure he knew the secluded corner of the garden where we would find Jesus. If it had been up to me, I would have just left Judas behind. I hate a traitor! But my master was emphatic he come. I heard he had been paid 30 pieces of silver to show us where his Rabbi was.

My master felt we had to arrest Jesus in this secluded spot rather than in Jerusalem proper. He was deathly afraid of the crowds rioting and the Romans getting involved. As a matter of fact, in my master's devious way of thinking, the best way not to get the Romans involved was to involve them early, which is why we had this cohort of Romans trailing us. It was still considered a Temple police action, however, which was why I led the brooding men.

Judas motioned me to stop, and he moved into the lead. At his signal, my men lit their torches, and we started moving forward again. A lone figure moved out of the darkness and approached us. To be honest, we all figured we were being led into an ambush. My master was afraid that in the darkness it would be difficult to make sure we caught the right man, so a signal had been arranged with Judas. Since he knew the Nazarene the best, Judas would walk up and kiss Jesus in greeting, and we were to rush forward and grab Him. But it was not working out like we had anticipated. There were no cowering, hiding, frightened men rushing around in the dark, but this lone figure walking calmly out to us. Judas approached Him and kissed Him.

"Judas, are you betraying the Son of Man with a kiss?" Jesus spoke calmly. Then, turning to us, He asked us in that calm, deep voice I had listened to for so long. So rarely I had understood a single word He said, but this time it was clear.

"Who are you looking for?" He asked.

"Jesus the Nazarene," one of the high priests behind me answered.

"I AM." At this forbidden name of God Most High, the entire crowd of Sadducees and Pharisees fell over backward to the ground.

As they sheepishly got to their feet, again, Jesus asked them, "Who are you looking for?" Again they answered, "Jesus the Nazarene."

"I AM," Jesus repeated, then He added, "Since you have found Me, let these others go." But while He was still speaking, the rest of His disciples rushed out of the night. We had come to the garden expecting a search and having to fight, but when Jesus walked out alone and was talking with us calmly, I guess we all let down our guard. I mean, He certainly did not look threatening. But one of the men rushing out of the night drew a sword. In the panic that followed when we realized he had a weapon, I stepped back and my foot must have turned on a rock, saving my life. As I was falling, instead of slashing across my neck where it was aimed with great force, I felt the sword slice down the side of my head. I was immediately drenched in blood and had such a ringing in my head I could not hear a thing. I saw our men grab the man with the sword, and in the light of their torches, I realized it was the disciple Peter. His face was twisted with fear and hate.

Others had rushed up and grabbed the Nazarene. I saw His lips moving and realized He was telling Peter to drop his sword. It clattered to the rocky ground, and my hearing came back in time for me to hear the metal clanging as it fell. "Put away your sword Peter. Should I not drink the cup My Father has given me?" I heard Jesus ask. Then my eyes opened wider as I heard

Him say, "Do you think I could not ask My Father for more than 12 legions of angels? But if I did, how then would the Scriptures be fulfilled that said it must happen this way?" I was dazed and bloody and, looking back, realize that I was in shock. I noticed that Jesus was staring at me.

I mean, at different times, Jesus had gazed at me, deep in my eyes, and it had always moved me in a way I could not explain. Now, as He looked intensely at me, I saw the compassion that I had heard Levi and John talk so much about. My world stood still. Although I am sure the confusion was still going on — with men yelling, running, and fighting — it all died down for me. My world existed with only the Nazarene and myself. Jesus reached down, and my eyes followed His hand down. I saw in horror that He was picking up a human ear—my ear! My eyes flew back to His face as He drew near me. Calmly, in spite of the roar of chaos going on around us, He reached over and gently pressed my bloody ear back onto my head. The ringing in my head stopped! As I continued looking deep into His eyes, it was if I could hear His deep, calm voice.

"Can you hear me now, Malchus?"

My eyes clung to His face. All my anger, fear, and shame were before me. Suddenly I knew that Jesus knew it all. He knew all about my sin and shame, and yet, I knew He loved me. As clearly as if He had said it out loud then, I remembered His words from His many stories: "Go, and sin no more!"

Then, with a roar, the world closed back in around us, and we were no longer alone. Jesus was roughly bound. Again, I heard His calm voice, "Why do you come at Me with torches and clubs as if I were a criminal? You never laid a hand on Me while I was with you daily, teaching in the Temple. But you do your work in the darkness since that is your dominion. Now, this is your hour. Go ahead." Somehow, in the confusion, His disciples were gone in the night.

They dragged the bound Jesus through the night, back across the Kidron Valley and up the other side, to a gate and into the house of Annas, the father-in-law of my master, Caiaphas, He had been the high priest before Caiaphas and was still the most powerful man behind the scenes in Jerusalem. We were only there for a short time while the Sanhedrin was called for an emergency meeting at my master's house. But while there, Annas wanted to question Jesus about His disciples and His teaching.

Jesus answered him by making a point of Law. "Why don't you question the ones who heard Me speak? I never spoke in secret but spoke openly in the synagogues and the Temple complex. If you want to know what I taught, ask the ones who heard Me."

One of the Temple police standing near Him slapped Him across the face. I closed my eyes, not able to watch. Annas then sent Jesus, bound, the short distance to my master Caiaphas' house, where the Sanhedrin had already gathered.

As we approached the gate to my master's house, I noticed my cousin John standing there. I motioned him to follow me inside, and he stood there warming himself by the fire. I was still in a daze about all that had happened. I was finally understanding what Jesus had told Nicodemus: that unless you were born again, you could not see His Father. I truly did feel born again. My heart was light—but then again, looking over at the bound and already bloodied Jesus, my heart sank. What could I do?

John, from his seat by the fire, caught my eye and looked over at the gate. Walking that way, I glanced out and saw a shaken

Peter hiding in the shadows. Nodding to John, I indicated that he should let Peter in. John walked over to a slave girl, who was guarding the gate, and showed her Peter, telling her I had said he could come in. The slave girl nodded.

Opening the gate, she motioned to Peter to enter. As he walked by her, she touched his sleeve. "Hey, you aren't also one of this man's disciples too, are you?" she asked. I was surprised to hear Peter's answer.

"No, I am not!" he exclaimed. Shaking her hand loose, Peter made his way over to where some servants and Temple police had a charcoal fire and were warming themselves. Peter walked over and sat down, rubbing his arms and trying to take off the chill of the night.

A short time later, one of the men took a closer look at Peter and accused, "You look like one of that man's disciples. Are you one of His disciples?" Peter shook his head. I was really surprised to hear Peter deny his Master again. "I am not!" Peter insisted.

Then, just a bit later, my brother-in-law, who also works for my master and who had been in the garden with us when we arrested Jesus, came out and saw Peter. He had of course seen Peter take a whack at me with his sword.

"Wait a minute!" he shouted. "What are you doing here? You were in the garden with Jesus!"

Peter jumped up and started cursing. "I tell you I don't know the man!" Just about that time, I heard a rooster crow. Peter stopped as if someone had slapped him. I saw him look over to where Jesus was still standing, bound, waiting to be taken into the Sanhedrin. Jesus turned His head and looked at Peter; His face was sad beyond belief. Peter's shoulders slumped, and, shaking his head, he stumbled to the gate and went out into the night.

Glancing around, I saw no one was watching me, so I slipped out behind him.

Hearing sobs, I made my way over and saw Peter slumped on his knees, crying. His body shook with deep sobs. I touched his shoulder, and Peter looked up at me with the most despairing face I have ever seen. At my questioning look, he started crying harder, if that was possible.

Finally, as his sobs subsided, he choked out, "I denied my Jesus. He said I would, and I did it. Just like He said I would. I denied my Lord. He said I would deny Him three times before a rooster crowed tonight. I am so ashamed. I had told Him I would go to jail for Him or die with Him. But He just shook His head. He told me I would deny Him." Peter's voice died, and his body shook with more tears. I looked around. I could not leave him out on the street like this. Someone who recognized him might come around, and he would really be in trouble. Touching him on the shoulder again, I shook him to get his attention. His tearstained face gleamed in the moonlight. "Come with me, Peter. You are not safe out here. Come." Taking him by the arm, I helped him to his feet.

We started walking. Unconsciously, I had decided to take him to my room. I realized it was not a bad choice. He could wait out the night there while I was on duty. In the morning, I could figure out some other place for him to go.

We arrived at my small room. There was no one in the vicinity. I am sure with all the commotion going on with the Nazarene—no, my Messiah, because I truly did believe in Him now. He was the Messiah, and I could not believe it had taken me so long to figure that out. I had no excuse. I had listened to Him for three years and had even listened to John the Baptizer before Him, so I should have known. I should have recognized Him. I was so sorry for all the time I had wasted. But I should have known. This was the reason my heart burned within me while listening to Him. This was the reason His direct gaze penetrated my soul. I shook my head at my blindness and my deaf ears. Subconsciously, I reached up and touched my ear. I had to smile as I remembered asking myself what I had to be healed from? If only I would have known! My heart was the sickest. My heart needed healing most, and He had even healed that. Then, He healed my ear.

I could not believe they could actually kill the Messiah, but I had heard enough of my master's planning to know that was exactly what they had planned. And why did it seem as if Messiah was resigned to being killed? Why did He predict His own death? My mind was going in circles. How could my Messiah be killed? It was more than I could handle.

Still supporting Peter, I helped him into my room and showed him to a chair. He sank into it, deep in despair. I explained to him that I had to leave but would return about daybreak, that he could use my bed and rest. He showed no indication that he had even heard me. I was worried leaving him in this state, but knew I had to get back before I was missed. Explaining again, I hurried out the door, making sure to lock it behind me.

I hurried on back to the courtyard, hoping no one had noticed my absence. I worried about Peter. I had never seen anyone so depressed in my life. I hoped he would not do something drastic, like try and take his own life, but I had to get back to my post. Tonight was going to be crazy.

I ran back to my room wondering what I would find there. I couldn't even bear to think of— let alone tell about—the mock trial I had witnessed. How none of the witnesses brought to testify against Jesus could make their stories agree. How the guards beat Him unmercifully and even blindfolded Him while hitting Him, then ordered Him to tell them who had hit Him. It was terrible. I could barely force myself to look at Jesus. His face was bloody, and as if that was not bad enough, there were great globs of spittle running down and dripping off His beard. How could anyone be so cruel?

Then, finally, my master got up and demanded Jesus answer him. "Are You the Messiah, the Son of the Blessed One?" he shouted in frustration.

"I AM," said Jesus, once again using the Divine Name for God, "and all of you will see the Son of Man seated at the right hand of the Power and coming with the clouds of heaven."

Then my master, the High Priest, tore his robes and said, "Why do we still need witnesses? You have heard the blasphemy! What is your decision?"

Jesus' words impacted me more than I would have thought possible. Remember, I had asked Nicodemus what the term "the Son of Man" really meant as relating to Jesus, and Nicodemus had quoted a passage out of Daniel. Now to hear Jesus quote that same passage as its fulfillment was almost more than I could comprehend. The large room filled with angry men was gone as my mind was back walking along the road with Nicodemus, his old voice strengthened as it did when he was talking about his passion, "... And behold, One like the Son of Man, coming with the clouds of heaven, He came to the Ancient of Days. And they brought Him near before Him. Then to Him was given dominion and glory and a kingdom, that all peoples, nations, and languages should serve Him. His dominion is an everlasting dominion, which shall not pass away. And His kingdom the one which shall not be destroyed."

I shook my head. I so wanted to believe the prophecies. Even though what I was seeing and hearing seemed to be direct confirmation of them, I could not reconcile this with what I knew my master had always taught about our coming Messiah King.

———————————————

They left to take Him to the Roman governor's mansion. This was the infamous Pontious Pilate. The hatred between my master and the rest of the Temple authorities was nothing compared to the contempt between them and Pontious Pilate. This enmity was well-known, but since they wanted to put Jesus to death, He had to be condemned and killed by the Romans. The priests' hatred of Jesus overcame their animosity toward each other and their Roman masters.

I opened the door to my room. In the predawn darkness, my eyes could hardly see anything. I looked at the chair where I had left Peter. He was still huddled there. I don't think he had moved a bit since I left him. I moved over.

"Peter," I said. "Peter!" I shook his shoulder. "Come on, Peter."

He moved away from me. "Leave me alone!" he whispered. "Leave me alone!"

"I can't, Peter. I have to be back on duty. They are taking Jesus to Pilate. They have condemned Him to death."

Peter raised his head. "I denied Him ... I denied Him three

times!" he cried. "I was going to die with Him, and the first time I was asked, I denied Him! I have nothing to live for." Tears welled in his eyes again. "Jesus told me I was going to deny Him. How could He have known? I tried to help save Him, but He would not let me fight for Him. What else could I do …?" His voice trailed off. I don't even think he was aware whom he was talking to. I mean, I was there! I felt his sword! But Peter kept talking.

"You should have been there at our last supper. He told us someone was going to betray Him. We did not know who He was talking about. We kept asking Him who it was going to be, but He never said, at least not in a way we understood. The next thing I knew, we all were arguing about who is going to be the greatest in His kingdom. Then, do you know what He did?" Without waiting for a reply, he answered his own question. "Here we were arguing, and without saying a word, the next thing we knew, Jesus quietly got up, took off His outer robes, and He wrapped a towel around Himself like an apron. Then, looking for all the world like a slave, He got a basin, poured it full of water, and started washing our feet. We were speechless!

"I watched in horror as He got down on His knees beside each one of the other disciples and carefully washed their feet. He even washed that traitor Judas' feet!" Peter paused as if remembering his own part in the previous night's happenings. His eyes misted over again, but with obvious effort he went on. "When He got to me, I was so embarrassed that I said, 'No Lord, You will never wash my feet! Ever!' Jesus looked at me with those eyes of His. Eyes that look right through you." I nodded. I knew that look. Peter went on. "Jesus told me softly, 'If I don't wash your feet, you have no part with Me.' I gasped."

Peter went on. 'Lord,' I said, 'not only my feet, but also my hands and my head.'

"I did not even notice when Judas walked out into the night. Jesus was talking about loving each other and yet, He had said we could not follow Him where He was going. He had spoken so much about His death, I thought He was referring to that again. So I asked Him. 'Master, where are you going?'

"Jesus looked at me sadly. 'You can't come with Me now; but you will join Me later.'

"I just could not leave it alone." Peter shook his head sadly, big tears once again welling up in his eyes. " 'But why can't I come now?' I asked, 'I am even ready to die for You.'

"Jesus looked like He was ready to start crying, 'Die for Me? No, three times before the cock crows tomorrow morning, you will deny that you even know Me!'

"I slumped down in despair. What could He mean? But Jesus went on talking to us. 'Don't let your hearts be troubled,' He said. 'You are trusting God, now trust Me. There are many homes up there where My Father lives, and I am going to prepare them for your coming. When everything is ready, then I will come and get you, so that you can always be with Me where I am. If this weren't so, I would tell you plainly. And you know where I am going and how to get there.'

"My friend Thomas—Thomas, he looks so much like Jesus we jokingly refer to him as the Twin—he said, 'No, we don't know where You are going. We haven't any idea, so how can we know the way?' "

"Jesus told him, 'I AM the Way, I AM the Truth, and I AM Life. No one can get to the Father alone. Only I can take you to Him. If you had known who I Am, then you would have known who My Father is. From now on you know Him—and have seen Him!'

"He talked with us at length, but all I could think of was Jesus thinking I was going to swear I had never known Him. Why would He doubt me? I had proven my love for Him. What could He possibly be thinking, was all I could think. But then after Jesus prayed with us and for us, we left to head to the garden. You basically know the rest from there," said Peter, letting me know that he did know who I was. His voice trailed off, and he slumped back down, disheartened again.

"Peter, I have to go back. Are you going to be okay here for a bit longer?" I asked the top of his head. "My master expects me to be there when he gets to Pilate's palace. I figured no one would miss me in the crowd, but he will know I am not there if he does need me and he can't find me, so I have to go."

Peter nodded without looking up. I rushed out of the room, again locking the door behind me. I began to run, taking a shortcut I knew. I hoped to arrive at Pilate's palace about the same time as my master and the mob.

I actually beat them there and backtracked just a bit until I saw the crowd coming. I moved into the shadows. It was still pretty dark, with the dawn only now having broken. No one saw me as they came abreast of my spot and passed me. I saw Jesus. His face was bloody and His eyes swollen shut. The men holding the ropes by which He was bound were tugging on them insolently, and I gritted my teeth in shame and anger. I looked at my master and the other chief priests and Pharisees. What a difference one day makes. Yesterday, I had served my master with pride and respect; but today, all I see is the hate of a little man.

The trial at Pilate's passed quickly. Pilate did not want to have anything to do with Jesus, but the chief priests and rulers of the Jews were more than a match at manipulating him into at least listening to them. Pilate even tried to pass the buck to Herod by sending Jesus to Herod, because Pilate found out Jesus was from Galilee. But after trying to get Jesus to do a miracle for him, Herod sent Him back to Pilate. Something funny seemed to have happened between Herod and Pilate. Their antagonism is well-known, but after this mock trial, a real friendship seemed to have developed between these two rulers.

Pilate, thinking he would appease the crowd, gave the order to have Jesus scourged. Jesus was led away. He was tied to a post and brutally flogged. This was not a beating with 39 stripes like we Jews do, using rods; His scourging was done with a flagellum, a lash made out of heavy leather straps with pieces of bone, brass, and even lead balls sewn into the straps. With the Romans, there was no limit on the amount of lashes a person could receive, only that the person would be flogged until the flesh hung from his back. I had seen prisoners literally disemboweled by Roman flogging. Thankfully, I did not have to watch them flog Jesus. My master asked for something and I had to run to retrieve it for him, so I was spared having to watch this spectacle.

By the time I returned to Pilate's courtyard, Jesus, wrapped in a purple robe, was led back up to the elevated area and was standing next to Pilate. He had been beaten so brutally He could barely stand. His blood dripped in large drops and pooled at His feet. I had the feeling Pilate had brought Him up there to display Him, hoping the Jews would see the blood-soaked Jesus and be satisfied. Pilate waved his arms to get the crowd to quiet down. Finally, my master gestured to the masses, and the rabble quit screaming.

"I find no fault with this innocent man!" Pilate shouted. "Behold the man!" But they screamed louder for Him to be crucified.

Finally, to try to get them to see reason, Pilate told the crowd that he would release someone for their Passover. He picked the worst thief and murderer he had in his jail and offered to release either the murderer Barabbas or Jesus. I don't think Pilate ever thought the crowd would clamor for Barabbas, but by this time, my master and the other Temple authorities had the crowd whipped to a frenzy. They yelled for Barabbas' freedom.

Pilate, trying to make the crowd realize they were killing an innocent man, had a large pan of water brought out. While the crowd watched, he washed his hands, showing them that his hands were clean of the blood of Jesus.

But my master screamed, "Let His blood be on us and on our children!" Then, seeing that Pilate was still trying to figure out a way to let Him go, they began to yell, "If you release this man, you are no friend of Caesar's!" Well, that did it. Pilate could not afford to have it be known that he had released someone who was a threat to Caesar's throne.

Finally, Pilate tried to make Jesus' trial and execution as legal as possible. To be honest, this whole trial had been a farce from the beginning! He was illegally brought before the Sanhedrin during His midnight trial, as our laws state plainly our court can only meet during the light of day. He was scourged by the Romans before being declared guilty. He should never have been beaten until he was formally tried and convicted. But this entire trial had been ugly. So now, to make it all nice and legal, Pilate went to the "High Place" or Gabbatha, as we call it. It was referred to as the Stone Pavement, and it was here that Pontious Pilate had his judgment seat outside the Praetorian. He sat down on the judge's bench and pronounced the formal sentence of crucifixion, "Ibis in crucem"—"You shall mount the cross!"

Pilate was not through with the Jews, though. If anything, I thought after this trial, he was going to hate the Temple authorities even more than he did before. He stood up, waving the unsigned order.

"What do I do with Jesus? What do I do with your King?" Pilate shouted. Their words still send chills down my spine.

"Take Him away! Take Him away! Crucify Him! Crucify Him!" the crowds screamed. "We have no king but Caesar!" Pilate hunched his shoulders as if he had been given a blow, sat back down, and signed the order. Jesus was led away.

The next few hours are too painful to write about in any detail. I had hoped to slip away from the whole thing, but my master insisted I attend him all the way until Jesus was on the cross.

His torment had only started with His scourging. After Pilate signed His crucifixion order, the soldiers took Jesus into the headquarters and stripped Him, then draped a military scarlet robe on Him. To further mock His kingship, they twisted together a wreath of thorns and jammed it down on His head. Mocking Him, they bowed to Him, saying, "Hail King of the Jews!" They spit and hit him until they tired of their game and the cross was ready. They took their scarlet robe back and forced Him to pick up His own cross. They led Him away to the place of the Skull to crucify Him. Gulgolet is Hebrew for skull, so we have our word Golgotha. The Romans say calvaria, hence Calvary.

On the way, due to the brutal beatings and the amount of blood He had already lost, it was obvious a weakened Jesus was going to have a hard time carrying His cross by Himself. The fact that the next day was a High Sabbath gave a sense of urgency to the Romans. They wanted Jesus to be on the cross as long as possible before He had to be removed before the Feast day. It was already almost nine in the morning. So a passing man, one by the name of Simon of Cyrene, was pressed into service by the Romans and made to carry Jesus' cross the rest of the way.

A huge crowd followed Him, including women who were mourning and lamenting Him. But turning to them, Jesus said, "Daughters of Jerusalem, do not weep for Me, but weep for yourselves and your children. Look, the days are coming when they will say, 'Blessed are the barren, the wombs that never bore, and the breasts that never nursed!' Then they will begin to say to the mountains, 'Fall on us!' and to the hills, 'Cover us!' For if they do these things when the wood is green, what will happen when it is dry?"

I kept thinking back to the mock trial. I was shocked at my master and the other religious leaders. I still found it almost impossible to believe that they had committed such an atrocity. How could they be so blind? It was obvious to anyone watching that Pilate did not want to condemn Jesus! I don't know if he had any thoughts about Jesus' claim to be God's Son; I doubt it. But I know Pilate talked with Him privately, and each time, after he spoke with Jesus, he did make an effort to have Him released.

I heard it rumored that Pilate's wife had a nightmare regarding Jesus and sent word to her husband to not have anything to do with "this righteous man," but I don't know where the rumor started. Whatever it was that caused Pilate's hesitation, I think Pilate got revenge on the Temple authorities. He ordered the "titulus"—this was a wooden plank nailed to the cross above the person's head to show to the world why the person was being crucified. Sometimes the board was painted with a white chalk-like substance to make the words stand out. And in this case they did, for in big, bold letters Pilate's sign read in all three languages of the area (Hebrew, Aramaic, and Latin), "JESUS OF NAZA-RETH, THE KING OF THE JEWS."

Two other men, criminals, were also led away to be executed with Him. When they arrived at the place called the Skull, they crucified Him there, along with the criminals, one on the right and one on the left. It was about the third hour when they nailed Jesus to the cross. Tears blinded my eyes again as I heard Jesus say, "Father, forgive them, because they do not know what they are doing." How could He have such compassion and love for these people who were torturing Him?

Standing by the cross of Jesus were His mother, along with her sister and two other women. My cousin John was supporting Jesus' mother. Since I was part of the Temple authority, I felt guilty to let my cousin see me. Thankfully, I only had to hang back in the crowd. John was oblivious to anything else around him except for his Messiah—and now, my Messiah—hanging on the cross. I remembered the time I had been offended for His mother when He had ignored her and would not go out when she called Him. Now, I heard Him speak to her with great compassion from the cross. I know it took Him much effort to get the words out, but He wanted to make sure His mother was going to be taken care of.

Looking down at His mother, He said, "Woman, here is your son." Then He said to my cousin, "Here is your mother." I knew Mary had four other sons, but from that day on, John took her home with him, and she was like his own mother in his house.

After the soldiers crucified Jesus and He was up on the cross, they took His clothes and divided them into four parts, a part for each soldier on the crucifixion detail. But holding up the tunic, which was seamless, woven in one piece from the top, I heard one of them say, "Let's not ruin this, but let's cast lots for it, to see who gets it." When they held it up, I saw Mary look over and cringe. I figured she had probably made the beautiful, seamless tunic for Him herself. She looked back up at her naked, beaten, bloody Son hanging there, and I watched a large tear slide down her face.

Since the place Jesus was crucified was right outside the city and near a busy thoroughfare, everyone entering or leaving the city saw Him there and could read the sign above His head. When the chief priests saw this sign, they were furious and stormed in to see Pilate, figuring they could brow beat him into changing his sign. They only wanted to make a small change—for the sign to read, "HE SAID, I AM THE KING OF THE JEWS." But by now, possibly knowing he was manipulated to carry out their heinous deed, Pilate would not budge. "What I have written, I have written!" he told them.

Those who passed by were yelling insults at Jesus, shaking their heads, and saying, "Ha! The One who would demolish the sanctuary and build it in three days, save Yourself by coming down from the cross!" In the same way, the chief priests with the scribes were mocking Him to one another and saying, "He saved others; He cannot save Himself! Let the Messiah, the King of Israel, come down now from the cross, so that we may see and believe." They shouted, "He saved others; let Him save Himself if this is God's Messiah, the Chosen One!" The soldiers also mocked Him. They came offering Him sour wine and said, "If You are the King of the Jews, save Yourself!"

Even those crucified with Him were calling out to Him. Hanging there, one condemned criminal began to yell insults at Him, taunting, "Aren't You the Messiah? Save Yourself and us!" But the other one rebuked him: "Don't you even fear God, since you are undergoing the same punishment? We are punished justly, because we're getting back what we deserve for the things we did, but this man has done nothing wrong." Then he said, "Jesus, remember me when You come into Your kingdom!" From where I was standing, I could hear Jesus say to him, "I assure you: Today you will be with Me in paradise."

From noon until three in the afternoon, darkness came over the whole land. About three in the afternoon Jesus cried out with a loud voice, "Elí, Elí, lemá sabachtháni?" When some of those standing there heard this, they said, "He's calling for Elijah!" But maybe because I was standing closer to His cross, I understood the Aramaic words. Although in Jesus' weakened state His voice was guttural with pain, I heard Him say, "My God, My God, why have You forsaken Me?" The pain and agony in His voice were soul-piercing. Then, in a quieter voice, He said, "I am thirsty."

It is funny what your mind does to you in a stress-filled time like this. My mind took me back to hearing Him in the Temple, telling everyone who was thirsty to come to Him to drink and out of Him would flow streams of living water. Now, He was thirsty. It broke my heart. Somehow, at a deeper level, I understood that He was thirsty physically so that I might never have to thirst spiritually again.

When He said He was thirsty, one of the guards ran and got a sponge, filled it with sour wine, fixed it on a hyssop branch, and reached it up to touch Jesus' lips with the sponge. I don't know if He actually drank or not, but then, Jesus shouted again with a louder voice, "It is finished! Father, into Your hand I commit My spirit." I was watching Him and saw His head fall down on His beaten and bloody chest. While I was still watching, He breathed His last. Jesus was dead!

At Jesus' final cry, a tremendous earthquake hit the land. The knoll where the crosses stood was rocked violently, and we were frightened! The centurion who was in charge of the crucifixion detail slowly sank to his knees, and I heard him say, "This man really was God's Son!" Those with him, who were guarding Jesus, saw the earthquake and the things that had happened; all were terrified!

Even with all this, there was more! I heard later that right at the same time Jesus gave up His spirit and died, the curtain of the sanctuary—the one dividing the Holy place from the Devir, the Holy of Holies in the Temple — was split in two from top to bottom. Many people said that the earthquake opened the tombs, and many who had died were brought back to life and claimed to have seen their loved ones! I don't know about that — I did not see anything. But I can tell you one thing: if I would not have been convinced He was the Christ earlier, I would have become a believer after living through the events of this last day. If only from hearing Him say, "Father, forgive them, for they don't know what they are doing." After all they had done to Him, it really would take God's Son to be able to forgive like that.

Then, later on, to hear Jesus tell that thief, "Today you will be with me in paradise," took such love and compassion. Only God's Son could demonstrate that depth of love in the face of His own rejection.

Since it was the preparation day, the Jews did not want the bodies to remain on the cross on the Sabbath. They requested that Pilate have the men's legs broken and that their bodies be taken away. So the soldiers came and broke the legs of the first man and of the other one who had been crucified with Him. When they came to Jesus, they did not break His legs since they saw that He was already dead.

I was surprised to see Joseph of Arimithea and Nicodemus approach the cross. They had not seen me, and I was not sure I wanted to be seen. I had no idea what they would be doing at this place, and I was shocked to see them. I knew they had secretly really liked and respected Jesus, and I had thought both of them believed He was the Messiah.

Quickly I realized they were there to honor Jesus' body instead of mocking and joining the crowd of haters. They must have asked Pilate for Jesus' body and were going to take it down and prepare it for burial. I was proud to be able to say I knew these men.

I noticed Mary, Jesus' mother, moving up to see what they were doing. I had thought it was going to kill her when she saw the men rush up with large mallet-like clubs to crush the knees of the two men on either side of her Son. But when they noticed Jesus already hanging lifeless on the cross, they did not break his legs. One of the soldiers, however, took his spear and pierced it up into Jesus' heart. I thought His poor mother was going to faint away, but John was holding her. She is a strong woman.

When she saw they were taking her Son down, she fell to her knees and, with tears running down her face, she silently watched them. John stood beside her looking helpless, so I walked up to him and nodded a greeting. He appeared happy to see me, and I knew he was wondering about Peter. Whispering, I told him Peter was at my place, but I had left there before dawn that morning and had not been back since.

"I have been worried sick," John told me. "He looked unstable when he left the courtyard. Let me take Mary to my house, and I will come by and check on Peter. I think I have time before the Sabbath starts." I nodded without seeing him. I could not take my eyes off my dead Messiah.

Up until now, neither Joseph nor Nicodemus had ever publicly come out as Jesus' followers. I knew that one time Nicodemus took up for Him on a point of Law, but none of the authorities thought seriously that Nicodemus "believed on Him." After some of our talks, I could perceive that both of them were believers in Him. It took a lot of nerve for Joseph to go directly to Pilate, especially, since by doing so, he would be going against the entire Temple authority. According to what I heard later, Joseph went boldly to Pilate, asking him for permission to take down and bury Jesus' body before the Sabbath. I think Pilate gave him permission partly to show his disdain for the other religious leaders. Nicodemus came with Joseph, bringing a mixture of about 75 pounds of myrrh and aloe, all very expensive: a burial fit for a king.

After they finished wrapping His body in linen cloths with the aromatic spices, they wrapped His head with a separate linen napkin. John and I watched. John was still supporting Mary, Jesus' mother. Joseph placed the body in a brand-new tomb he had hewn from rock there in a nearby garden. Everything was done quickly, as it was almost evening, the start of the Sabbath. This was not a normal Sabbath. Rather this was the High Sabbath day of the Feast of Unleavened Bread, which is always the day after Passover no matter what day of the week Passover falls on. This meant that on this week we had two Sabbaths in a row: the Feast of Unleavened Bread, which is a High Sabbath, followed by the regular week's Sabbath.

My heart ached with my loss. I needed to have some time to myself to really analyze everything that had happened — not only to my Messiah, but to myself. So often I had ridiculed Levi and John and the rest of Jesus' disciples. Oh, how I wish I could have been one of His chosen! No wonder my heart always burned in me while listening to Him. How could I have been so deaf and so blind?

As Nicodemus and Joseph headed back into the city, I walked with them. How I needed to talk to Nicodemus to tell him what had happened to me! But I did not know where to start. Also, they were in such a deep conversation, I did not want to interrupt them. Joseph believed that the place Jesus was crucified was the exact same mountain where Abraham almost sacrificed Isaac! I wondered at his thinking. We took the long way around, so we could walk with Joseph to his house first, and stood there for a bit until they finished their conversation. Then we started for Nicodemus' house.

"Master," I said. "What happened? I am so confused! I know you thought He was the Messiah. What happened?"

Nicodemus looked at me. His old face was seamed with age, but his eyes were bright. Although the marks of tears were still on his face, his eyes gleamed in anticipation. "My boy," he said, "do not misunderstand me. This was a terrible day! The worst day of my life! But on the other hand, if it had not been clear to

Joseph and me before, today was the absolute proof needed that Jesus was indeed the Messiah!

"Remember when John called Him 'the Lamb of God which takes away the sin of the world'? Remember those passages in Isaiah we looked at where it says, 'He was beaten, smitten of God and rejected, a man of sorrows and acquainted with grief'? Do you remember what Jesus cried out from the cross right before He died?" He stared at me intently.

With tears blurring my eyes, I whispered, " 'My God, My God why have you forsaken me?' "

Nicodemus nodded, "The entire phrase goes, 'My God, My God, why have You forsaken Me? Why are You so far from helping Me and from the words of My groaning? My God, I cry in the daytime, but You do not hear; why are You so far from helping Me?'

"This passage is out of our Psalms. It was written by the Shepherd David. We have long held it to be a direct reference to our Messiah, although it did not paint a picture of our Messiah that we wanted to accept, so we pushed it back and ignored it. All those prophecies and more were fulfilled today. What day is today?"

I looked at him blankly; everyone knew it was the Passover. But I answered dutifully, "Master, it is the Passover."

"Yes, you have spoken correctly. Remember the instructions given by Moses before the children of Israel left Egypt? They were to separate a lamb four days before they killed it, for observation. This way, they knew it was spotless without blemish. Well, Jesus, as the Passover Lamb, provided by God Himself, came publicly and was hailed as the Messiah on Sunday, exactly four days ago. Today, right at the hour the priest was killing the

Passover lamb for the Nation, God's own Passover Lamb cried out with a loud voice, 'My God, My God, why have You forsaken me?' He then said, 'It is finished!' and died. Joseph and I have studied this extensively, and we had come to the conclusion that there could be no other outcome. Jesus was the Passover Lamb, as the Passover Lamb He had to die. By His death on our Passover, He proves He is our Messiah. Do you remember what you told me John had told you Jesus said? Remember, it was when John and Peter were getting the donkey for Jesus. You told me that John and Peter both looked so sad. Do you remember?"

I thought back. It seemed a lifetime ago, so much had happened. But Nicodemus was right, it was only four days ago. John's words came back to me. "Oh yes, Master. He said that Jesus took the 12 disciples aside and told them, 'Listen! We are going up to Jerusalem. The Son of Man will be handed over to the chief priests and scribes, and they will condemn Him to death. Then they will hand Him over to the Gentiles to be mocked, flogged, and crucified, and He will be resurrected on the third day.' "

"What do you think? Did that happen?" asked Nicodemus.

I blinked … it almost took my breath away. When I had heard John say those words, they were just words; but now, in light of all we had lived these last days, it was uncanny how accurately Jesus had foretold everything that was going to happen to Him. He had been handed over to the Chief Priest, my master. They did condemn Him to death through a mock trial. He was handed over to the Gentiles, to Pilate, and He was mocked, flogged, and crucified. I shook my head as tears came back to my eyes.

"But wait!" Nicodemus said gently. "Don't give up yet! What was the last thing He said? Do you think if He could predict everything right up to His death, might He be right about the third day as well?"

I thought about Jesus' words that day — a lifetime and yet only four short days ago, I wondered if I could believe Him. I looked at Nicodemus and answered, "He said, 'He will be resurrected on the third day!' "

Nicodemus nodded in agreement, "I believe it! I believe Him!"

Now instead of dread and despair, I had hope. Funny: I, who never had time for Jesus while He was alive, now found myself hoping in His words even after His death.

"Master, one more question, if you don't mind." I hesitated to keep bothering Nicodemus; he looked especially frail right now. But he smiled and nodded for me to go on. We were almost to his house, and I knew he was tired and anxious to get in for his own Passover celebration— although how anyone could celebrate at this time was beyond me.

I continued, "Master, everyone was talking about the thick curtain separating the holy place from the the Holy of Holies, ripping. What could have caused this, and what do you think it means? I have seen this curtain, and it is thick and strong, made with many layers and almost three feet thick! Nothing could just rip this curtain — and from top to bottom, no less? What does this mean?"

Nicodemus hesitated and seemed deep in thought. "My boy, it is the symbolism. That curtain separated God's presence for our nation from normal access. Once a year, only on the Day of Atonement, could the High Priest go into the Holy of Holies. In our Torah, the instructions to the High Priest were very clear. But when Jesus said 'It is finished!' as the Passover Lamb of God, His blood was enough. No more did the curtain have to divide the Holy of Holies. Now, because of Jesus finishing the sacrifice on the cross, I believe it means we can have direct access to God. God Himself ripped the veil down to show there was now no more barrier between Himself and man. His Son, Jesus, paid the final price as the Lamb of God for the sins of the world. Now, we can go boldly before God. At least this is what I believe. My boy, this has been an amazing day, and I don't think we have seen anything yet!" The old man shook his head. I saw tears in his eyes, but he appeared far from disheartened. I think they were tears of joy!

Suddenly, I remembered Peter. "Master, I have to go back to my room. Peter is hiding there." At Nicodemus' startled look, I quickly explained all that had happened in the garden, with Jesus' arrest, and Peter slicing my ear.

"Jesus bent down and picked my ear off the ground!" I recalled, enjoying Nicodemus' look of shock. "Can you believe it, Master? We were coming to arrest Him, and He still took the time to heal me. I became a believer and a disciple right then. Master, I believe He truly was the Son of God." Nicodemus beamed, and I gave a quick explanation of Peter's actions and why he was hidden away.

At Nicodemus' nod, I took off running. I only had a short time to get back to my quarters anyway, as it was almost officially evening time, the start of our High Sabbath Feast day. I opened my door, and Peter rushed at me, his eyes wild.

"What has happened? Tell me everything! I have been sick with worry," he demanded in one breath. At my own look, he backed up, his face stricken.

"Oh no!" his voice faltered. Peter sank back down into the chair he was in when I had left him at dawn. Such a long, long day. So much had happened, it was hard to believe it had only been one short day.

"What happened to Him?" I could barely hear Peter's whisper. "I have to know; please tell me." He looked up with tears once again running down his face and glistening in his beard. I really felt sorry for him, and I wished John would get here. I hated to be the one to give Peter the terrible news. Peter looked near collapsing. I knew he had not eaten anything all day. Perhaps if I gave him something to eat, it might distract him until John could get here.

"Peter?" I touched his arm again. "Peter, may I get you a little something to refresh yourself? It has been a long day."

Peter shook his head. "No, just tell me all that happened today. Don't leave out anything. I don't deserve to know. I surely did not show much love for Him at the end, but please tell me."

Just about then, I heard a soft knock on the door, and I rushed to open it. I was so relieved to see John. He came in and hurried to Peter's side, though Peter refused to look at John and kept his head bowed in shame.

"Peter, Peter! We have to go. I want you to come with me. I want us all to go and wait out the High Sabbath in the upper room where we had our last supper with Jesus. I have sent word to the other disciples to meet us there. But we have to hurry if we are going to get there before the Sabbath starts," John instructed, practically turning to leave before he was all the way in the room.

Peter started sobbing at the mention of the last supper. I looked at John. Tears filled his eyes, too. I knew this day had been brutal for my young cousin. I felt my own eyes tearing up. I could not believe that Jesus was really dead. For some reason, I had thought that He would do something to save the day, another miracle at the very end — the greatest of all. But He had died like a common criminal there at the end. His agonizing cry of "My God, My God, why have You forsaken Me?" haunted me. I tried to concentrate on what Nicodemus said, but the brutal reality of what I had seen with my own eyes was too harsh. Jesus was dead. The end of the story!

John motioned me closer. "Malchus, we have to get Peter out of here. I want him to be back with the rest of the disciples. He is getting too depressed here by himself. Can you help me? Why don't you come with us? You can help me get him over there. I know today was hard on you, too. I saw what Jesus did for you and how you looked at Him after He healed your ear. I feel in my heart you are one of us now. Will you come?"

My tears were coming in earnest now, and I could not talk. I felt so honored to have my cousin want me with him and the rest of the disciples during this terrible time. I suddenly realized I did not want to be by myself either. I nodded through my tears. John turned back to Peter and, taking him by the arm, helped him to his feet.

"Come on, Peter." While not answering or even acknowledging John in any way, Peter allowed himself to be helped to the door. I grabbed a few things and rushed to the door behind them. We hurried through the quiet streets. We were really going to have to rush to make it to the upper room before the Sabbath officially started.

I sat back against the wall. I looked around at the 11 disciples and a few other close friends of theirs. I noticed another friend of mine, Cleopas, was there as well. I knew he had been a follower of Jesus from the beginning, but I had not realized he was in this place. I wanted to talk to him, but my first concern was Peter. He was slumped down beside me, not engaging in anything. I was really worried about him. He was totally locked away in his own guilt and shame and had walled himself away from everyone. All the disciples had tried to engage him since we had arrived, but with no success. He looked suicidal, as far as I was concerned. He had to have known the news was terrible, but to hear about it in all its gory detail — and to really know that Jesus had died and was buried — was almost more that Peter could handle. I hoped the other disciples would try and help him some more instead of ignoring him. Although, that thought was not fair. I didn't think anyone was ignoring him. I kept seeing everyone looking over at him.

I was not sure if I even believed it, but seeing how depressed Peter was I decided to try and share with him what Nicodemus had told me about Jesus being the Passover Lamb.

I shook him, but he groaned and turned away from me. I decided to keep talking anyway. I knew even with his back to me, he could still hear me.

"Peter," I said gently. "Do you remember last Sunday when you and John were going to get the donkey for Jesus? Do you remember that I met you both on the way and walked with you to pick it up?"

I saw Peter nod his head, so, encouraged, I continued on. I recounted the story of the donkey and what he had told me about Jesus saying He would be "mocked, flogged, and crucified … but resurrected on the third day." At these final words, Peter raised his head and saw me.

"Do you remember Jesus telling you this, Peter?" I asked.

Now, Peter sat up a little straighter. "Yes," he whispered. "I remember. I think I remember every word He ever said to me."

Again, tears welled up in his eyes. "But do you know what I remember the most? I remember Him telling me that I would deny Him three times before a rooster crowed. That is what I remember, because I am shamed. I should have done what Judas did. I should have hung myself. Malchus, I have nothing to live for now!" Peter slumped back down.

I had hoped Peter had not yet heard that Judas had tried to give back the money from my master and the Temple authorities just laughed at him. I had hoped Peter had not heard that after throwing the money at the priest's feet, Judas had gone out and hung himself. But I should have known there was no way of hiding a story like that. I pressed on.

"Peter, do you remember the rich Pharisee, the old man, who came to Jesus one night almost three years ago? I came with him, remember? I stayed out in the room with you all while Nicodemus went into the inner room and met with Jesus. Do you remember him?"

Peter nodded again.

"Do you want to know what he believes?" I asked him.

Taking his silence for a yes, I kept on with the story. "I was just talking with Nicodemus on the way back from the cross." At the mention of the cross, Peter physically cringed, but I kept on. I decided to try and tell it just like Nicodemus had told it to me. "Peter, do you know what day it is today?" Again, Peter raised his head and looked at me blankly. I asked him again. "Do you know what day it is today?"

Peter nodded his head. "It is Passover," he whispered.

I kept on. "Do you remember when John called Him 'The Lamb of God which takes away the sin of the world'?" Peter nodded again. "Well, Nicodemus took that to mean Jesus had to die as the sacrificial Lamb of God. He brought in passages from the old prophets like the passage in Isiah that says, 'He was beaten, smitten of God and rejected, a man of sorrows and acquainted with grief?' Well, according to Nicodemus, all those prophecies and so many more were fulfilled today."

To Peter, I recounted Nicodemus' words about Moses and Jesus as the Passover Lamb, his eyes widening. "Jesus as the Passover Lamb had to die. By His death as our Passover, He proves He is our Messiah," I concluded enthusiastically. I thought I saw a gleam of hope in Peter's eyes, so I went on with my own thoughts.

"Peter, you were with Jesus when He told you, not once, but —according to John — three times, that He was going to be arrested, convicted, and turned over to the Gentiles. According to John, Jesus' exact words were, 'We are going up to Jerusalem. The Son of Man will be handed over to the chief priests and scribes, and they will condemn Him to death. Then they will hand Him over to the Gentiles to be mocked, flogged, and crucified, and He will be resurrected on the third day.'"

I looked at him intently, and questioned him just as Nicodemus had done to me: "As you think about His words, does this sound like what happened today?"

Slowly Peter sat up straighter. "Yes, this is exactly what happened."

"So do you think the last thing He said is going to happen as well?"

I could see Peter thinking back over the words in his mind and mouthing the words, "He will be resurrected on the third day."

He looked at me, agony covering his rugged face. "It would

not make any difference to me. I denied I even knew Him." His face settled down into the deep lines of depression I was getting used to seeing on his normally smiling face. I wish I knew how to help him.

I set there in silence for a minute. "I know one thing. Nicodemus believes Him. Nicodemus believes He is going to rise again. He says He has to be raised from the dead in order for the old prophecies regarding Messiah to be accurately fulfilled."

By this time, hearing our conversation, most of the other 10 disciples were loosely gathered around us listening to us talk—well, actually listening to me talk, as Peter was once again slumped down in despair.

John sat down beside me. "Do you think Nicodemus really believes Jesus is going to rise from the dead?" he asked.

I nodded. "Yes, I asked him point blank and he, with no hesitation, affirmed that he and Joseph believe that what happened yesterday and today is the only thing that makes sense based on the prophecies in our Scriptures. It's also obvious that Jesus Himself believed He was going to rise from the dead."

John shook his head. "I wish I could believe that. His death was so final. I was there. I saw Him die. I saw the spear thrust into His side after He was dead. I watched them take His naked, beaten, and bloody body off the cross. I watched Joseph and Nicodemus wrap His body in a beautiful white linen and anoint it. I saw Nicodemus carefully wrap His head. I was supporting Mary all the way to the tomb as they gently laid His body into Joseph's tomb. I am sorry, Malchus. He is dead!"

XIV

The feeling of despair was so palatable that I found myself wishing I would have just stayed home. I had thought it would be easier on my sorrow to be around Jesus' closest friends, but it seemed Peter's depression had taken over the whole group. We were together, but all alone in our grief.

Finally, I couldn't take it any longer. I got up and walked over to where Levi, my good friend—now Matthew—sat with his head on his arms at the table. I took a chair beside him.

"What do you think, Matthew?" I asked, making sure to use his new name for the first time. "I wish I knew Jesus as well as you all did. I only knew Him as someone trying to find information for someone else."

Matthew looked up sharply. "What do you mean? Who were you getting information for?" I swallowed. I had never let it slip before that I was only ever getting information for my master. I was a spy, so to speak. It looked like everyone was tired of just sitting around because John, hearing us talking, walked over and sat down with us. They were both looking at me.

"Yes, Malchus. What are you saying?" John snapped.

"Well," I looked at each of them in turn. "Now, don't yell at me. You all know who my master is. You know he was always asking me questions and sending me to keep track of what was going on. How do you think I feel now?"

"Malchus, I can't believe you would spy on us and give information against your own cousin!" John's eyes reflected his hurt.

"John, I am sorry. I never believed it was going to turn out like it did. You have to remember, I even warned you and asked you to caution Jesus against coming to Jerusalem. Remember, I told you that my master was planning a trap. I did not know how they were going to do it. To be honest, I saw Judas visiting the Temple after Jesus raised Lazarus from the dead; then, I saw him again in the Temple a few days ago. I really did not know what he was doing. My master never told me. I found out about Judas betraying Jesus the night we went to the garden to arrest Him." I couldn't look either of them in the eye.

"I still can't believe it!" John shook his head.

Matthew nodded in agreement. "We should have known it was coming. Looking back, Jesus kept trying to tell us, but we never understood Him. I remember one time …" He stopped abruptly and looked over at Peter with concern in his eyes. Then he continued on in a whisper. "I remember one time, Jesus went into a lot of detail about what was going to happen. Peter took Him off to one side and basically rebuked Him. Peter has really been our leader in so many ways. It hurts to see him so beaten. I am really worried about him …" John's voice trailed off. I, too, looked over at Peter, still slumped down with his head on his chest, his face hidden.

"What happened when Peter rebuked Jesus?" I whispered.

"You remember, I told you about when Jesus took us to Ceasarea Philippi?" I nodded.

"Remember, while there, Jesus had asked us who people said He was? Then He asked us who we said He was? Peter spoke right up and said, 'You are the Christ, the Son of the Living God!' Jesus congratulated Peter and told him that he did not just know that in and of himself, but that Jesus' Father in heaven had shown that to him. He again, affirmed that he was Peter, and on this rock He was going to build His church. Peter really became our leader that day.

"So then Jesus took that moment and started telling us that we were heading to Jerusalem, where He would suffer many things from the elders, chief priests, and scribes. He would be killed, but be raised the third day. Looking back, I realize that every time we heard Him say anything about being killed, a cross, or anything like that, we must have just quit listening.

"Peter took Him aside and told Him, 'No way, Lord! This can't happen to You!' Peter was still hearing Jesus' blessing and the glory he was sure was going to follow that blessing. I guess we all were," John said sadly.

"What did Jesus do?" I asked.

"Jesus' response shook us all up. He reacted harshly, I thought. Because Jesus told Peter, 'Get behind Me, Satan! You are offending Me by trying to stop Me. You are not thinking about God's agenda here, but man's!' Then He told us. 'If anyone wants to follow Me, he has to deny himself, take up his cross, and follow Me ...'

"There was more, but what difference does it make now? I can't believe it all ends like this." John lowered his head.

"John, didn't you see it happening? I mean, you all spent a lot more time with Jesus than I ever did, but even the little you have told me about Him, it seems He was always talking about being taken and killed. I remember the first time I went to where you all were staying and Nicodemus talked to Him. Way back then — over three years ago — He told Nicodemus that 'as Moses lifted up the serpent in the wilderness, even so must the Son of Man be lifted up.' See, my problem was, back then, I did not know who the Son of Man was. But I tell you, Nicodemus told me that Jesus had to die. He had to die to fulfill all the prophecies." Feeling sick, I added, "I wish I would have stayed home!"

Matthew looked up. "No, I am glad you are here. This is a hard time. I won't deny it: I ran like a thief being chased by the guards in the dark. But no one was chasing us. I was embarrassed. I need to try and make Peter see that we were no better than he was. Peter at least tried to do something. I was so frightened I did not know what I was doing and just ran like a coward."

By this time James and a few of the others had joined us.

I thought of another story I wanted explained. "Hey, Peter told me that Jesus washed your feet? What did that mean? When Peter told me about it, he was crying so hard he did not make a lot of sense."

Matthew picked up this story. With a solemn shake of his head he said, "Malchus, you would have had to have been there! I can't even begin to tell you how that made me, and I am sure all the rest of us, feel. What started the whole discussion was Jesus told us that one of us was going to betray Him that night. That news shocked us. We kept asking each other what He meant. Finally, one of us turned to John, since John was sitting at the place of honor beside Him. Getting John's attention, Peter whispered, 'John, ask Him who it is.' But then, somehow, I don't even know how, we were all of a sudden arguing about who was going to be the greatest in His kingdom. Remember, we had just had an incredible high when He was declared King and our Messiah that Sunday. I mean, we had no idea what was waiting for us that night."

Matthew got a pensive look on his face. "You know," he continued, "that was not the first time we had argued about it either, and we all knew Jesus did not like, nor appreciate, us squabbling about being the greatest. But I think the rest of us were jealous of Peter, James, and John, because Jesus seemed to treat them like He liked them better than the rest of us. Then, we all heard that James and John's mother had come and asked that her two boys be allowed to sit one on each side of Jesus when He came into His kingdom, so I guess we just got carried away." His voice trailed off.

John picked up the story. His voice sounded rough, and I looked at him. Tears welled in his eyes. "It so shocked me!" he whispered. "All of a sudden we realized Jesus had gotten up and taken off His robe. That beautiful tunic of His they were gambling over today." He swallowed and lowered his head to hide the tears now running down his face. Wiping his eyes on his sleeve, he looked up and continued with his story. "Picking up a towel, He wrapped it around His waist and He filled a big pan of water. Taking the pan, and with another towel around His arm, He looked for all the world like a common slave. I was mortified. He came to each of us in turn and washed our feet. I was so ashamed of myself. You know what I thought of when He did that?" He looked around, but no one had an answer. "I remembered the Baptizer being asked if he was the Messiah? Remember, Andrew?" Andrew nodded. John continued on, his voice gaining in strength. "The Baptizer answered, 'I am not the Messiah, I baptize you with water for repentance, but the One who is coming after me is more powerful than I. I am not worthy to remove His sandals.' "

Here John paused and took a deep breath. "So the Baptizer was not even worthy to do the work of a slave and take off Jesus' sandals; and we, we kept wanting to be the first and the highest. Our Rabbi, our Messiah, came and washed my feet." He shook his head. Here John's voice failed him completely, and he bowed his head as his sobs shook his body. All of us, by that time, had tears freely running down our faces.

I was surprised to see Peter get to his feet and come over and kneel down beside John. "But at least you had the sense to keep your mouth shut, John. I had to open my big mouth and declare He was not going to wash my feet! Ever! Then, can you all ever forgive me? I denied I even knew Him! After all we had been through, all the stories, all the miracles ..." Once again, Peter was overcome with his grief and began to sob.

But with Peter joining the conversation, I felt the mood shift. We were still grieving, but our stories changed to remembering Jesus' life and the good times they all had with Him. How I wished I had more to offer the group. I touched my ear. I am sure no one would be interested in hearing how I had gotten my ear chopped off — because I had the nerve to go out and arrest Him. I decided to just listen.

It was not long before we were all smiling and laughing in spite of ourselves and our grief. Such wonderful stories! Each one was trying to outdo the others with a favorite story of Jesus.

Andrew started, "I just loved how He was so thoughtful. I mean, if you look at it, He did not need me to go and find a few barley loaves and fish. He could have just made the meal out of nothing. But I think He wanted to involve that boy who was able to give his lunch—such a humble little lunch and yet, Jesus smiled so beautifully at the boy, it just made his day. Then, I have to tell you, I have eaten barley loaves before and they never tasted like those loaves that Jesus had us pass out. My point is, when everyone was totally satisfied, there was just enough for each of us. Jesus was so thoughtful!"

Everyone nodded. "Seems like I never understood Him," Thomas said, "but He never tired of explaining everything to me so I could understand." Again, the other 10 guys agreed.

I was surprised to hear Peter join the conversation. "My favorite story about Jesus was in the boat when we were heading across the lake to Genesaret. Remember that storm? I have spent my whole life on that lake, and I had never seen a storm like that. I honestly thought we were going to drown. I had already seen Him do miracles. I knew He was a prophet and probably more, but this one! I mean," Peter's eyes glowed with wonder, "who can control the weather? If there was one point in time when I really realized He was the Messiah, it was when He defied that storm, climbed up on the front of that crazy bucking boat, and shouted, 'Peace! Be still!' Such an incredible calm." He looked around and singled me out, I guess because I was the only one in the room who had not been there in the boat with him. He repeated, "Such a calm, and it was instantaneous. It did not slowly die down. I mean, one minute I thought the boat was going to break apart; the next, the storm was gone!"

All of a sudden, Peter seemed to remember another story,

"No, wait. My favorite story has to be when we saw Him in all His radiance up on that mountain. James and John, you all remember. He looked so radiant I knew we were looking on the very face of God. I just knew we were all going to die." Peter smiled. "And as usual, I had to open my fool mouth." He shook his head sadly as tears once again filled his eyes.

Everyone nodded. John looked up, his face still streaked with tears, but he had a smile on his face. "What about the time during the storm you got out of the boat, Peter?" Everyone laughed, Peter harder than anyone.

"I don't know what came over me. I mean, that storm was crazy! Not as bad as the first one, but still ... then to see a ghost walking on the water!" His voice lowered. "Then, to know it was Him out on the surface of the water and not sinking, and to hear the forbidden name of God! I tell you, I don't know what happened to me when I heard Him say, 'I AM, Don't be afraid.' Everything in me desired to go to Him." His voice faltered. "It was something to walk out on that water with those waves. But it was awful to start sinking out there, I will admit that!"

Everyone laughed again. Peter got really serious. "He caught me as I was sinking. I wish He were here now; surely I am sinking again." Once again tears flowed freely from his eyes and down his beard.

Trying to change the subject, I decided to ask the group something I had overheard Nicodemus and Joseph of Arimathea talking about on the way back from the cross. I wanted to be careful, because I did not want to distress them anymore than they were, but if they look at things in the light of how those two old Pharisees were talking about it, it might cheer them up. I mean, if God had this whole thing planned out since Abraham, it was no one's fault that Jesus had been arrested. There was no way any one of us could have stopped it. I know when I heard them talking, it sure took some of my guilt away, unless it is just wishful thinking on my part.

I decided to go ahead and tell it. "Hey guys," I started. "Do you know what Joseph and Nicodemus believe?" They all looked at me. "Well, as we were walking back from the place today," — I could not force myself to say the crucifixion site, —"As we were walking back into the city, I was walking with Joseph and Nicodemus. Joseph was telling Nicodemus about something he had just studied. See, Joseph and Nicodemus were convinced Jesus had to die. They were convinced Jesus had to die today! According to what they were saying, this last Sunday when Jesus was recognized as the Messiah, that was a day foretold by the prophet Daniel to the very day! So, if that was the case, then, Jesus had to die today on this Passover.

"But the point Joseph was explaining was, he believed that the crucifixion site was the exact same mountain, possibly the exact site, where Abraham was commanded to sacrifice his son, Isaac. Abraham obeyed God, but at the last second, God provided a different sacrifice. So God stopped Abraham from sacrificing his son, but no one stopped God from sacrificing His only Son, Jesus. I don't remember all of Joseph's line of thinking, but if that is the case — you all and Peter — there was nothing we could have done to stop it. Sure we are all guilty—according to Joseph, it was for the sins of the world that He paid the penalty and became the sacrificial Lamb of God—but it was not because you all," I looked at Matthew, "ran away and didn't defend Him, or because Peter denied Him, or even because I was a spy for my master and led the arresting party." Here, I could not go on, but started my own fountain of tears.

I finally got my tears under control and decided to tell my own favorite story about my Messiah. I got everyone's attention. "You all might not want to hear this story, but it is a story that involved both Jesus and me. I was in the garden last night with you all, but not as one of you." I paused. I knew John, Matthew, and Peter knew my secret, but I wanted to come clean with them all. "I have been a spy for the High Priest. He is my master, and I go do his bidding. He had me shadowing the Baptizer first, then Jesus, ever since they started their ministries. It was easy for me to fit in and be one of the crowd, so to speak, because I also was from Galilee. I listened to Him and gave my master reports on what was happening and where He was going, what He was saying and everything. I was proud of my position and proud of my work. I listened to Him talk and reported on everything I heard. But the funny thing was, I could never understand a word He said. I kept asking John and Levi — I mean Matthew — what He meant. They did not know I was a spy, so they tried to make sure I understood Him, hoping that I would decide to follow Him as well. Levi especially kept trying to get me to believe on Him, but I always shrugged him off.

"Then, last night, my master commanded me to take the Temple guards and, backed up by a contingent of Roman guards, go and arrest Jesus. You all know that one of you, Judas, had already come and sold Jesus out. He was going to guide us to where Jesus was spending the night. My master was secretly hoping that you would put up a fight, and we could manipulate the Roman solders into attacking and killing you all, especially Jesus, and that would be the end of my master's problem. He only saw Jesus as a problem. A huge problem. My master thought he was going to lose control of the Temple.

"So we went out into the night. A night almost as bright as day because of the huge Passover moon in the sky. We walked as quietly as we could; my master was emphatic that we not let anyone know what we were doing. If there was one thing my master was more afraid of than the Romans, it was a Jewish mob, and he knew if the common folk found out he was arresting Jesus, there would be hell to pay. We crossed the Kidron Valley and got to the garden of Gethsemane. Judas took the lead. We lit our torches and followed Judas. It was darker under the trees in the garden.

"You don't need many details now, as you were there. All I will say is it really shocked us when Jesus walked right out to us.

" 'Who are you looking for,' He said in that calm, deep voice of His.

" 'Jesus of Nazareth,' one of the Temple priests said.

"I forgot to mention, along with the Temple police and the Roman guards, many scribes, Pharisees, and other Temple authorities came along with us. I think my master sent them along to ensure something would happen in order to kill Jesus outside of the city. The last thing in this world my master wanted was to have Jesus brought back into the city and delivered to him there in the Temple.

"When they said they were looking for Jesus of Nazareth, Jesus calmly said, 'I AM.'

"In their shock and fear at hearing the Name of God Almighty spoken, the Temple authorities fell over backwards. We were all shocked, and this happened twice. Then, Jesus said, 'Since you have found Me, let My disciples go.'

"Before we could even answer Him, Peter rushed out roaring

like a lion and took a huge swing at my head with his sword! I tried to move back, but my foot rolled on a rock, probably saving my life. It made me fall, but Peter's sword still hit me a terrible swipe on my head that almost killed me! The swipe cleanly shaved my ear off! My head was ringing, and blood was pouring down my face. I was on my knees, hardly aware of anything going on around me. I noticed Jesus looking at me. Matthew, do you remember trying to tell me and explain to me Jesus' look of compassion? I never knew what you meant. But suddenly, I knew. I saw Jesus' look. Such compassion and love!

"He bent down, and I saw Him pick up my bloody ear and gently bring His hand to the side of my face. I felt a gentle pressure as He pressed my ear back on. My head instantly cleared up! You won't believe it, but something I always told Mathew and John was that I could never hear Him, meaning I could not understand Him, but as He was pressing my ear back on to my face, I was looking into His eyes and I could hear Him as plainly as if He had said it out loud: 'Can you hear Me now, Malchus?' And boy, could I ever! My life changed at that minute. How I wish I would have known Him longer. How I wish I would have accepted Him when I first heard Him. How guilty I feel now because I was the one in charge of arresting Him. But how honored I feel to be one of the ones He healed." My voice trailed off, and my own tears came with a rush now. John put his arm on my back in sympathy.

———

With the High Sabbath giving us two Sabbaths in a row, we had two long days to sit and tell stories. But finally the long Sabbaths were over. So right at dawn on the first day of the week, a friend and I decided to get an early start. I refused to go back to the Temple right now, and I figured in all the confusion, I would not be missed. I decided to travel home and visit my family, and since my friend Cleopas needed to go to Emmaus, just a short seven miles from Jerusalem, we decided to walk together. Dawn was only a red slit in the dark sky, but it was dawn as far as we were concerned, so we were getting our things together when some women came running in saying they had gone to the tomb and Jesus' body was gone! An angel had told them He was alive! I saw Peter and John starting to run to the tomb, and for a minute I almost started running with them, but I just could not handle any more drama! I had to get away.

My friend agreed, so we continued preparations to leave. Peter and John ran on to the tomb, and we were just leaving when they got back. Peter was quiet, but John seemed like he was convinced of the women's story. I asked John what made him change his mind.

He had a pensive look on his face. "I saw Him die," he said. "I saw them spear Him, and I watched Joseph and Nicodemus take Him down from the cross. And — and this is the big one — I also watched them wrap His body. Malchus, you were there. Remember, they wrapped His body in a large linen sheet, but around His face and head they wrapped a smaller piece of linen. Well, when I stooped down to look into the tomb, I saw the cloths still laying exactly the way I had seen those two old guys wrapping Him. I remembered the way Nicodemus had wrapped the linen napkin around His face so lovingly and carefully. Those two pieces of linen were still wrapped exactly like I had seen them wrapped, only the body was gone. It had not been unwrapped and taken away, it was obvious the body had just disappeared from inside the linen. I saw it. I believe He is alive!"

I shook my head. I wished it could be true, but all my optimism of the two days before was suddenly gone. I was discouraged and tired beyond belief. I knew my master would be looking for me, but I had decided to just go home. I'd had enough.

Cleopas looked like he wanted to stay and keep listening to all the talk, but I couldn't take any more. The last three years had worn me out.

We finally made it out to the gate of the city and started on the road to Emmaus. Frankly, I was happy to be gone. I would have walked in silence but Cleopas was still full of questions. I was trying my hardest to explain, so we were deep in conversation about all that had happened that week. I was doing my best to fill in Cleopas about all that I knew. He, of course, also knew most of it, but did not have the inside story like I had. We had been only walking for a short time when we caught up with another man walking alone in the early-morning mists.

Sidling along with us silently for a few minutes, He then asked us, "You all seem to be talking about something important. What happened that has you both so concerned?"

We both stopped walking. I looked at Cleopas, his face etched with sadness, as I am sure mine was. "Friend, You must be the only man in Jerusalem who has to ask about the terrible things that happened there this week!" Cleopas told him.

"What things?" the man asked him.

"Everything that happened to Jesus, the Nazarene. He was an incredible prophet and a great teacher doing mighty miracles. We thought He was approved by God and man, but this week, our chief priests and our leaders arrested Him and turned

Him over to the Roman authorities to be condemned and crucified. We can't believe they could have killed Him because we thought He was the promised Messiah. We honestly thought He was going to rescue Israel," Cleopas told Him.

"Then, if that was not enough, some women from our group who were also His followers, went to His tomb early this morning and came running back saying His tomb was empty! They even said they had seen some angels! These angels asked them why they were looking for someone who was alive in a tomb!"

"Then Peter and my cousin John ran to the tomb, and sure enough, it was empty," I added. "Peter told me that John outran him but did not go inside. Peter, not caring if he were made unclean by going inside the tomb, went right on in; he just had to know for himself what had happened. Finally, my cousin John went in behind him. They looked at the linen cloths, and there was no evidence of the grave having been robbed, according to both of them. The cloths were laying there, undisturbed, like the body had just disappeared from inside of them. Peter said the cloth napkin face covering was laying still wrapped beside the other cloths right where the head would have been, with the body linen laying right where the body would have lain. John told me that was all he needed to see. He knew Jesus had risen from the dead. Anyway, of all of the disciples, I think John is the only one to believe that Jesus has indeed risen." My voice trailed off, and I took a deep breath.

"But who knows what happened!" I finished, frustrated and hearing the anger in my voice. I had spent the last three years not believing John, and now, I still couldn't take the step to believe like him that Jesus had risen from the dead! "I figure there are going to be people saying they saw Jesus for the rest of our lives!

I can't take any more!"

Cleopas and I were both surprised when the man said, "Oh you foolish, foolish men! Why do you find it so difficult to believe what the prophets said about the Messiah? The prophets clearly wrote that the Messiah had to suffer. He was going to be rejected and crucified before He would enter His glory."

Then the man started at the beginning of our Torah and went all the way through, quoting the passages of Scriptures that told all the Messiah had to go through. As He quoted the different passages, He explained how the man Jesus fulfilled each prophecy. How I wish I could remember all the Scriptures He used! But I have to admit that in spite of all I was hearing, my grief had my ears closed. My mind kept going back to all I had heard Jesus say and how I had just rejected it out of hand. I could not believe how blind and deaf I had been when listening to Him.

I do remember one of the prophesies He brought out, because—let's face it—I had just witnessed it firsthand. This prophecy was from our book of Songs, from the Psalms of King David. When I got home, I looked it up to read it for myself, as I could not believe how accurately King David had described what I had witnessed happen to my Messiah.

> I am poured out like water,
> And all My bones are out of joint;
> My heart is like wax;
> It has melted within Me.
> My strength is dried up like a potsherd,
> And My tongue clings to My jaws;
> You have brought Me to the dust of death.

For dogs have surrounded Me;

The congregation of the wicked has enclosed Me.

They pierced My hands and My feet;

I can count all My bones.

They look and stare at Me.

They divide My garments among them,

And for My clothing they cast lots.

By this time, we were almost to Emmaus. I had decided to sleep at Cleopas' dwelling. Our friend moved to keep going, but we begged Him to stay as it was already late. Funny, we had gotten so interested in all He was telling us that the short seven miles had taken us most of the day. Our friend agreed, and we went on home with Cleopas. We sat down to eat, and our friend assumed a position at the head of the table. It just seemed right. After He asked God's blessing, He took a loaf of bread and, breaking it, passed it on to us. The simple act of breaking the bread suddenly opened our eyes. It was Jesus! HE WAS ALIVE! But as soon as we recognized Him, He disappeared!

We looked at each other. "No wonder our hearts were burning as He was talking! Why in the world did we not recognize Him?"

We hurriedly got ready and rushed back to Jerusalem. With the lightness of our hearts, our trip back did not take us any time at all. We were running when we got to the upper room. We almost crashed through the door. As we ran in, we saw nothing but smiles. "He's alive!" they all shouted. "He already met and talked with Peter!" I stared. Peter's face told it all! Whatever they had talked about, Peter was at peace.

Then, I remembered our news. Cleopas and I were almost

yelling over each other in our excitement. "We spent the day with Jesus, and He explained everything to us! We rushed back to tell you the good news!" We were still talking when, all of a sudden, Jesus was right there with us! We froze, then shrank back as if we were seeing a ghost.

"Why are you so afraid? Why can't you believe it's Me? Come closer. Look at Me. Look at My hands! Look at My feet. It is really Me. Come here, you can touch Me! I am not a ghost! Ghosts don't have bodies like I do!" My eyes dropped down to His outstretched hands, and I was shocked to see the jagged, round holes from the large nails through the base of His hands. Slowly, I fell to my knees, and it was only then that I realized everyone else in the room was also on their knees. I even heard a few sobs — from fear or joy, I didn't know.

Suddenly I heard Him chuckle. "You know, I'm hungry! Do you all have anything to eat?" I am not sure who ran and got Him a piece of broiled fish and bread, but we watched Him as He ate it and obviously enjoyed it.

"Don't you remember all the things I taught you about the Holy Scriptures being fulfilled in Me?" He asked us. "Remember I told you that everything written about Me by Moses, the prophets, and the Psalms had to come true? Remember I said I had not come to do away with Moses and the prophets but to fulfill them?" Then, like He had done for us earlier on the road to Emmaus, He carefully explained the passages and how they applied to Him. Amazing how everything fit together so beautifully once it was explained. I couldn't believe I ever doubted He was the Messiah.

I felt so honored to even be in the same room with these men. I mean, I had gone and arrested Him. Yet, as I watched

Him look around at everyone, He gazed at me with the same love He gave anyone else in the room.

Jesus went on, "Yes, long ago, the prophets wrote that the Messiah had to suffer and die, but would rise again on the third day. And this is the message of salvation that you all will take from Jerusalem to all the world. There is forgiveness of sins for all who believe in Me."

We all nodded, now that we finally understood. We truly were hearing Him now.

I did finally make it back to Galilee. While it was still agonizing in poverty, I had to admit, it was good to be home. For all the times I had come on spy missions for my master, I had never recognized it as coming home. But now, I was here with all the disciples and I think we were all getting on each other's nerves, because it was a relief to hear Peter say, "I am going fishing!" I had not been back on the lake since my childhood, but I was one of the first to say I was going with him. By the time we got down to where the boat was pulled up on the beach, there was Peter, Thomas, Nathanael, James, John, one of the other guys, and me.

After fishing for hours and catching nothing, I remembered why I had been so ready to leave life here and move to Jerusalem. I looked around. Some of the guys were already asleep, either using the small cushion in the back or just sitting at their oars with their heads on their chests.

We were just drifting with our net out, but it was hanging empty. John was still awake, so I left my place and moved over beside him.

"John," I spoke quietly, "tell me more about Jesus. I feel so left out. I know I shadowed you all everywhere, but back then I was on the outside looking in. Now I want to know things I missed."

John grinned. "Where do you want me to start?" he asked.

"At the beginning!" I begged him.

John got a pensive look. He stared out over the water with the moonlight reflected on his face. "I have really been thinking about this. I wish I would have written things down, and one day I plan to, but where do I start right now?" He repeated almost to himself. Then looking at me, he said, "Malchus, when I do write everything down, I want to start by saying: In the beginning was the Word and the Word was with God, and the Word was God."

He paused deep in thought. "I am not sure how to bring everything out, but when I write this down, I want to include something about creation, because I know now Jesus was with God in the beginning. I know that all things were created by Him and without Him nothing was created. Especially since I saw Him rise from the dead, I know Life is in Him and His life is the Light of men. His Light shines in the darkness and the darkness could not put out His light."

I was amazed at John's passion, and I said, "I remember when I was following the Baptizer around, spying for my master, you were looking for Jesus then."

"Yes, the Baptizer was always telling everyone who would listen that he was not the Light, but he only came telling about the Light so that people would be ready for the Light when He came. Then one day, I remember him telling us, 'Behold the Lamb of God which takes away the sin of the world.' Andrew and I were standing there. We dropped everything and fell into step behind Jesus." John shook his head. "Seems a lifetime ago."

"Once you found Him, how long did it take you to realize that He was God?" I asked him.

"I think it was as soon as John pointed Him out to us! We followed Him and spent the night talking with Him. I knew! I just knew. Sure, there were times I disappointed Him by doubting, but really, looking back, I knew He was our Messiah."

"You know," John paused with a sad look on his face. "You know, He was in the world, and the world was created by Him, yet the world did not recognize Him. I think one of the hardest things for Jesus to accept was that although He came to His own, His own people did not receive Him. But to all who did receive Him, He gave them the right to be children of God, to those who believe in His name, who were born, not of blood or of the will of the flesh or of the will of man, but of God. The Word became flesh, and took up residence among us."

I had never heard John speak so eloquently. I nodded, unable to speak, with tears flowing down my cheeks and a big lump in my throat. I swallowed and cleared my throat. Blinking my eyes and finally wiping them with my sleeve, I said, "I heard Jesus say something to Nicodemus that night so long ago: that 'unless a man is born again he can not see the kingdom of God.' I did not understand Him then, and barely do now, but this is what you are talking about, right? 'Being born, not of blood or of the will of the flesh or of the will of man, but of God,' right?"

John nodded in the moonlight and went on. "Yes, remember I told you about seeing Him transfigured on that mountain? I can't tell you what that was like. Words can't convey what seeing Him like that did to me." John's voice dropped to such a quiet whisper that I had to strain to catch his words. "We have seen

His glory, the glory of the One and Only." He looked up and his voice strengthened, "I know it did the same thing to James and Peter. We actually saw His glory! We saw Him in His glory as the One and Only Son from the Father," John repeated in amazement, as if it was hard to really believe what they had seen. "Jesus said a number of times that He did not come to abolish the Law but to fulfill it. I realize what He meant was that Moses gave the Law. It was impossible for us to keep it. Jesus kept the Law in its entirety, and by His keeping of the law, we can have His grace and truth. Yes! We have all received grace and truth from Jesus! He has fully revealed God the Father, because He is the One and Only Son!"

I sat there quietly thinking about all this. My heart was bursting with love for my Messiah. Looking out over the water, I watched the sky slowly turning light as a new day was dawning. In the early morning mists, John and I noticed a man standing on the shore.

"You don't have any fish, do you?" the man called to us.

"No," Peter answered, shaking himself awake from where he was supposed to be tending the net.

"Pull it up and throw your net on the right side of the boat," the man shouted. "There are fish there."

I am not a fisherman, but for some reason, we all jumped up to obey this strange command. As soon as our net stretched out, it was so full of fish we could not even begin to pull it in. We were afraid our boat would swamp, so we decided just to pull toward the beach and bring the net up on shore.

As soon as John realized the net was full to bursting, he told Peter, "Peter, it is the Lord!"

You should have seen Peter! Grabbing his cloak, he wrapped

it around himself, dove into the cold water of the lake, and started swimming to shore. It must have been at least a hundred yards to shore, but Peter could not wait for the slow boat. He had to get to Jesus.

The rest of us finally got the boat and the net full of fish to shore. Can you believe it? With a catch like this, Peter and my cousins could go right back into business as fishermen! I wondered what they might do.

We all gathered around Jesus. I looked at His disciples. They were shy around the risen Lord, as if no one knew what to say, but Jesus, smiling broadly said, "I have already cooked some fish and bread, but bring some more fish. I'm sure you all are hungry!"

We all jumped to obey, but Peter beat us to the net and hauled the thrashing, jumping, and splashing net full of fish to shore. There were over 153 fish in that net, and the net did not break! We had a delicious meal of broiled fish and bread there on the beach.

While we were finishing up, I saw Jesus motion Peter to come walk with Him down the beach. It was funny watching John meander a bit behind them, as if he just could not stand to be separated from these two heroes of his. I would have loved to hear what Jesus told Peter, but I respected Peter's privacy too much to pry. I was sure one day he would tell us what the Master said to him.

One day, not long after, Jesus led us out of the city toward Bethany again. Getting as far as the Mount of Olives, Jesus stopped us. "I have been given all authority. With My authority, go into all the world and preach the good news about Me to everyone! Make disciples of all who believe, baptizing them in the name of the Father and of the Son and of the Holy Spirit, teaching them to observe everything I have commanded you. Never forget! I am with you always, even to the end of the age."

Listening to His beautiful voice, my heart was full, because now I heard Him plainly and truly understood Him. Jesus spoke a berakah, a blessing, then, while we stood there amazed, He was taken up into heaven. We watched Him go out of sight, straining to catch one more glimpse of Him in the clouds. We were still standing there dumbfounded when we realized we were not alone.

There were two men in shining clothes, and they asked us, "Men of Galilee, what are you doing here staring up at the sky? Jesus has gone away and one day will return just like you saw Him."

Remembering Jesus had told us to wait in Jerusalem for the gift from His Father, we ran back the short distance to the upper room, and there waited in prayer and praise for His Promise.

After Jesus was gone, I jokingly asked John if he was writing his book yet. He grinned.

"Malchus, if I tried to write down all the things that Jesus taught us and told us, why—" John's eyes got big with expression. "Why," he went on, "I don't think the entire world could contain all the books. I wish you could have heard Him all those quiet nights as we would sit around a fire, or out in the boat crossing the lake, with most of the guys asleep and Jesus just talking. How I enjoyed those times!" John said wistfully. I nodded, wishing I could have heard Him then as well. But one thing you can't take away from me. I, Malchus, did hear Him say, "And remember, I am with you always, to the end of the age." How honored I was to hear those words!

THE END

AUTHOR'S NOTE

Looking back, I am surprised at this story. It almost seemed to write itself at times. As I typed, the dialog just flowed.

I have to be honest and say, however, I had no intention of ever trying to write a story about our Lord. The idea came about while speaking via WhatsApp with my son, Joshua.

"Dad," he told me, "I have an idea for your next book. I've been thinking a lot lately of the guy who got his ear cut off by Peter." He continued, "I just keep thinking how this man's life would have changed forever after Jesus, someone he probably thought very little of, healed him on the spot! How could he ever be the same? I was thinking we could call it, Can You Hear Me Now?"

I remembered his name being Malchus, especially since I show The Jesus Movie/Passion of the Christ in villages 4-5 times a month down here! We started talking about what we did know about Malchus, and to be honest, it wasn't much. Here's what we know.

We know his name was Malchus as John, in his Gospel, called him by name.

We know he was a servant of the High Priest Caiaphas.

We know John had some kind of connection to the High Priest's household.

Those are the facts, and my mind started filling in the blanks. Might it have been possible for John's connection in the High Priest's house be a relative working for the High Priest? Why else might John still remember the servant's name after almost 50 years when he was writing his Gospel? Also, in thinking about John telling us his name after so many years, I began to wonder — would John have bothered to tell us the name of someone who did not become a believer?

So began this incredible journey of trying to retell the story of our Lord and Savior Jesus Christ through the eyes of someone unknown.

I pray you get as big of a blessing from reading it as I did from writing it. I learned more from writing this story than I can tell. I have to admit in reading the Gospel accounts, the stories can seem disjointed. I am afraid that in the past and even after many readings, I had gotten the mistaken idea the discourses and actions took place almost in a vacuum, whereas in really studying it out, the stories can only be understood if you take into account His location, His audience, and even the season or Feast that might be taking place during His discourse.

Up until right before publishing, the name was still Can You Hear Me Now? until my youngest son Stephen texted me asking, "Dad are you aware that Can You Hear Me Now? is copyrighted by Verizon?" As we progressed with the book further, we thought it might also be distracting calling it something people are so familiar with, so we decided to go with Malchus instead.

The main idea remains — how many times do we have to be at the breaking point in our lives for us to no longer simply listen to the words of God and finally experience the Word of God, to finally hear Jesus?

Made in USA - North Chelmsford, MA
1104783_9780999524510
05.12.2020 1721